Love's Bequest

Adam J. Ridley, Blake Allwood

Blake Allwood Publishing

Cover designed by Samrat Acharjee

This book is a work of fiction. Names, characters, places, and incidents either are products of the author's imagination or are used fictitiously. Any resemblance to actual persons, living or dead, events, or locales is entirely coincidental.

Blake Allwood

Visit my website at www.blakeallwood.com

Printed in the United States of America

Box Elder, SD

First Printing: August 2021

E-book ISBN: 978-1-956727-16-6

Paperback ISBN: 978-1-956727-17-3

Library of Congress Control Number: 2021920812

Content Warnings

Depression
Contemplated Suicide
Kidnapping
Violence

Join Blake's email list to get advance notice of new books and receive his occasional newsletter:

www.blakeallwood.com

MM Romance
By Blake Allwood

Transitions Series
Aiden Inspired
Suzie Empowered (MF Romance)
Bobby Transformed

Chance Series
Love By Chance
Another Chance With Love
Taking A Chance For Love

Romantic Series
Romantic Renovations (1)
Romantic Rescue (2)
Romantic Recon (3)

Melody Series
Melody of the Heart
Melody of the Snow

Road to Rocktoberfest Anthology
Changing His Tune - 2022

Coming Home Series (2023)
A Long Way Home
Family Home
Down Home
…and many more

Novellas
Tenacious
Moon's Place

Romantic Fantasy
By Adam J. Ridley

Big Bend Series
Love's Legacy (1)
Love's Heirloom (2)
Love's Bequest (3)

The Witch Brothers Series
Emerald Earth
Diamond Air
Ruby Fire
Sapphire Water

A special thank you to
Samrat Acharjee
Renee Mizar
and
John Gilchrist
for his work on the family tree
and being a great Beta-reader.
And of course, a big thank you to my husband who encourages
me to keep going down these rabbit holes never knowing where
I might end up.

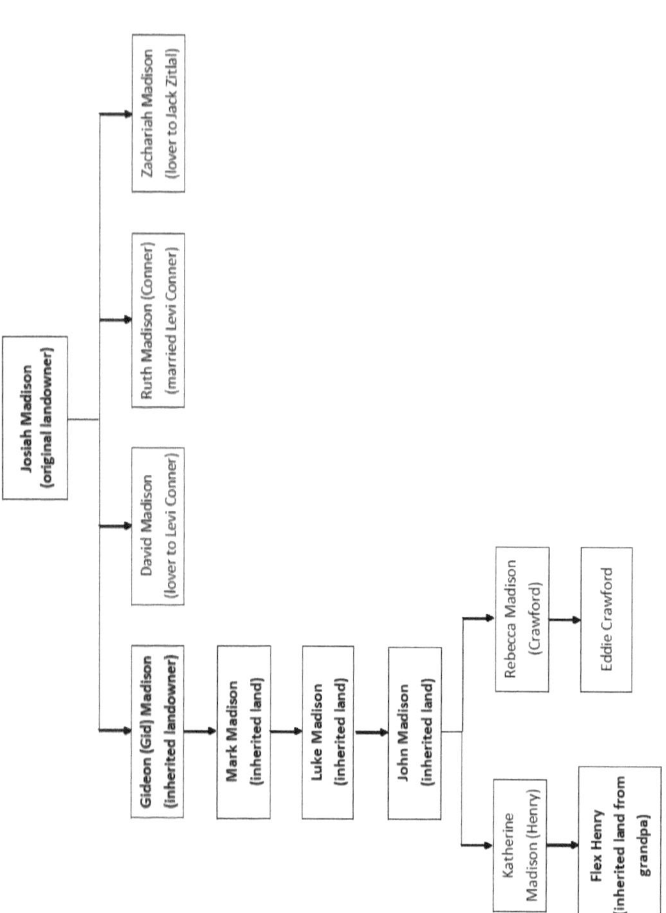

Josiah Madison (original landowner)
David Madison (lover to Levi Conner)
Ruth Madison (Conner) (married Levi Conner)
Zachariah Madison (lover to Jack Zitla)
Gideon (Gid) Madison (inherited landowner)
Mark Madison (inherited land)
Luke Madison (inherited land)
John Madison (inherited land)
Rebecca Madison (Crawford)
Eddie Crawford
Katherine Madison (Henry)
Flex Henry (inherited land from grandpa)

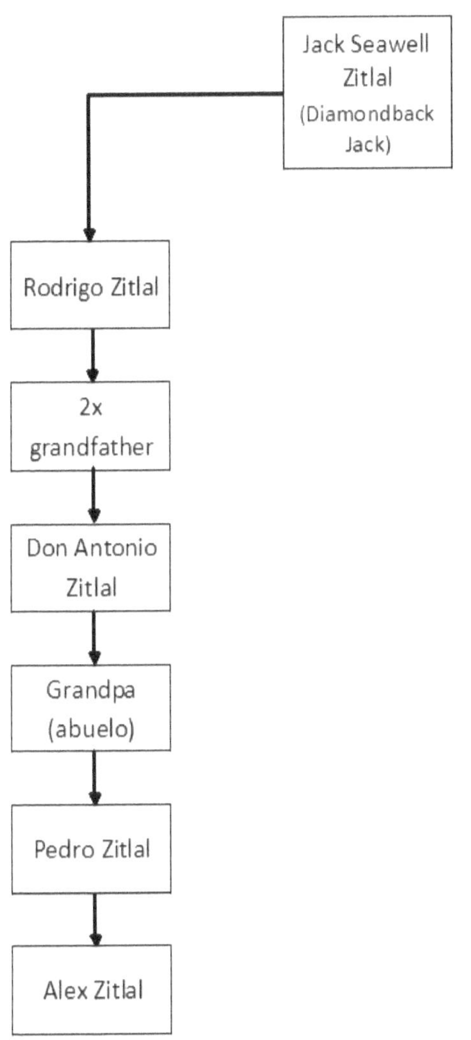

Jack Seawell Zitlal (Diamondback Jack)
Rodrigo Zitlal
2x grandfather
Don Antonio Zitlal
Grandpa (abuelo)
Pedro Zitlal
Alex Zitlal

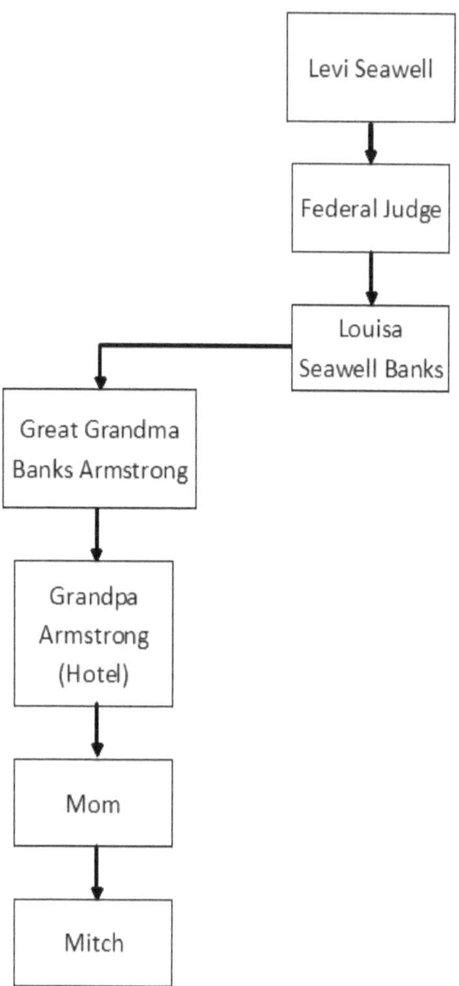

Levi Seawell
Federal Judge
Louisa Seawell Banks
Great Grandma Banks Armstrong
Grandpa Armstrong (Hotel)
Mom
Mitch

1

Steve

I SAW THE BLUE-CLAD figure walk around the driver's side of the RV and was shocked at seeing someone there. I'd intentionally parked my forty-foot motorhome, which doubles as my research vehicle, down at Croton Springs, a primitive campsite in the park I'd chosen this spot because it was secluded and other than the occasional hiker I'd probably have the place to myself.

I waited for the figure to come to the front of the vehicle, so I could get a better view. When he didn't emerge, I decided to look around. When I didn't see anyone, the needle-like sensation spread across my body like it did when I was seeing someone from the *other side*.

I sighed. Spirits were something I'd seen and felt all my life, and I honestly preferred to avoid them if at all possible. I rarely felt them when I was in Big Bend, though. The Native's spirits had long-ago transitioned; or they just weren't interested in dealing with me. Occasionally, when I was around springs or down by the Rio Grande river I'd catch the feeling of other presences, but they were rare and uninterested as well.

I sat back down at my computer, determined to log the items I'd found and photographed while hiking along Emery Peak earlier in the day. The moment I sat down, I began to feel a familiar tug, something I often felt when I encountered a spirit that wanted to show me something. Spirits could be persistent, and I knew from experience that if I didn't comply, the sensation would become – intense.

"Okay, okay, let me put my hiking boots on," I said out loud so the entity could hear me. The spirit was a playful one, and there was no malice or negative emotion, so I knew this was likely to just be a nature walk. More often than not, I found the spirits that reached out to me wanted company more than anything else.

When I stepped out of the RV, the tug was stronger and I followed it toward the path labeled Croton Springs Trail. I hadn't had time to explore it yet, but because the entity seemed to be in a hurry, I didn't take time to grab my camera or notebook.

I followed the tug along the trail and my *spectral friend* flashed images into my mind, letting me know to keep my eye out for snakes. "Don't worry," I said aloud. "I'm *always* on guard for snakes." I could almost hear the entity chuckling.

From my earlier glimpse of him, I guessed he was in his early to mid-thirties when he'd passed away. The clothes he was wearing appeared similar to the miner's gear I'd seen in so many photos while researching the nearby Little Bird Mine from the 1800's. He probably died in a mine accident like so many others; but he didn't seem too upset about it. So, I decided to go with the flow and see where he led me.

We walked downhill and came to a wash that led to a larger dry creek bed. The pull became stronger as I got closer, and had I not had the spirit's guiding tug, I wouldn't have known which way to go. I turned left and walked along the creek bed. Since I'd heard the warning, I kept a close eye out for snakes that might be hiding among the rocks. Spirits were odd and tended to communicate randomly, almost like you were in their minds without a filter; so I wasn't sure if the snake thing was a message, or just a thought.

As I came to a bend in the creek, I saw a hole filled with water. Immediately, I heard the words 'watering hole', and I smiled. The place must have water most of the year, and I wondered if maybe this was the spring that was labeled when we came onto the path. Probably not, though, since I didn't see any evidence that an actual spring was there. The tug pulled me out of the creek, and up to a huge flat-topped limestone rock.

When I arrived, the tugging stopped, and I turned around taking in my surroundings. I saw my RV in the distance, and knew why the entity had seen me and come to check me out. I felt my guide standing next to me.

"So, this was your place, huh?" For a moment, I could smell horses, and knew the guy must have snuck away and ridden a horse up to the spot when he'd been alive.

I understood why someone would want to make this their spot. It was hidden away, had access to water, which was rare for these parts, and the view of the Chisos Mountains and the surrounding terrain was amazing. It was a peaceful, wild, and beautiful place.

I waited a bit longer, spending time with the sweet spirit, who was clearly missing companionship. "Have you thought of moving on?" I asked, but there was nothing to indicate he'd heard or was paying attention to me. I decided to leave it. Most spirits transitioned on their own when they were ready, and clearly, he wasn't.

When I stood to leave, he didn't try to stop me. "Thanks for showing me this. It's a nice spot. I saw a lot of tracks around the water, so I bet you get to see everything while you are here, don't ya?" Again, I didn't feel or hear anything. I was alone. Maybe he'd just needed a little company. Spirits were hard to read.

I headed back up the trail and thought about all of it. My dad's family was from West Texas, and his mother, my granny, still had her old Southern ways. She told me early in my youth that I was *touched*, which was the old people's way of saying someone had the sixth sense when it came to spirits. I didn't let many people know about my ability, because few people understood it.

The sun was beginning to approach the horizon when I got back to the RV, and I was disappointed to see I had a new new neighbor who'd pulled up while I was out following the spirit. He had one of those car-top tents that seem to be pretty popular with a lot of hikers.

I went inside and put on a pot of water for tea, then turned my computer back on and began working on logging the different archeological finds I'd photographed on my morning hike.

Big Bend was one of my favorite national parks. When the Friends of the Park had asked the Archeological Society to help develop a grant proposal to survey and document the park's archeological areas, I readily volunteered for the job. Now that they'd secured the grant, and I'd completed my work at the Little Bird Mine, I was free to take on the project.

Who cared if it only paid half what I was used to getting? I got to stay in my favorite park, I got access to back areas that most tourists would never find, and best of all, for the most part, I got to soak in the solitude I craved. Until I needed to get into the research elements of the job, I didn't have to worry about the stuff archeologists working in academia did, like students, lectures, or university faculty and all their drama...it was just me, the silence, and because Big Bend was sparsely settled, very few spirits. It was the best place on earth for me to spend the winter.

Before turning in for the night, I pulled out my maps and double checked all the sites around the Mariscal mine. After seeing the entity, I wanted to go there, and see if maybe that's where he'd come from. I packed the supplies I thought I would need for the hike and decided to turn in. I hadn't spoken with my new neighbor yet and hoped they would be gone before I got up in the morning so I could have my privacy back.

2

Eric

I GOT UP EARLY the next morning and quickly put some supplies in my day pack for a hike to a nearby mine. I was happy to see there wasn't any movement in the RV that was parked next to me and hoped they would leave this morning before I got back from my hike. I decided to leave my car with the attached tent where it was and walked out to the road to hitch a ride from a tourist driving through the park.

When I arrived at the trailhead, I thanked the family that had dropped me off and grabbed my pack from their trunk. Finally, being alone for the first time since leaving Oregon, I let the anger and frustration flow freely. I stomped heavily down the path, enjoying the dust cloud my little hissy fit was causing.

"Life is fucking shit," I said to myself... I wanted to yell it, but even here in the desert separated from the world, I still felt the need to control every freaking emotion I had.

I shook my head as I walked along. How had things fallen apart in such a short time? In the last year, my wife had left me, my dad and brother had all but kicked me out of the house, I'd lost both of my jobs, *and* my friends were too busy to notice.

I was in full-on self-pity mode when I heard someone coming up the path behind me. *Fuck,* I thought, *glad I didn't yell after all.*

I quickly pushed down my annoyance. I admit, I was enjoying my pity party, but damn, I'd held it in for a long freaking time... *and who the hell could blame me?*

I turned around and found a man standing behind me. He, too, was a hiker, and had his gear loaded heavily on his back.

I ignored the funny electrical pulse that shot up my spine when I got a look at him. Tall, refined, but rugged, was that a thing? I argued with myself inside my head, then realized the man was looking at me. I smiled and stepped out of his path.

He walked past me and stopped, then turned around with a perplexed look on his face. "Do I know you?" he asked.

I shook my head, the strange electrical pulse now darted into my heart, causing it to pick up speed. "I doubt it," I said. "I'm not from around here."

He nodded, then turned around again and continued walking along the path. I waited a moment to let the man get further ahead. As I forced myself to enjoy the beauty of the landscape, I pondered on the strange feeling the man gave me. Finally,

I decided it was because I was desperate for another human's connection.

"God, I need to find more friends," I whispered to myself as my mind wandered to my two best friends, Flex and Eddie. They owned a sprawling ranch just outside the park border, and I had come down to spend time with them. Unfortunately, a movie production had taken over the ranch so the friendly support and seclusion I sought wasn't really available there. Anyway, Flex was so head over heels in love with Alamito Motel owner Mitch, that he didn't really have time for me...and oh, this was truly a surprise, Eddie and the movie producer, Alex, were now boyfriends. I had no idea Eddie was gay or bisexual, or whatever.

Oh well... like you're one to talk, I chastised myself, your sexuality is all over the damned place.

Ignoring the irritating voice in my own head, I thought about the ranch. It had been my refuge after my mom had died while I was still in high school in Houston. When my dad and brother decided to ostracize me during the holiday, I'd immediately thought about staying with my friends at the ranch. When things got ugly, it was the place I could count on. A place where I could go to hide and lick my wounds.

Unfortunately, with the filming on the ranch, the whole place was in chaos. I figured I was better off not interfering. Apparently, this was the new theme of my life—try not to interfere in other people's lives. Disappear, get out of the way, don't be a nuisance.

Alone, bored, unemployed, totally feeling sorry for myself, and with nothing else to do, I'd decided to spend some time in the national park bordering the ranch.

I'd found a couple of local books about the history of this part of Texas at the visitors' center, and decided to check out the old Mariscal mine, where a lot of the trouble in the area had stemmed from. They'd even had a big shootout there. A couple douchebags who had been fired by the mine owner were killed when they confronted the mine's security guard. It was almost like reading a Zane Grey novel. Besides, focusing on historical people's problems let me forget my own.

Even when I wasn't trying to avoid my own life, I loved history. For me, history was about the people, their stories, their struggles, and how they overcame them and survived. Maybe if I was lucky, I could take a page from their books, and figure out how to survive my own disaster of a life.

When I figured the stranger was far enough ahead, I started walking toward the mine again. Upon my arrival, he was sitting on a rock and appeared to be listening to someone. Of course, there was no one there, and I knew no phone coverage reached out here, so I must have been wrongly interpreting his expression.

"Beautiful day," I said, startling the man.

He turned toward me, confusion covering his face. He quickly masked it and smiled. "It is a great day for a hike."

I sat down near him and pulled out my water bottle. I wasn't particularly looking for company, but he seemed friendly enough, and it would probably do me some good to get out of my own thoughts.

"How long are you here?" I asked him.

He chuckled. "Well, for the foreseeable future. I just got hired by the Department of the Interior to document the history of the area."

That intrigued me. "You're a historian?" I asked.

"Yes, archeologist to be precise."

"And you're writing about this area?"

"I'm charged with updating the history of human settlement in the park. I'm studying the archeological sites currently, but I'll be going through the Spanish archives about the area to see what the conquistadores wrote about it, and then follow through up to modern day."

I smiled. "Maybe this is providence. I am... or rather was a high school history teacher and adjunct professor at my local community college, but I'm only out here visiting friends.

In fact, you may want to speak to them when you get to the nineteenth century. Their family reaches as far back as you can get in this region, including the Natives, Spaniards or Mexicans, and the other Europeans after the Civil War."

He looked genuinely surprised. "I'd like that actually. It'll be a while before I'm ready to tackle that, though. Right now, I'm focused on the Natives of the area."

"How far back are you going?" I asked.

"Well, as far as I can. I'll start with the Late Paleo period. Most of that is references to what's been found in the area, or in Mexico, but I've done quite a bit of research there."

"That's the late Ice Age people, correct?"

He nodded. "Yeah, from eight thousand to sixty-five hundred BCE."

"Do you need a history assistant?" I asked, and flashed him my brightest smile.

He chuckled. "I don't have the money to hire anyone, but if you are looking for volunteer work, I could use some help. I was going to try to get a few students from the university in Alpine, but if I could get a professor, that would be much better."

I shook my head. "I have absolutely no access to anything like internet." I held up my phone. "Or phone coverage even."

"If you're serious, you can use my internet in the RV I've been using as a research vehicle."

"Woah, you have a research vehicle? You are the real thing then?" I asked, genuinely impressed.

"Don't be too impressed, I bought a fifteen-year-old motorhome and the Archeological Society I work for retrofitted with satellite internet and phone."

"It's better than what I've got at the moment," I said begrudgingly.

"Where did you teach?" he asked me.

"I worked at a high school and community college in downtown Portland, Oregon, until a couple weeks ago, then my grant dried up. Now I'm footloose and fancy free."

He smiled. "What brought you down to Big Bend?"

His smile sent that same infuriating zing into my heart again. Ignoring it, I answered, "I grew up in Houston, and my best friends recently took over a ranch not far from here. They're the family I told you about."

"Oh, cool," he replied.

We sat for a few moments, enjoying the gentle midday breeze. This part of the park could be unforgiving when the sun was pounding, and even in winter and late spring, a soft breeze was always appreciated.

"So, if you're serious, you'll need to sign up with the society as a volunteer. Of course, as I said, I can't pay you, but it might look good on your resumé if you want to teach at another college or university. I've had a few volunteers that worked for me just for that reason."

"I mostly just want something to occupy my time. My specialty is the US after the World Wars, so I have a lot to learn about prior US periods. Maybe you can convince me to go back and get my degree in archeology... although, I've never been patient enough to scratch the earth with art supplies."

He laughed. "I've never heard anyone refer to it that way, but I don't do many digs. Mostly, I search the internet or old reference books for information. I'm more a research librarian than a field archeologist."

"That I can do," I said, and looked toward one of the vistas. Without turning back toward him, I continued, "I thought about going into anthropology after I took a cultural anthropology course in school, but I'm more into individual stories than I am society as a whole. Not that I don't like culture, but the individual's story is what inspires me the most."

"Deal, you're hired for free labor!" he said, and stood up. "Do you know where Croton Springs Trail is?" he asked. I nodded and said "Yes, that's where I'm camped. Is that *your* RV there?"

"Yes, what a weird coincidence. Wait...your car was still there when I left to come here. How did you get here? That's about twenty-five miles away."

"Yeah, I didn't feel like putting away my tent to drive here so I just hitched a ride. I didn't really plan for how I'd get back, though."

Steve chuckled, "I'm going to spend some time exploring the mine, then I guess you can ride back with me. Unless you really enjoy hitchhiking in the desert," he said still grinning.

Again, with the strange uptick of my heartbeat, I knew I was feeling an attraction for this man. What was strange was as a demisexual person, I didn't tend to feel like this upfront. I usually only liked someone after getting to know them. I rubbed the center of my chest, and quickly responded, "That sounds perfect," and swallowed the lump that'd formed in my throat, "if you're sure you don't mind the company."

He thought for a moment. "I'm usually a loner, but if you're volunteering free labor, who am I to say no?"

I chuckled, not sure how to take that, but I'd just been thinking how much I needed to spend time with other humans, and since Eddie and Flex were locked down tight as a drum with all the goings-on at the ranch and motel, I really wanted this potential project to work out. I'd never really spent much time in the field. I was an academic all the way, but it would do me good to expand my horizons.

"Then let's check out the mine," I said.

3

Steve

I WOKE UP A little later than I'd expected and rushed to head out for the mine I wanted to I'd only come to this mine because I wondered if the spirit that made contact with me this morning had worked here or perhaps he'd somehow died in the mine. When I came up on the hiker, it was more than just a little disconcerting that the ghost looked so much like him.

Mariscal was opened in nineteen hundred when a rancher discovered quicksilver. So, by the look of the spirit's homespun clothes, I knew he couldn't have died here. The only other logical place, of course, was Little Bird. I knew that already, but I thought it was strange after the time I'd put in at that mine, that I hadn't seen him until now.

Not that this was the strangest thing to ever happen to me, but there was something serendipitous about seeing the spirit today, then meeting a living man who looked almost identical to him. I just had to assume my ghost friend had wanted me to meet this guy. I wondered if we were looking at some kind of relative, maybe a descendant.

It took me a moment when I saw the man on the path to realize this wasn't my ghost. I mean, you could tell the difference. Spirits were often translucent or had a feeling about them that often caused you to feel off... maybe even a bit afraid... and people, well, they didn't, they were just there.

Just to be sure, I turned and asked the guy if I knew him. Of course, I didn't, but when he responded like a living person, I knew I had a live one on my hands—pun intended...

What really threw me was when I was sitting below the mine ruins. The spirit was sitting next to me, even trying to talk to me, although I wasn't really able to hear him, then the guy came up, and for a moment, I was in both their presences at once. That was a new experience for me.

Luckily, my spirit friend decided to take his leave, and I didn't have to try to pretend like he wasn't there. I'd rather avoid any discomfort if anyone figured out my secret while on the job. For the most part, I'd kept my secret hidden my entire adult life. My mom and dad were always skeptical, and in middle school when I'd been plagued by a kid who'd drowned in the school pool, I'd been sent to therapy. At one point, even put on medication following a diagnosis of schizophrenia.

I learned from then on to keep my abilities a secret. I knew I didn't have schizophrenia, because, well, every time I saw an entity, I could do a minimum amount of research and find the person's history. Schizophrenics saw things that weren't there, not entities that existed in historical reality.

I was deep in my own thoughts, when the man came around the old building left standing at the mine, and asked me if I was ready. I shrugged. "I'll need to come back when I'm researching the area for documentation, but for now, yeah, let's go."

"I'm Dr. Steve Fowler," I said, and stuck my hand out. "But, Steve's fine."

"Eric Anderson, no Ph.D., I'm afraid."

I smiled at him. "Just a few more years of school and a ton more writing, and that title can be yours too."

He shrugged. "Hasn't seemed worth it for me yet. Besides, I thought I was going to be a high school teacher until I was let go, so a Ph.D. seemed like overkill."

"The field of history can be difficult. There aren't many jobs out there unless you want to teach or do research, and even if you do those, our jobs often depend on grants, and it appears you already know the precarious nature of that firsthand."

"Unfortunately, I do."

"Weren't you under a contract?" I asked. "Usually, high school teachers are protected for the entire school year."

"No, I worked in a charter school, and because I was paid directly through the grant, my terms of employment were those of the grant. So, I sort of knew the end was coming. I was just hoping it'd get renewed, or the district would provide the money to prolong the position at least until the end of the year."

"I see," I said, and I did. I always worked through grant funding. Even this job was based upon the grant process. I'd helped write the grant myself, and I'd only just begun the project, but once it was done, I'd either have to have a new grant started, or I'd be out of a job.

"Welcome to the wonderful world of grants," I said, and we both laughed in understanding and shared misery.

We finally made it to where I'd parked my car, and when he climbed into the passenger seat, I asked, "Are you wanting to keep teaching?"

He shrugged. "Honestly, I don't know any longer. I enjoyed it, but it's all-encompassing, especially working in the inner city. I often felt like a therapist more than a historian." He thought for a few moments, and said, "I'd have to go back to school to get a teaching certificate, neither the grant nor the school I worked at had required it. But, I doubt there'll be any more grants like the one I've just finished, it was sort of a one-off. If I want to teach at the university, I'll have to go for that Ph.D. like we were talking about earlier, but I don't really know what I'll do with that either. The truth is, I'm on a fact-finding mission. I'm looking for facts that will tell me what the hell to do with my life now."

I nodded my understanding as we pulled onto the main road and up toward Panther Junction.

"It took me a long time to find my footing, and I knew archeology was the field for me. I enjoy the intricate elements of the work, even the digs, although that isn't my strongest skill. I tend to do better on the research side of things, and I've always enjoyed writing."

"Have you been published?" he asked.

I hated this part. People were always easily impressed when I told them my background and who had published me, so I tended to minimize my success.

"Yeah, I've had a few things published."

The man looked at me for a moment, then shook his head. "I just put it together, you are Dr. Fowler from the Institute of Historic Research and Preservation. You were a major hero of one of my college professors. He used your journals on European history instead of a textbook."

I didn't know what to do, other than shrug. "I'll just apologize now and get it out of the way."

He laughed. "No, I enjoyed them. I wrote my master's thesis on how the dissolution of Roman occupation had a direct influence on the world wars."

I looked at the man, trying to piece together how he justified that. I agreed that Rome influenced and continued to influence modern Western culture, but even I would have to stretch to tie the world wars to the ancient culture.

"How did your thesis come out?"

"I received honors," he said smugly, and then laughed. "But it was a war proving my point with the committee. Ultimately, it was your journals that linked Rome and their organized war machine to the way Europe has evolved over the centuries that gave me my pass, so thank you."

I shook my head. "It's an outlandish theory, and I've had my most ruthless criticism come from that journal, so don't thank me, just be ready to defend yourself if anyone ever gets access to that paper."

He laughed. "Warning noted," he said. "Although, I seriously doubt anyone will ever read that thesis again. Hell, at this point, I don't know if I could easily put my finger on it, at least not without digging through a storage unit."

It felt good to just chat with someone. It was rare that I found another person interesting enough to want to indulge in small talk with. More often than not, I felt uncomfortable with others, and that usually came from fear of someone finding me out, but this guy was easy to be with. It felt as if he was naturally laid back, which caused me to think again of the entity he looked so much like. Maybe having spent time with him had helped smooth the transition to the living version. Either way, it was enjoyable to hang out.

When we got to the visitors' center, we walked in and he reserved his place at the campsite. As I guessed, it was still available. One of the rangers, Kyle Smith, who'd shown a great deal of interest in my project, cornered me with several questions.

The ranger was young, probably no older than mid-twenties.

When Eric came over, I introduced him to the ranger. "Mr. Smith, this is Mr. Anderson. He is considering working as my volunteer assistant."

I noticed the young ranger blush a bit, and it hit me. I'd been missing some obvious signs that he might be interested in more than my knowledge of history. Eric seemed to notice as well, and politely excused himself, walking over to the books.

"It's always a pleasure, Mr. Smith," I said, and made a mental note to figure out how to avoid the man from now on. I liked men, and although I never embraced any labels, when the urge for companionship struck me, it was always a man's company I sought. But this guy was not my type. Rugged, bearded, young. No, when I pursued a guy, which was like maybe once a month, if that, I looked for sleek, smooth, and dare I say delicate? I looked over at where my assistant-to-be Eric was standing and thought, *Yeah, like that.*

I felt my face redden as I realized I'd just had a sexual thought about a guy I'd just met. I looked at him again, and my blush deepened. Oh yeah, I was totally thinking of him like that. Maybe his volunteering was a bad idea after all. I was in no position to date someone. Fucking a stranger when the urge was too strong to resist, that was okay, but one look at Eric Anderson, and I knew that was not what he was about.

I erased the fleeting thoughts of lust and tried to focus on reality. This wasn't the first time I'd worked with someone I'd taken a sexual interest in, and having pursued that once was enough to cockblock any future thoughts on the matter.

23

4

Eric

THE TENSION BETWEEN US shifted on the walk to Steve's car from the mine. I could've been knocked over with a feather after discovering this was the guy I'd referenced when writing my thesis. I searched my memory of Dr. Fowler, and remembered he was a sort of protégé. He'd been homeschooled, so he graduated early from high school, then he finished his Ph.D. before he was twenty-one. It had been quite a big deal in academic circles, and my professor harped on about how talented and gifted he was as a historian. My classmates and I had laughed thinking our professor had a bit of a crush on the man. Now that I saw him, I understood why someone could. He was what you'd call academic looking, about the same height or just a little taller than me, but broad shoulders and a strong chin. He wore glasses, which gave him a professor look, but he was younger than I expected him to be.

My mom was a serious Doogie Howser fan back in the day, and as a result, we were forced to watch reruns from time to time. Steve had that same kid-turned-professional look about him. He looked to be about thirty, but he had the credentials of a fifty-year-old. Yeah, it would do me a lot of academic good to work with him, even if it was as a volunteer, but since we were probably about the same age, it might also be nice to have a buddy that shared my love of history just to hang out with.

Flex and Eddie were engrossed in their own stuff, not to mention relationships, and I was lonely. So, if the good doc was willing to let me shadow him, then I considered myself lucky on all fronts.

I had to really work at not smiling when the young ranger began flirting with him. I couldn't quite see the young Grizzly Adams—yeah, my parents made me watch reruns of that too, this time, my father being the culprit—and the professor looking good together. But, you know, opposites do attract, and maybe it would work out. Once I got to know Steve better, it might be fun to tease him about it. Would we be those kinds of friends?

I was overthinking things again and I hated being needy. Friendships had always been important to me, well, relationships in general. I thought that was why it hurt so much that my father and brother had dropped me from their lives.

Over the holiday, I'd found out my brother Keith had moved in with dad. It stung that they hadn't told me about it. But what really hurt was finding out my dad was dating a woman, and they were serious enough that she'd moved in too. When I confronted them about them not communicating with me, they got mad. "You're the one who left," my brother had said.

I'd been reeling since then. I made a point of calling my dad and brother once a week since I'd moved away, but clearly that hadn't been enough.

I was also hurt that Flex and Eddie hadn't confided in me about their relationships and how they'd progressed. Yeah, of course, I knew that was as much about their lives being insane. I'd flown down when Eddie called me about Flex being shot and had stayed with them for a week afterward. Eddie had been good about texting during that time, but he'd been in El Paso and had better coverage. After he moved back to the ranch, the texts and communication slowed down, eventually stopping altogether.

I'd allowed myself to get caught up in my own life too, and now that all that had come crashing down, I felt estranged.

I pulled into the tent space that was just off to the right of Steve's RV. When I got out, he invited me in to show me his home.

It was impressive. He had a nice desktop computer set up on a custom-built cabinet that looked like it might have replaced the original table. There were books everywhere you looked, which felt right for a college professor, even in the modern day.

He'd turned the captain's chairs around, and they worked as nice living room furniture. I hadn't been in many RVs in my life, but this was much better than I would've ever expected.

"Do you want a glass of tea?" he asked.

"No thanks," I replied. "Too hot for tea."

He chuckled. "It's iced tea."

"Oh," I replied. 'Sure."

He opened a refrigerator and poured us both a glass. I was curious. "I didn't see electrical hookups outside, how do you have electricity?"

"I have solar panels on the roof, and a generator I can use to charge my batteries up at night, in case the solar doesn't do the job for me."

"So, even out in the middle of the desert, miles from civilization, you have electricity?"

He nodded. "Thankfully... I don't love roughing it."

"Went into the wrong field then, didn't you?" I asked sarcastically.

"You'd think so, but then I have this," he said gesturing around him.

"Have you taken this to any dig sites?" I asked.

He nodded again. "Yeah, I've surveyed a few mound builders' sites throughout the Southeast of the US, and they didn't have... well, anything, but I could park this up close to the worksites. It was very convenient, since my colleagues were often sleeping on the ground, or had to drive to motels in the area."

I chuckled. "I'm sure you were popular."

He smiled back. "Actually, my RV often became the head-quarters, so yeah, I made friends fast."

He invited me to sit across from him at the desk that extended from the wall and handed me a form. I'd seen similar ones. Basically, it released everyone under the sun from liability in case I was injured. I read through it while he waited. "Pretty boilerplate, huh?" I asked, and he nodded.

I signed it and handed it back to him. He immediately went over to his printer, made me a copy, scanned it, then emailed it to what I assumed was his main office.

"You are official," he said. "Let the grunt work begin."

I laughed. "So, what first?"

He sat back across from me. "Well, you need to brush up on your Late Paleo and Archaic periods. Our first adventure will be to document a transition between the time this area was forested to when it became arid."

"How do we do that?" I asked.

"Well, it's tough, because since the area became a park, people have been stealing artifacts. They didn't make that illegal until the year I was born, so we are working with limited documented artifacts. But, I have my ways. That usually involves a whole bunch of research. We'll also need to access areas along the river that haven't been as corrupted by recent human occupa-tion. Once we've exhausted our research, we'll go knocking on doors."

I sighed, then smiled. "Okay, well, you said you have internet, so shall we begin?"

Steve pulled an old laptop out of a drawer and set it up for me. "You won't be able to do much on this, sorry, but it's what I've got. If you have a better one, feel free to bring it with you next time," he said.

We worked side by side for about an hour before he recommended we stop for the day. "I'd offer to make you dinner, but I usually eat cereal or oatmeal, I'm afraid. You may be better off driving into town."

I laughed. "Yeah, I usually carry a few protein bars with me when I'm out hiking, so I didn't really plan to eat anything extravagant myself. I am really careful what I pack in this area, because they do have bears, and I'd rather not wake up with one of them pillaging my pack."

"Very wise of you," he chuckled. "Come on then, I'll help you set up your tent."

It had been so long since I'd had someone who I just enjoyed hanging out with, and of course, that was making me feel a bit goofy. I came on too strong with people, it was just my nature. When I liked someone, I didn't follow social norms well. I was more likely to be direct, which more often than not made me come off as an asshole. I was working hard not to be a dick with Steve, though. I was sure someone as famous as him was constantly being bombarded with student admirers. For once in my life, I needed to stay cool, or at least not be so overbearing.

By the time we got the tent set up and a small fire going in the fire pit, we began hearing the sounds of the desert's wildlife start to emerge. "I'm glad I didn't bring my little poodle with me." I shivered as a coyote howled in the distance.

"Probably best," Steve agreed. "What kind of poodle?" he asked.

"Well, the vet says she's technically a standard poodle, but she's only sixteen inches tall, not small enough to be a miniature, but certainly not as big as most standards."

"I wouldn't have pegged you as someone with a poodle."

I laughed. "You were thinking of someone who was more 'prim and proper?'"

He laughed with me. "Well, you do think pedigree when you think standard poodle."

"Wait until you meet her. Puddles is not your typical poodle."

"Puddles?" he asked. "Puddles the poodle?"

"Hey, I didn't name her," I said in my defense. "There was a family who lived next to us in Portland. The little girl who initially owned her had cancer, and they simply couldn't take care of the dog any longer, but the little girl couldn't bear to lose her, so my wife and I volunteered to take her until the little girl got better."

"It isn't a story that's going to end well, is it?" he asked.

I sighed. "It was tough for everyone involved, but in the end, the family couldn't deal with their grief and the dog, so they just never picked her back up… well, after. Do you know dogs mourn just like people?" I asked.

He shook his head, the story sobering our conversation.

"This little dog just somehow knew when she'd passed. For weeks she refused to get out of bed, unless Lisa or I picked her up and took her out, and she refused to eat. I'm sure she'd have just died if we didn't force her to eat and drink. Even as we were pushing food into her mouth through a syringe, she was lethargic and barely swallowed."

"How did the family deal with seeing her in the neighborhood?" he asked.

"They didn't. After the girl passed, they sold everything and moved. She was their only child, and I think it pretty much destroyed them. One of our neighbors who'd been particularly close to Lisa told her they divorced soon after they moved."

'Yeah, that's sad," he said. "Death really affects everyone differently. And why wouldn't dogs grieve? Domestic dogs depend on their people for everything, from physical to emotional needs."

We sat silently staring at the fire and listening to the howls of coyotes in the distance.

"Where's your dog now?" he asked.

"She's staying at a dog groomer in Portland, until I figure out what I'm doing. They have a daycare as well as grooming. Puddles is spoiled rotten there, and I swear she'd rather be with them than with me."

He chuckled. "I've never had a dog. My parents were not fans of indoor animals, and we were in a small subdivision, so they said we didn't have enough property for a dog to run like it should be able to. As an adult, I spend all my time on the road, usually in this thing." He waved his hand around the RV. "So, I haven't gotten a dog as an adult either."

"I couldn't imagine life without a dog," I admitted. "After my divorce, Puddles was all I had. Maybe, because she understood grief as much as she did, she understood how sad I was. She'd cuddle with me for hours, night after night, until I began to crawl out of my depression. Had it not been for that contact with another creature, I think it would've taken a lot longer for me to recover. Have you ever been married?" I asked, before realizing I'd crossed a social boundary. "No, sorry, that's none of my business."

He smiled at me through the firelight. "It's fine, and no, I've never been married. I think it's hard for anyone to find a relationship when they travel as much as I do and being mostly attracted to men... well, that just adds another layer on top."

I nodded, thinking of the young ranger. "Well, there was a certain ranger who might be willing to try," I said, deliberately poking at my new friend.

"Yeah, today is the first time I figured out he was interested in more than just talking about the history of the park. It was rather awkward. Unfortunately, he isn't my type at all. Sweet guy, but seriously not for me."

"What is your type?" I asked.

He looked down bashfully, and I couldn't help but smile. The guy was shy.

"Well, let's just say not quite as... hairy," he said, but wouldn't look me in the eye.

Interesting, I thought. *Does this man like me? Do I like him?* If the heart zings were any indication, I probably did. *No!* I shook my head to get rid of the preposterous thought. He was embarrassed because I was picking on him.

We sat staring at the fire for a while before I went into my tent and pulled out two Clif Bars.

"My stomach is beginning to complain about being empty." I tossed a Clif Bar to him, and said, "Dinner's on me tonight."

He chuckled as he tore into it.

"What did we do before energy bars?" he asked.

"It's my understanding hard tack was the food of choice. Nothing like a little lard, salt, and flour to keep a person running on all cylinders."

"Geez, give me a Clif Bar any day," he said.

We tossed the remains of our snacks into the flames to rid ourselves of any food smells that might tempt the bears down from the Chisos Mountains.

The fire had died down enough that the stars were brilliant. "It's amazing to me how much brighter the stars appear from this area. I remember coming out here for the first time when I was a kid and looking up in wonder at them. My friends and

I would go lie on top of one of the sheds at their grandparents' ranch, and stare at them for hours."

When he didn't respond, I looked over at Steve and saw him staring at me. The look on his face made me blush. It wasn't a look you gave a new friend or acquaintance. It felt... hungrier.

I knew I was being a coward, but I pretended to yawn, and excused myself saying I was tired. However, once I lay on my sleeping bag, I'd admit, the man's expression of hungry desire stayed in my mind. I didn't think anyone had ever looked at me that way, and I was pretty sure I liked it. Too bad I was too chicken to act on it.

5

Steve

W ELL, I FUCKED THAT up. He'd probably be packed up and gone by tomorrow morning. He'd been upfront with me, telling me about his nasty divorce, and sharing his personal life like we were lifelong friends, then I all but fondled him with my eyes.

I had no idea what had gotten into me. Sure, I wasn't a stranger to my attraction to men. Hell, I'd been out with plenty of guys on dates, and many more had warmed my bed, but I just couldn't shake the feeling there was something special about this one. Not only the similar features between my astral visitor and him, but the warmth and friendliness that seemed to radiate from him.

As he looked up at the stars, I could see the long sensual lines of his neck. His Adam's apple slightly protruding as he leaned back. I could almost feel what it'd be like to let myself kiss him right there, then run my tongue up alongside that Adam's apple to his ear. Unfortunately, he looked at me just as I was contemplating what he'd taste like, and even in the dim light, any fool would be able to see I wanted him.

Not surprisingly, he did the straight-guy yawn and ducked for cover. It would've been funny if I didn't feel so fucking awful about it.

After he went to bed, I sat a while longer staring at the fire and kicking myself for having fucked things up so badly.

I was about to get up and go to bed myself, when I caught sight of something from the corner of my eye. When I turned to see what it was, I wasn't surprised to see my ghostly buddy had returned. He was too far away for me to see his expression, but I could feel that he was sad. I couldn't be sure why, of course, but it was probably to do with seeing someone who looked so much like him sitting with me.

Had Eric not been in a tent right next to me, I'd probably have invited the spirit over, but I needed to keep secret the knowledge that I could see and speak with people on the other side of the veil. I ignored the spirit, and fetched the bucket of water I'd put aside and tossed it onto the flames, causing the fire to steam and hiss. When I turned back toward where I'd seen the ghostly figure, he was gone. Just as well, I wanted my bed and to wallow in self-pity because of my stupidity. Tonight wasn't a good night to hang with ghostly friends.

I assumed the next morning would be strange and awkward, but it was fine. Eric met me at the RV door demanding coffee. "Free labor requires free coffee. I should've handwritten that into the contract," he teased.

"Lucky for you, I have a Keurig," I replied, and went to turn the generator on. "My solar doesn't make enough electricity to handle coffee-making, and I didn't want to turn the generator on until I knew you were awake. It can be loud."

"If you're making coffee, you can turn it on and wake me up. I never complain where coffee is concerned!" he chuckled.

After we each had a cup, we got to work on the research. I showed Eric what I needed him to do.

My workspace was small, and Eric and I sat shoulder to shoulder as we perused reams of documentation. Occasionally, Eric would point out to me something he'd found in the research. For the most part, it was information I'd already had access to but I made a note of it, nonetheless. I'd need all the references I could acquire once I had some grasp on the sites and the events that occurred there.

More than once, we bumped shoulders as we worked, and each time it sent a spark through my system. It was almost painful to sit this close to a man I wanted to touch. Or... if I was honest... do a whole lot more than just touch.

He didn't seem to notice, however, and even though I was wound tight as a drum by the time lunch rolled around, he seemed laid back and happy. *Good enough*, I thought. Now, to use the move to the campground and dump station at Rio Grande Village as an excuse to spend some time getting myself under control.

I got the RV ready as Eric packed his tent. I pulled the RV up and attached my car to the back, encouraging Eric to follow behind me. "You can find a tent site when we get to the campground," I said. "It isn't very full right now, so you should have plenty to choose from."

Eric ended up pulling into a site right next to mine. It sat fairly far back from the river, which I guessed was good for flooding, but I really would've preferred to be right on the water. The Rio Grande was a lovely surprise as it ran through the desert.

When Eric came in after I finished setting up and putting out my slides, I shared with him how I liked the area for getting a perspective of the time we were studying. Without the river, we'd never be able to grasp the feel of a forest in this region. Even with the river, it was strange there were trees here.

"Did they plant trees like this on the Mexican side?" Eric asked.

I shook my head. "I honestly don't know. I don't think so, and if they did, they aren't there now. It does seem the Mexican people were better prepared to accept the land as it is. Unlike the Anglo-Americans who seemed to be hell-bent on forcing the land to conform to their needs, like they did in this area."

"Would you say that's because Spain has so many arid areas?" he asked.

"Again, you have me on that. It might be worth doing some research and making the argument, if you want to pursue an anthropological comparison between the two colonizing countries, Spain and England," I said, letting my mind think about the varied Spanish landscapes.

"Let's stick to this project for now," Eric teased. "I'm guessing you've got more than enough work to keep me busy for the time being."

"Speaking of," I said. "I was wondering how long you planned to be in the area."

He sighed. "To be honest, I can probably afford to be here until the middle of next month. After that, I need to collect my belongings, close my storage unit, and pick up my dog. I also need to get a job," he added.

"Money is always such a buzzkill," I remarked, which caused him to chuckle.

"You can say that again," he replied cheerfully.

"I have a phone call in fifteen minutes," I told him. "You can walk down the trail next to the campground to get to the water. If you haven't spent time on the river before, you'll be surprised at how amazing it is."

He smiled. "I spent a lot of time on and in the Rio Grande," he admitted. "My friends Flex and Eddie's ranch runs right along the edge. Most of it is co-opted with the state as a protected site and part of the state's wildlife preserve, but they have full access to the property, and when we were kids, we'd go down there and play."

"That sounds cool. I wouldn't mind having the river to myself for a while. I always feel... invaded in the park, even in the slow months. It seems there are always people in boats floating down, visiting, or swimming in the river."

"Again, once their guests are done with the ranch, I'll be happy to set up a time for you to meet them. At the moment, they're hosting a film company who're doing some kind of film about the national parks separated by the Rio Grande and the international line."

"Really?" I asked. "That sounds interesting and challenging."

He chuckled. "I'm sure it is, but the film's producer seems to have it under control. The fact the property sits right next to the park helps; I think. They can film without having to deal with all the red tape and tourists in the park."

"I can imagine," I said, remembering all the red tape involved in getting permission just to survey and record the historical elements of the park, and I was part of a grant *from* the Department of the Interior that ran the park.

Eric took the walk I suggested down to the river, while I took my phone call. I was excited the conversation with the Mexican archeologist gave me something to go on. The Mexico City museum did have significant data about the people who lived here after the Ice Age, but I'd have to travel there to get access to the documentation. The information wasn't online, and they weren't too keen on letting people know what they had. I'd be able to go through it, but only if I was discreet about the artifacts and archeological knowledge.

Once again, I was struck by the nuances between the two countries. I couldn't blame them for keeping their documentation of the borderlands a secret. The US was known for being a bully when it came to things they determined were rightfully theirs. I walked a thin line politically as I perused this part of the research, and I'd have to protect my relationship with Mexico if I ever hoped to work with them again, even if secrets hampered my documentation and research.

I was warring with a headache as I contemplated these issues, when Eric knocked on my door. "Come in," I said, massaging my temples.

"What's wrong?" he asked.

"Oh, nothing, just trying to work through political strife between two governments," I admitted.

"Ouch," he replied, and then came over and put his hands on my back. "I'm pretty good at this if it doesn't make you uncomfortable."

I assumed he meant a back rub, and I just nodded. "I'd be stupid to say no." He chuckled behind me as his hands began to massage my shoulders. "Dear God, that feels good. I forget how good a massage feels, so I never get them. Maybe once I finish this part of the work, I can go have a full body massage."

I could feel him smiling behind me, even though he didn't respond. As his hands moved along my tense muscles, I all but fell asleep. I'd put my elbows on the desk and allowed my head to rest on my hands as he worked.

When he moved from my shoulders to my neck, I moaned. If I'd been thinking, I'd have realized I sounded very sexual as he worked my muscles over. He pulled my head back then, and let me rest my head on his stomach as he worked my scalp and temples.

"Dear God, I could die now and go happy," I said.

He didn't respond, so I cracked an eye open. He was staring at me as he worked, and the look he was giving sent shivers through me and struck me right in the crotch.

I reached up and put my hand on his, stilling him.

"Eric, this might be a bad idea," I said. "I like you and want this to be a long-term working relationship, but if you keep touching me, I'm afraid I'm going to want to pursue something else entirely."

Eric moved to the chair beside me and turned the seat, so we were facing one another.

"I'm not afraid of pursuing that option too," he said. "But, I'm vulnerable right now. I can't promise if we get involved with each other in that way, I won't run away tomorrow."

Excitement coursed through me with the realization that Eric would consider something... anything with me. But, I didn't want to be a jerk either. So, I forced myself to be calm as I responded. "I get it, and I don't want you to be uncomfortable, but I need to be upfront. There's something about you that... well, let's just say, there's something about you."

Eric smiled. "Let's throw caution to the wind, shall we?" he asked.

All I could do was nod as Eric leaned over toward me and moved his hand to the back of my neck, pulling me into a kiss.

I was ready for the disappointment I tended to feel when I kissed another man. Usually, kisses with previous partners were just a formal step that got in the way of the sex. How fast could we get the other stripped and fucked.

That wasn't the case with Eric. His kiss was electrifying, but below the sexuality, there was something different, something more.

I let myself go with it, allowing the man to lead the charge, to push the energy levels up. My cock was pressing against my jeans, and I desperately wanted to take control, pushing him back and into my bedroom. I wanted to feel his skin next to mine, to take him and use him.

My instincts told me to take it slow and allow him to take this at his speed. I wasn't disappointed by his interest. As his mouth explored mine, he began to tug at my shirt, lifting it up and over my head as his hands moved across my torso.

Eric embraced me and lifted me up, continuing to kiss me as he did. I was slightly taller than him, but that just made it feel better, more right somehow.

When we got to my bed, I stumbled and fell on my back as Eric crawled on top of me and kissed my neck.

As I moved away from him to scoot up fully onto the bed, he lifted his shirt off and undid his jeans, tossing them to the side. When he moved up me again, he ground his underwear-clad cock into mine, and began to kiss my nipples, then softly nibbled at them, sending shockwaves through my entire body.

This felt different from my other sexual encounters. More sensual, more attentive. He wasn't desperate to get to my cock, rather, he seemed to be enjoying the foreplay.

I had to fight the urge to throw him on his back and fuck his tight little ass into the bed. I wanted this man like I hadn't wanted another in a very long time.

I was about to say something to that effect, when Eric began to slip my pants and underwear off of me. When he tossed my clothes onto the floor next to the bed, he came back over me and took my cock into his mouth.

"Oh fuck..." I said, causing him to chuckle.

I moaned as his amazing mouth explored my cock. He began licking my balls and jacking me off at the same time, and I knew if he didn't stop, I was going to blow here and now.

I stopped him before I did, and gently pushed him back on the bed. "I don't want to come too fast, not before I can taste you too," I said, and he smiled back at me.

I immediately pushed my face into his underwear. He smelled very male, a scent that caused my heart to beat faster. I pulled his underwear down then and assaulted his cock, giving into my pent-up desire for him.

He moaned and arched his back into the bed. I decided I wanted to hear him moan louder. I wanted to make him to lose control, so I sucked him deep into my throat, and swallowed.

That had the desired effect, and he yelled out, "Fuck, oh fuck, yeah! Shit. I didn't know it could feel like this." I moved up so his mouth would have access to my cock and began to suck him again. He immediately got the idea and began sucking me off as well.

He tried the same maneuver I'd just done on him, and he gagged and choked. I pulled back and smiled at him. "Easy there, buddy, that's an expert move," I teased.

That seemed to spur him on. He took me deep again, and this time swallowed as I'd done to him. When he didn't gag, he pulled back and winked at me before drawing me in and doing it again.

"Fuck, that feels so..." I stammered when he began to deep throat me.

"Oh God," I cried as I lay back, enjoying the sensation of him taking me so hard and so fast.

"Eric, I'm gonna come," I said, and pushed his head back so I didn't assault him when I unloaded.

He knocked my hand away and pushed my cock deep into his throat, and when he lifted back up, I shot inside his mouth, shuddering as the orgasm poured over me.

I looked down as he pulled back and, using his finger, pushed the last of the cum into his mouth.

"That was... that was... fuck, that was awesome," I said.

He smiled at me, and I was glad I hadn't overwhelmed him.

"My turn," I said. This time, I pushed him onto his back, and more aggressively than I had before, I assaulted his cock.

It didn't take long for him to begin to crest as I used my finger to play with the sensitive area below his balls.

"Oh shit, oh fuck, I'm coming..." he managed to say as he ejaculated into my mouth. I was amazed at how much cum could come out of anyone. He just kept coming and coming, until he shuddered twice.

"Shit... oh fuck..." he said as he emptied into my mouth.

I moved up and rested my body next to his. Damn, if that wasn't some of the best sex I've had in a while!

6

Eric

I HONESTLY SHOULD'VE SAID no and forced myself to leave when the massage switched from me wanting to help, to me really wanting to do more. I wasn't in the frame of mind to be fucking anyone, but I was lonely, and Steve was so handsome, so kind, and we'd hit it off so well.

Making love, and yes, that's what I'd done with him, was so amazing, so touching that I was left feeling wrung out emotionally.

When Steve looked at me with those delicious, kind eyes, I lost my shit. "Fuck," I said as I scrambled to get out of bed. I couldn't believe I'd just turned a friendship into a freaking relationship—again!

Steve looked confused and upset, and that just made me more mortified.

"I'm an idiot, Steve," I said, "I'm an emotional basket case. I shouldn't have dragged you into this."

I was pulling my clothes on when Steve got up and gently pulled me into an embrace. "Hey, it's okay," he said, stroking my back. "You don't have to be freaked out. Everything's fine," he said, and continued to hold me.

I should've pulled away then and left, but instead, I let this man I'd just met hold me and nurture me in a way I'd needed from my family and friends.

When he pulled back, he used his thumb to wipe away the tears that were streaming down my face. "Tell me what's happening," he said, comforting me.

I shook my head. "I've had so much shit going on. Divorce, family stuff, friends all coupling up, and losing my job, and even my home. I just..." I couldn't continue. It was mortifying to have such an amazing sexual experience, then turn it into a pity fest. I laughed, wiping at the tears. "I'm too much of an emotional mess to get involved, not that you wanted to get involved," I said, trying not to sound like one of those crazy people who thought a tryst in the hay meant marriage. "You probably want me to go, and I probably need to."

I began to pull away when Steve put his hands on my shoulders, and gently held me in place.

"I'll tell you what I want, and you don't have to worry about my feelings, okay?" he asked, and I nodded. "I've been in emotional slumps in the past, and I get it. You don't have to be embarrassed with me. I like you, and I like what we just did. In fact, as soon as you feel up to it, I'd like to do it again."

Steve smiled at me then, and I couldn't help but smile back, even though I was still feeling self-conscious.

"I'm going to be here for a few more days before I have to go down to Mexico City. Let's hang out and see what happens professionally and personally. Does that sound good?" he asked.

I nodded, still trying to work out my emotions, but I liked the idea of having someone to cuddle with and make love to, instead of feeling so alone. I thought the fact that he had to leave in a few days made this more bearable. I could play sexual partners with him, then if things were over when he left, I could go on my way, and we could part having enjoyed each other while it lasted.

"Yes," I finally said. "That's perfect... but I still wanna help with your research. I'm really enjoying that."

He nodded and pulled me back onto the bed with him. I rolled over and he spooned me, holding me from behind as I snuggled into him. The physical and emotional comfort almost caused me to lose it again, but I'd embarrassed myself enough for one day, so I stemmed the tears, and before I knew it, I was out.

I heard the soft breathing behind me when I woke, and Steve's arms still held me as he slept.

I allowed the feeling of being embraced and feeling loved—even if it was by a stranger—to linger as long as I could.

I drifted in and out of sleep as we lay there. When I finally heard him stir, I pulled away from him and sat up.

When I turned around, the man, who was sexier than anything I could imagine, was staring at me with his sleepy eyes, then smiled and asked if I slept well.

"Better than I'd have thought. I don't usually sleep well in my tent, so I was already tired."

"I didn't sleep well last night either, but it was because I thought my giving you googly eyes was going to chase you off."

I laughed. "Apparently, it didn't," I said smiling.

I leaned over and kissed his mouth, and before I knew it, he pulled me closer, deepening the kiss and melting my bones.

When he reached down and began playing with my ass, I froze. "Um, sorry, I've never done that before," I admitted.

"No problem," he said, and rose above me, reaching over to a small drawer next to his bed, and pulling out lube and a condom. "You ever been a top before?" he asked.

"Um, yeah, I was married," I said, feeling my face blush.

He chuckled. "Ever topped with a guy?" I shook my head, then he leaned down, and whispered, "Wanna try it?"

I nodded vigorously cause, *fuck yes*, I wanted to try it.

He rolled the condom onto me, all the while whispering how beautiful I was to look at, and how much he wanted my cock inside him.

After he lubed my cock, he straddled me, and reached behind himself to line my cock up with his ass.

Within moments he began to slide my cock inside him.

"Oh, fuck," I said. "You're so tight. Fuck, that's amazing," I moaned

I had no idea what anal sex entailed, but I knew this was beyond amazing. I began to buck inside him, and he held my hips down, smiling. "You gotta give me a minute to get used to it. It's been a while for me."

I nodded, but it was taking everything in me not to just fuck into him, savoring the tight feeling around my cock.

He worked himself up and down a few times before he sat down, taking me fully into his ass.

"Oh, fucking hell, that's so... that's so..."

He smiled mischievously and asked, "Hot?"

I nodded as he lifted up this time and began to fuck himself on my cock, slowly at first, then picking up speed.

He released my hips, and demanded, "Now fuck me, Eric, fuck me hard."

He didn't have to ask twice, my libido took over, and I slammed my cock into his tight ass as hard as I could.

"Yes, that's it," he hollered out. "Yes, fuck me, Eric."

I did as he commanded, not like I had a choice. This was truly the most amazing sensation I'd ever experienced.

When he crawled off me, I thought I might cry. *No, it can't be over so soon, not when...*

I was about to whine when he got onto all fours. "Now, fuck me like this."

"Yes," I said, and immediately crawled up behind him, putting my cock up to his ass and slowly massaging his guardian muscle with the head.

He moaned, and that sensation was enough for me to ache with need.

My head penetrated him again, and I moved slowly this time, not wanting to hurt him, but as I was gliding in the second time, he reached behind him, grabbed my hip, and thrust me inside.

"Now!" he demanded.

I pushed into him, letting my cock rest there for a moment, before I pulled back and thrust inside again.

His moans just pushed me to be more aggressive, demanding more and more from him. I'd honestly never felt anything so intense as I did fucking Steve in the ass. He was tight, and at the same time, responsive to my thrusts.

I pounded into him. I'd never felt more like a caveman, like someone who had no control over their actions. All I could think of was this man and his fucking tight ass.

I was about to come when I leaned to the side. Steve arched up. "Yes, that's it! Fuck me there!"

I wasn't sure what I'd done, but I continued thrusting in that position until he emptied onto his bed. I'd had lots of sex with my wife, but I'd never felt a sensation so amazing as I did with this guy. When he came, he clenched down on my cock, making the intensity of his tight hole something impossible to explain.

I reacted immediately by coming into the condom as I rode the pleasurable sensation.

I collapsed over his back, and we stayed like that for several moments before I pulled the rest of the way out and collapsed on my back, staring up at the ceiling.

Steve fell next to me, leaned up on his shoulder, and asked if I was okay.

"Oh, no, I may be ruined for life. I didn't think sex could feel so…" It took me a moment to find the words. "I didn't know sex could feel so amazing."

Steve smiled at me. "Anal sex is pretty amazing."

"Now I know," I said, then pulled him on top of me and into a deep kiss.

"Let's do it again," I said happily, and Steve winced.

"Not for a while, I'm afraid. It'll take a moment for me to recover."

I frowned, then asked, "How does it feel?"

"It's amazing, if you do it right."

"Really?" I asked. "Can you show me?"

"Sure, when you're ready, but don't force it. My first time was a bad experience, and I didn't have anal sex for a long time because of it. You'll know when it feels right, and when it does, I'll promise to make it feel perfect for you."

I nodded and rolled over and let him pull me back into a spooned embrace.

The next few days were perfect. We worked during the day... well, mostly, but we did a lot of other stuff too. I could honestly say I'd never been this sexually active in my entire life, not even with my wife.

I couldn't seem to keep my hands off this man, and he was just as into it as I was.

We hiked the area scoping out sites Steve said he had to make a note of and survey, and he'd ask me to make observations.

"What makes this a historic site?" he'd ask.

When we first started, I honestly couldn't tell, but he had a keen eye. He'd point out the most obvious things first. "Notice how we are on a ridge above the river, so we'd avoid being caught in a flood, but also remember West Texas, and especially Big Bend, was a forested area at that time, so we want to look for clues as if we were in an eastern part of the country.

Then, he'd point toward more detailed parts of the site. He'd show me signs of earlier humans, such as the arrowhead that was located in the area. "We know it's here, because the rangers documented it," he said when we were at one point along the river.

"If you look at the arrowhead, it has fluted points which are longer and rounder than those from the Archaic period. This tells us the Clovis people were here, so of course, we call these arrowheads Clovis points...

Listening to the man talk was fascinating. It was almost like he had a personal relationship with the people who lived here then.

Steve made me feel included and wanted all at the same time. I knew he was renowned in historical societies, yet he embraced me as an equal. The time I spent with him was balm to my emotional wounds.

After moving the RV down the service road deep into the countryside, not far from the latest site Steve was cataloging, we made a fire, and laid out our blankets on the ground next to it.

It wouldn't do to sleep out here all night, since it still got pretty cool. We had learned that the hard way after finding three tarantulas in our blankets the morning after we fell asleep under the stars. Regardless, there was nothing more wonderful than lying on the ground next to Steve as we stared up into the heavens.

Steve was leaving the next day, and I was doing my best to ignore the sadness I was feeling. Neither he nor I had spoken about it, but it was clear this was a big parting. When, I couldn't ignore the inevitable any longer I finally said, "So, tomorrow is coming fast," causing him to turn toward me.

"Yeah, are you okay?" he asked.

I laughed. "I'm a big boy, Steve, but I'll be sad to see you go."

Even though it was dark, I could tell he was nodding. "I'll miss you too," he said, and snuggled close to me, laying his head on my chest.

I ran my fingers through his hair, enjoying how silky it felt. Steve leaned up on his elbow and looked at me. The fire painted his face in a warm orange glow and the reflection of the flames in his eyes made them dance.

He moved up my body and cupped my face with his hand, then kissed me. "I'm really gonna miss you."

I rolled him over, and seeing there was a different kind of fire in his eyes, I worked my hand down his torso and into his pants. He was hard and throbbing. I wrapped my fingers around his thick cock and gave it a squeeze.

"Show me," I said.

Steve undid his pants while my hand kept hold of his cock. He yanked his pants and underwear off, then pushed me back and straddled me, allowing me to lie on my back as he fucked my mouth.

This was one of my favorite ways to give him a blowjob. The ecstasy of allowing him to use my mouth for his enjoyment brought me to the edge.

He pulled out of my mouth and after jerking off his shirt, he slid his naked body down me, until his cock pushed up against mine still constrained by shorts.

"Get naked," he demanded.

I hustled to tear my clothes off, and when I'd finished, he rolled on top of me, grinding his hard cock into mine.

Naked under the stars, we kissed, licked and loved on each other that night.

Over our short time together, the sex between us had become stronger. It was hard to explain. It was just something greater than it had been before.

We lay there until it got too cold, then moved to his RV and made love again, before we fell asleep in each other's arms.

I woke up to the sound of Steve taking a shower. I got up, turned the generator on and made coffee. I turned my attention to the eggs and ham we'd bought at the local store near the campground.

By the time Steve stepped out of the shower, I had the eggs and ham cooking, and he took over while I climbed into the shower myself. It was incredible how in just days, we'd settled into a routine. It felt good and right, and way too fast. Well, maybe not for me, but it had to be disturbing for Steve.

We ate when I'd finished showering, then I followed him as he drove the RV to Alpine to store it while he was gone. I drove him to the airport, and kissed him as he prepared to board his plane. It was like we'd been married for years, and I was seeing him off for a business trip or something.

Even though the kiss was passionate, even though I knew we'd both enjoyed each other, I also knew this would probably be the last time I'd kiss him. When that plane took off, it ended the short love affair I'd so thoroughly enjoyed.

7

Steve

MEXICO CITY WAS EXCRUCIATING. Except for a weekend I'd spent in New Orleans, I'd never been confronted with as many otherworldly spirits. And, just like New Orleans, these spirits weren't shy. They were partying, and dancing through the streets. I could hear their music and feel their exuberance. Not all were playful and happy, though. There was darkness there as well.

The archeologist I met when I stepped off the plane was as exuberant as the entities, and ready to show me the town. If left to my own devices, I would've probably crawled under my bed and hidden until I was free to leave. Instead, I was traipsed all over the old part of Mexico City, which, if anyone asks, is by far the worst area in the fucking world for spirits.

Apparently, no one who died here left. There were conquistadors, Aztecs, spirits from all the ages, all occupying the streets that were already overcrowded with the living. The noise was unbearable. Usually, I didn't really hear the spirit world, but here it was different, everyone was speaking at once.

When we finally went into the Museum of Anthropology, the noise at least died down, but the hauntings didn't. Spirits clung to the exhibits, and more than a few were menacing. I could see many items had been protected by these entities long before they'd become part of the museum. I felt much of their anger and frustration regarding these items being removed from their original sites.

By the time I was in the archives, the spirit movement had minimized, and so did my senses. Señor Flores, my archeologist guide, showed me the multiple artifacts and documentation he had of Juarez. Most of the artifacts had been removed in recent years, and the documentation was thorough, allowing me to place the different eras.

Unfortunately, there wasn't much about the Big Bend area. When I questioned whether there were plans to explore the Native American sites in Canon de Santa Elena, I was quickly put off, which meant yes, they were considering it, and it was not something he was supposed to talk to me about.

Knowing how archeology worked, I doubted there would be any activity soon enough for me to look forward to. Maybe in fifty years, or so, they'd get around to it.

I did find a couple of fascinating accounts from a Mexican archeologist from the nineteen twenties who did site work on both sides of the Rio Grande. I assumed this was the stuff señor Flores didn't want me to share with the US government, as there were more than a few Clovis points as well as skeletal remains of bison.

I didn't want to hurt his pride any, but we already knew bison were one-time residents of the park. I'd have loved to be able to use the documentation about the Clovis points, but it wasn't worth instigating an international crisis over, so I didn't bring it up.

I did, however, want to use the archeologist's documentation from Canon de Santa Elena and planned to use it as a reference point to the Clovis culture, along with pictures of artifacts he'd collected on that side of the international line. I showed my guide, and when he nodded approval, I began taking photos of the work, as well as making notes.

Fortunately, using this research, I'd be able to make a much more definitive association with the culture using these artifacts than the one lone Clovis point the rangers told me about that I'd shown Eric just a couple days before.

The thought of the man I'd been working with, and having ridiculously wonderful sex with, filled me with lust and caused me to blush. Señor Flores must've taken that as a sign that I was concerned about the issues between the two governments, and quickly assured me there was no claim on that information except Mexico's, so I should be fine to use it. I nodded my thanks and was escorted out of the archives.

Señor Flores took me to one other exhibit in the museum, saying he was sure I'd be interested in it. I laughed when I saw what he wanted to show me and clapped the man on the back.

A couple years back, I'd become obsessed with linking the mound builders with Mexican Indians and had been at war with a few of my colleagues who said I was being overzealous in my assumptions. In the end, I was able to collect enough data to show that they were clearly trading up and down the continent.

The exhibit señor Flores took me to had several Mississippian artifacts, including the shell gorget I'd used in my research. I'd forgotten this and other artifacts that'd proved my point, were in this museum. I was thankful my guide had done enough research on my work to know I'd want to see this in person.

"¿Te gustaría tocarlo?" he asked.

I beamed. "Yes," I replied enthusiastically. "I'd *love* to touch it!"

We went behind the wall where the exhibit sat, and a guard was there waiting for us. He unlocked the display, and señor Flores took the gorget out and handed it to me. I was surprised they didn't required gloves before allowing me to handle it.

The second the artifact touched my hands, I saw the image of a young man sitting beside a river, carving the figurine. As quickly as the image came to me, it vanished.

"Muchas gracias, señor," I said, with as much sincerity as I could muster. The image caused me to become emotional, and again my response was probably misinterpreted as nostalgia over the artifact.

As we walked away, both my guide and the guard were smiling. I knew word would get out that seeing and touching the artifact had left the mysterious Dr. Fowler in tears. I didn't really mind. If they thought I was this passionate about artifacts, it could only help to improve my chances of getting to artifacts when I needed them in the future.

There were few words to express how happy I was to get back to West Texas. I almost crawled out of the plane and kissed the ground, knowing I'd escaped the spiritual chaos that was Mexico City.

My first thought was to call Eric, but I resisted. *Remember Mexico City*, I told myself. There was absolutely no way someone could've been with me on that trip and not figured out that I had the abilities that I did. It was simply impossible to hide my skill when there were that many spirits around.

Do you want this man to know you see dead people? I asked myself. No, the answer to that is no. You had a good break, let it be what it is.

I bummed a ride from a couple of college students who were going into downtown. That way, I avoided walking all the way back to the storage area where I'd kept my RV while gone. It was late, so I just stayed where it was stored, which was technically against the rules, but the owner told me as long as I didn't start up the generator, or something that drew attention to myself, it'd be fine until morning.

I lay on my bed, exhausted from the trip. *You're old enough now, you should have some grasp on dealing with these spirits,* I chastised myself. For the millionth time, I wondered why I couldn't just tune them out. Why were they such an intense part of me?

When I finally dozed off, I dreamed of strange-looking ghosts wandering around the RV, all staring at me. I felt for a moment like I was the museum exhibit, and the persistent staring was making me sweat.

When I woke up, I was drenched in sweat, but luckily there were no spirits staring at me. *Note to self, avoid Mexico City!* I needed to be back in the desert, back in the remote parts of the national park, where there were almost no spirits to plague me.

I got up, and even though it was the wee hours of morning, I made myself a cup of coffee, thanking the powers that be that I'd found a storage unit with fifty-amp electrical service to plug into.

I sat down at computer, then went through the different artifacts I'd photographed, and decided to spend the next few nights camping in the documented Clovis sites in the park. I'd have to let the Park Service know where I planned to camp, but since I already had permission from the Department of the Interior, I doubted they'd give me much trouble.

I thought again how nice it'd be to have Eric by my side keeping me company or making love to me under the stars. Memories of his perfect body flooded me. I quickly shook it off, though, using the excuse that if he were with me, I would certainly be unable to concentrate on the sites, and therefore, unable to *feel* anything that might still be there.

I ended up falling asleep as I sat in my chair, waking up to thoughts of Eric's body on mine. Unfortunately, even though the dream was a hundred percent better than the last one, I had a horrible crick in my neck from sleeping upright. I also had a hard-on that was giving me blue balls. I'd take care of one with my hand and the other with a good hot shower. Too bad Eric wasn't here with those amazing hands to work out the kinks. After fixing the blue balls problem, I ruthlessly forced thoughts of Eric out of my head.

8

Eric

ONCE I DROPPED STEVE off, I drove over to the ranch and found Flex. I wanted to see him before I left, having decided I'd rather begin the process of moving back here from Portland than sit around sulking because the best sex I'd ever had was with a guy I was almost sure I'd never see again.

I'd decided I was done with Portland, my ex, and all that was associated with that chapter of my life. I wanted to move back to be around friends while I figured out what was next in my life.

Flex was concerned about me driving back from Portland alone, and I told him I was more than capable of handling myself on the road. I planned to stop by a few of the other national parks on the way back, including Yosemite, Crater Lake, and Sequoia. He shrugged and told me I had to agree to text him every day, if not call, to keep him informed of my progress.

"Like you can get a text or a call out here," I teased him.

"You can try," he said. "Besides, I spend most of my time at Mitch's now anyway, at least until Alex is done filming."

I smiled. "You and Mitch are getting really close. When's the wedding?"

"Not everyone needs a wedding. Two guys can enjoy each other without wedding bells." I just looked at him until he laughed. "Damn, you know me too well. We're talking about it, but we've not made any plans."

I smiled. "I give it six months," I said as I walked out of the room.

Flex called me a jackass as I walked away, and I flipped him off. At least some things between us never seemed to change.

I spent the next couple of days tracking down a place to move my stuff into when I got back. After I went through the limited supply of rental housing in Alamito, I gave up and rented a large storage unit. Luckily, it was less than half the price of the one I was paying for in Portland, and it was at least twice the size.

I'd also set up with Mitch to stay in one of his extra RVs for the time being. The rent was more than affordable, and I could have Puddles with me as well.

I dropped my rental car off in Houston, after going over to try one more time to clean things up with my dad and brother, before leaving for Portland. Fortunately, I was booked to leave later in the day, because they both refused to see me. I ended up having a layover in Denver, then again in Seattle before finally making it to Portland. By the time we landed, I was beyond exhausted.

I'd left my Subaru Forester at the airport, so I stopped at the doggie daycare and picked Puddles up before going back to the business hotel I'd stayed at after Lisa got the house.

Puddles seemed happy to see me, which surprised me with as much as she loved the place. "At least someone missed me," I said as I let her kiss me on the nose.

Puddles and I snuggled into the full-size bed and watched TV like we tended to do when I got home. We both ended up falling asleep cuddled together. When I woke up, it was to her pawing, telling me she needed to go out. I'd forgotten the night before, so it was no surprise she'd woken me up in the wee hours of morning.

When I came back after taking her out, it was almost like I could feel Steve. I was sure he was awake and thinking about me, and if my reaction was any indication, he was thinking about me in very interesting ways.

"All in my imagination," I told Puddles as I crawled back into bed. All the same, I ended up thinking about him as I lay there. No, I wouldn't be calling him again. The ball was squarely in his court. If he wanted to see me, he needed to make the next move.

For some reason, I wasn't neurotic at the thought. It was going to be alright. I knew it was, and it didn't matter if Steve or any other love interest was a part of my life again. To be happy, all I needed were friends and a job I enjoyed. The rest would fill in as it was supposed to.

The trip from Portland to Alamito was long and even though I'd enjoyed parts of it, especially the national parks, a cloud of sadness seemed to accompany me the entire trip.

The sadness did have respites though, it had been amazing to see how different Yosemite and Sequoia were from Big Bend. It captured my imagination to think about the people who visited these landscapes, and knew the American public needed to preserve them for future generations.

By the time we pulled into Alamito, both Puddles and I were ready to be off the road. I ended up renting one of Mitch's nicer rooms for a few nights, just so Puddles and I had a chance to freshen up in style. The day after we arrived, I took the U-Haul to the storage place I'd rented and dropped off all my stuff. It never ceased to amaze me that our whole lives could be easily transferred into a few small rectangular boxes.

I'd ended up going over to Flex's for a visit one night, but Alex had been hurt, so Eddie was with him in El Paso. Flex and Mitch were mostly dealing with an upswing in business at the motel, and at the last minute he had to cancel, so I ate with only Emma Jean and Jimmy.

The meal was good, and Jimmy was, as always, full of life and colorful stories. I'd begun feeling more and more down during the past few days since I'd gotten back from Portland. It seemed like nothing felt right anymore.

"What's going on with you these days?" Emma Jean asked as I stared out into the distance.

"Oh, just, you know, figuring out stuff," I said off the cuff.

"And how are you really doing?" she asked.

I took a deep breath. "Well, besides my life being shit, both Flex and Alex almost dying... you know, good."

She looked at me from the corner of her eye, and I knew she'd have pried deeper, but the phone rang, interrupting her before she could. I took this as my opportunity to dash off the porch and say my goodbyes.

She'd seen too closely, and I didn't want to burden them with my pitiful emotions. The truth was, I was depressed. The world was feeling very dark and bleak. I'd felt depressed before, but I didn't seem to be able to snap out of this. I wasn't sure why, but it felt almost like I was dying but to be honest, I wasn't too upset about it. Dying didn't feel all that horrible to me, not when everything I cared about seemed to be out of my reach.

9

Steve

I WASN'T SURPRISED AFTER getting back to Big Bend that my ghost friend hadn't returned. I was almost certain he was somehow attached to Eric, both figuratively and spiritually. When I didn't reach back out to Eric, I got the distinct feeling the entity wasn't pleased with me.

I'd set everything up to spend the nights at the various Clovis sites, and had documented what I could about them. Unfortunately, very little spiritual activity remained. If the people of this area had died here, they'd crossed over long ago.

Even though I didn't always see spirits, I usually got a sense of the area, but even that was almost impossible here. It had been too long since these individuals had lived here, or maybe it was just because I was distracted. Either way, I was stuck using the more traditional ways to learn about the people, instead of any other senses I possessed.

With the help of the Museum of Anthropology, who'd decided to give me access to the information they had, I was able to write a fairly detailed account of the Clovis culture in the Big Bend area.

I was far from happy with my work. In fact, nothing I'd written hadn't already been discussed in detail prior to my research. However, I had no choice but to move on. The requirements of the grant were crystal clear. I was to write a brief description of the different eras, and each era had a very clearly defined timeline to meet.

As I began to dig into the Archaic period, it became significantly easier to find information about the cultures who lived here during that time. The Archaic period began as the Ice Age ended, and Big Bend became arid.

I had to admit, it was the era that most fascinated me about American prehistoric times. I was anxious to see how the shifting climate affected the people.

I began to think about Eric, and how he'd probably be able to help me individualize the process, help me look past the group, and see how it must have impacted the people who had, up until that point, lived in a lush environment.

I sat on an isolated mesa where a variety of artifacts had been found and documented by the National Park Service, one of the few areas that hadn't been pilfered prior to the 1970s. I could feel the people who'd lived here, connecting with them on a personal level. Like the Clovis, I didn't see any of the people who'd been here before, rather, I could conceptualize what it would've been like to be here, what it felt like to live here.

The people were happy, although confused about why the land was changing. I could feel religious beliefs forming during this time, but I didn't have a strong enough connection to understand what those beliefs had been.

As I dug into the era, the weeks swirled away from me, and I was confident my writing on the Archaic period would at least not embarrass me. I lay awake in my bed thinking about Eric. It had become a nightly thing since I'd returned to the area.

I was just wondering what he must be up to, when I felt a sick feeling in my stomach. Suddenly, my head was filled with images of the ghost that looked like Eric. He was in the cave, and the ceiling was falling in on him. I immediately knew Eric was in trouble.

I didn't think, or I'd have stopped myself from picking up my phone, but there was such urgency, I couldn't stop myself. I flipped the screen on, found Eric's number, and dialed.

I thought the phone was going to go to voicemail, but right before it did, Eric answered. There was wariness in his voice.

"Hello?" he asked.

"Hi... Hi, Eric, It's Steve. Are you okay?"

There was silence on the other end of the line then, "I'm okay, why do you ask?"

I was stuck, and I knew it. I'd let my emotions get carried away with the heat of the moment. What was I going to say now?

"Um, I had a really funny feeling about you. I was concerned."

Eric sighed. "Things just feel like... too much," he said.

There were no more questions about how I knew, just an acceptance that somehow, I did.

"Do you want me to come over? Where are you?" I asked.

Again, there was silence before he responded, his voice tentative. "Steve, I haven't heard from you... it's been weeks... why now?"

I didn't know how to respond. Honesty seemed the best route, but, obviously, not too much honesty.

"I think you need someone," I said, and held my breath.

"I do, but I can't..."

I let that sit, I knew what he was saying, and I deserved the sting I felt as a result. Although we weren't ever really more than a sexual fling, I knew Eric wasn't someone who played around sexually. Yet I'd treated him like he was just that.

"I'm sorry, I just didn't know what to say. I thought it would be better to let things go."

Eric sighed. "That was probably the right decision, Steve."

"Did you miss me?" I asked, letting the moment take me away.

Eric's breath caught a little, and I felt like an ass. "Yeah..."

"I know. It wasn't fair of me to ask. Are you still in this area?" The line was silent, but I knew he was nodding. "Okay, are you in the motel you were staying at before? The one in Alamito?"

Although I wasn't clairvoyant, I felt strangely connected to Eric. I guessed it was somehow spirit-related. Again, I could tell he was nodding. Although I trusted my intuition, I knew it would be too much to let Eric know I had that kind of connection. I waited until he responded in the affirmative, and I said, "I can be there in about an hour. Do you think I can stay with you when I get there? It might be too much to drive back in the dark."

"Yeah, I'm in the camper at site number three. You'll see a Subaru Forester parked in front."

I hung up and immediately grabbed my toothbrush, a change of clothes, and my toiletries bag. When I stepped outside, the ghost who looked so much like Eric, but had been missing since I came back from Mexico City, stood leaning against my vehicle.

"So, *you're* back, I see," I said accusingly.

The spirit stared at me with a blank expression, just watching me.

"I'm not going to hurt him," I said, and when the spirit's expression seemed to challenge me, I added, "Well, I'm not going to hurt him on purpose."

I walked to the driver's side of the car, ignoring the spirit, and got inside. When I turned the engine on, I looked to where he'd been standing, but I knew even before looking, he was gone. Well, his image was gone, but the feeling of displeasure that I'd not connected with Eric before now was certainly still there. I'd seen spirits attach themselves to relatives before, and although I didn't know who this guy was to Eric, he was protective of him. I guessed, if he was a long-lost relative, he would be.

I leaned back before driving to Eric. "Okay, I promise, I'll do a better job at communicating. Is that better?"

I saw a flash of the color blue out of my peripheral vision, and knew I'd been given a second chance.

"Thanks," I said as I pulled out and drove the hour to Alamito, and to the man I hadn't stopped thinking about since I'd last seen him.

My other senses had taken over, and I drove right up to Eric's camper without having to look for the signs. Something about him had clicked inside me, and I knew I could find him anywhere. I didn't take the time to analyze how. It scared me too much, and I was afraid if I looked too closely, I'd just run away and never return.

I knocked on the door, and Eric opened it. He looked exhausted.

I immediately pulled him into my arms. "Eric, what's wrong?" I asked, and he melted against me.

When he led me inside, I saw a bottle of pills sitting on the table. I instantly knew what that meant. I pulled his weary eyes toward mine. "Were you about to hurt yourself?" I asked.

Eric shook his head, but then in a quiet voice, said, "I was considering it, but I just couldn't. No matter how bad things are… it… it just didn't feel right."

He slumped into the camper's little dining booth, and let his head fall into his hands as silent sobs racked his body.

I scooted into the booth with him and held him against me. "It's okay. Most of us have been here at some point in our lives. I promise it'll get better."

He didn't look up, but rather snuggled into me, letting the tears take him.

When he seemed wrung out, I lifted him out of the booth and moved him toward the bed at the back of the RV. I helped him take his clothes off, folding them and putting them on a little chair in the corner of the room. I helped him into bed, undressed and slid in next to him. I didn't ask, but then again, I didn't need to. I was here because he needed me. Somehow, his spirit had called out to me, and I had heard him.

We slept curled into each other through the night. Occasionally, I'd wake up to him crying, but he never said anything, just lay there. His spirit was in tatters.

The next morning, I could feel something had shifted. Even before Eric woke up, I knew he was going to be okay.

I pulled away and went to the little kitchen to cook us breakfast. When we'd spent time together, he seemed to enjoy ham and eggs, and wasn't really fussy about how they were prepared.

By the time the ham was finished, he was leaning against the wall facing me.

When I faced him, he was flushed with embarrassment.

I went over to him, but before I could embrace him, he shook his head.

"I need a moment," he said, so I just stood facing him.

Finally, he looked up at me. "Thanks, I really needed you... err, someone last night. I don't know how you knew, but I'm glad you did."

I didn't respond. Instead, I continued standing in front of him, waiting for permission to hold him again.

Finally, he sighed and moved into me.

Holding Eric was like seeing the sun after being stuck in a cave for days—relief, warmth, and a strong feeling of right all wrapped into one person.

"Are you hungry?" I asked, wanting to give him a moment to catch his breath before we had to talk about the evening before.

He nodded into my chest, and I chuckled. "Good, I made a hell of a lot of food. You're probably going to need to go shopping again if you want any more breakfast food."

Eric chuckled against me, reassuring me he was much better today.

He slid into the booth and I put the plate, piled high with ham and eggs, in front of him, and inwardly cheered at the smile on his face. "You know the way to make a depressed man feel better, don't you?"

"I seem to recall something about the way to a man's heart is through his stomach. Maybe it's the same with depression."

Eric's face changed then, but I turned from him, piled up my own plate, and sat across from him.

"Wanna talk about it?" I asked.

Eric stared at his food, then shook his head. "Not until I eat this, then yeah, I can."

We ate in silence. I watched him, unable to take my eyes off of him. The connection that had linked us the night before seemed to pulse inside me. Had I known him longer, I would've called it love, but I couldn't be in love with a relative stranger, so I told myself to accept it as just a strong connection.

When he'd finished most of the food on his plate, he sighed. "Steve, I'm mortified and grateful all at the same time. Last night, things in my life came to a head. After you left, I went back to Houston and confronted my dad and brother about why they'd kept me out of the loop about their lives. My brother was so angry, and accused me of throwing them out of my life, how could I expect anything else?"

He looked at me and took a deep breath. "I didn't, I didn't throw them out of my life, but when I said as much, he admitted then that Lisa had told them to keep their distance. I had no idea she'd done that. I mean, if they'd told me, I'd have..." he shook his head. "I don't know what I'd have done. Lisa was hard to be around...

"Keith, my brother, told me I'd made my choice and that I should just leave them alone. I looked at my dad, and his face was as set and angry as my brother's.

"I'd lost, my wife, Flex almost died when he'd been shot, then Eddie's boyfriend was half dead, trying to survive. My life is in shambles, I have no family, my friends are fighting some war they're barely winning, and I'm no fucking help at all. Even my poor dog is sick of me."

I looked around the camper, and seeing no dog, I looked at Eric, and he shrugged. "She's with Mitch and Flex. I told them I needed a quiet night for myself, and they said they'd take dog duty for me."

I reached over and put my hand on his. "It's going to be okay. You just have a lot on your plate. Like I said last night, almost everyone's been where you are at some point in their lives."

He sighed. "I have to admit, concern for my friend's boyfriend was certainly something that bothered me, but I was really just jealous that he'd met someone he loved that much. I hate that my first reaction was jealousy and not happiness for one of my best friends, but I think that might've been the part that pushed me over the edge."

Eric looked like he could break down again, so I began rubbing his hand. "We all want a connection. You have no reason to feel guilty over that."

Eric looked over at the bottle that still sat on the top of the table but had been pushed to the back as we sat to eat. "I wasn't going to go through with it. I wanted to, don't get me wrong, but it felt so wrong. You'll think I'm nuts, but it was almost like my mom was standing here telling me to stop."

I looked around the room, almost expecting to see her here, but there was no one with us. Then, I remembered the spirit who'd definitely been the one to warn me, and almost told him it wasn't his mom but another ancestor, when I caught myself.

"How did you know?" he asked.

I'd been thinking about my response, and even though I knew it was dishonest, I said, "I didn't really, just had a strong impulse to call you. Who knows why?"

That seemed to mollify him, because he stood, took the two plates to the sink, and washed them. When he was done, he turned to me. "Thanks, Steve, but you don't have to stick around. I'm not going do anything stupid, and after all that drama, I'm sure you're chomping at the bit to get away."

I chuckled. "Well, you'd think that, but I want nothing more than to be here with you. I've missed you more than I should've, and I've been an idiot by ignoring it and not calling you sooner."

Eric smiled, and the light seemed to reflect in his eyes. "Yeah, I should've stopped being too prideful myself and called you."

"Well, in that case, let's get cleaned up and go for a long walk. I'd like to get out and into the countryside without working for a change."

"Where do you wanna go?" he asked.

I smiled. "Well, I had a job at the Little Bird Mine before I started this one, and it's beautiful up there. Want to walk with me to see it?" I asked.

"Never heard of it, but sure, why not?"

He showered while I finished cleaning up the table and counter from breakfast, then I grabbed a quick shower myself.

We drove hand in hand to the mine, which had been abandoned for years. The owner had hired me to write up a history. I think they'd hoped they could get a historical designation, or could attract people to the property, but I didn't think there was much there that would be interesting enough to attract tourists.

We pulled into an inconspicuous space, which technically belonged to the Bureau of Land Management. The new owner, who'd inherited the property from his father, had shown it to me, saying it was the closest access to where the old mine was.

When we hiked far enough to find the trail that led to the mine, I said, "You should probably promise not to show anyone where this is. Technically, I shouldn't be back here myself without the owner's permission, but if we run into him, I'll tell him I'm still doing some research on my own terms."

Eric nodded, but I could see he was skeptical. I had a feeling this one was usually a rule follower. I wasn't necessarily a rulebreaker, but I'd long ago stopped worrying about doing everything by the book. Most of the time, it was a waste of time... at least, in my opinion.

We walked about a mile when I finally spotted the discreet entrance. I pointed it out to Eric, who smiled. "I doubt anyone would find this on their own, even if it wasn't on private property," he said. "When did it shut down?"

I shook my head. "Not sure, before the turn of the twentieth century, but it'd never been very productive. The original owner found a few specks of silver in the entrance of the mine, but nothing more came of it. The details are mostly lost in time, but according to what I could sniff out, there was a raid of some sort and one guy ended up in the mine when it collapsed, killing him. He's still buried in there, somewhere," I said, and Eric looked up at me sadly.

"It feels like a gravesite, doesn't it?" he asked.

I nodded, having thought the same thing, but unlike a lot of other areas, this only felt like something tragic had happened. It didn't feel horrible, just sad.

"Follow me. This is what I wanted to show you," I said.

We wound our way up a steep incline, and I kept my eyes on Eric, making sure he was okay. He seemed to be used to hiking and made it up behind me with little effort. When we crested the ridge, I waited for him to join me.

He sucked in a breath when he saw the view. "This is remarkable," he said. "You can see for miles. Is that the national park?"

I nodded. "Yep, we're technically between the state and national park. Somehow, this land was never pulled into either one. I'm guessing it's because even during the nineteen twenties, the owners of this property were politically powerful in Texas."

"Well, it's one of the prettiest places in the area," he said. "The only view I know that comes close is on my friend's ranch. They call it the buttes. But, this is a very close second."

He turned to me smiling, and I couldn't help myself. I pulled him into a hug, then kissed him. We clung together, staring out over the landscape. My eye settled on a place several miles into the park, and I immediately knew what I was looking at. The spirit I'd met hadn't seen me from the flats, he'd seen the flats from here. When I turned around, he was standing just to the right of us, staring into the distance.

I would've talked to him, but I had Eric in my arms. When he looked over at me, I nodded, letting him know I understood. The man who'd died here, the one who looked so like the man in my arms, was the same one who'd visited me when I'd first begun working in Big Bend.

Of course, I wanted to know why he didn't reveal himself to me before, when I was coming to the mine and researching it for the owner, but the truth was, this was a sad place. The flats, next to the watering hole, that was a place of happiness, and I knew without asking that the spirit had met me there because he'd been happy in that place.

Eric looked up at me inquisitively. "You seem to be lost in thought," he said, and I smiled.

"Oh, I'm taken with the spirit of the place," I said, rather tongue in cheek.

Eric returned my smile and hugged me tighter. "Thanks for bringing me here. It feels sacred and important." Then, he scoffed, "I think I'm still overly emotional from last night. Just ignore me."

I wanted to confirm this was indeed a sacred place that was significant for someone in his history, but I was far from feeling comfortable enough with him, or anyone, to ever admit why I knew that.

We hiked back down the path, and were about to come out in the clearing where I'd parked my car. I heard him before I saw him, and for some reason, the warning bells went off in my mind. I was afraid all over again. "Danger," I could've sworn I heard someone say, before I looked up to see the mine's owner step in front of me.

I smiled, even though I really wanted to run and protect Eric. "Mr. Brice, good to see you."

The man didn't smile but looked at me warily. "Why are you here, Dr. Fowler?"

I shook my head. "This is Eric Anderson. He's a historian doing research on the area around here. I was hoping he'd have some information that would help us chase the leads I couldn't seem to find."

Eric looked at me and then over at the man and smiled. "Nice to meet you," he said.

The man looked at Eric, and his expression changed from curiously angry to feral. That expression was definitely *not* one you'd want to see aimed at someone you cared about.

"Did you find anything?" he asked Eric.

Eric looked confused. "No, I've just begun discussing the area with Dr. Fowler. I'm afraid it'll take some digging to figure out if there are more leads worth pursuing. I'm visiting friends in the area, though, so I should be able to dig around and find out what folklore is floating around. Maybe some of the locals will have some information..." Eric looked up and smiled. "Sorry, I'm rambling. I tend to do that when I'm pondering a project."

The man's face never left Eric's, and I wanted to pull him behind me more and more. I didn't like this man all of a sudden. When I met him, he'd felt a little off, but nothing had jumped out at me. Seeing him look at Eric, I knew there was something not right. I needed to get Eric out of here as soon as possible.

"Well, Mr. Brice, I've monopolized more of Mr. Anderson's time than I should've. If you'll excuse us, I'm going to get him back to his motel, so he can get back to vacationing. I'll be in touch with any new developments."

The man seemed to snap out of a dream and turned toward me. "That'll be nice, Dr. Fowler, make sure you do."

We got into my car and drove away.

"Well, he's creepy as shit," Eric said, and looked over at me.

"Yeah, I was thinking the same thing."

"Was he that creepy when you worked for him before?" he asked.

"Not that I noticed. I thought he was a little off, but the way he was looking at you made me feel like I was watching Hannibal Lecter or something." When I looked over at Eric, he'd gone white. "Oh shit. Sorry, Eric, I didn't mean it like that."

"Yeah, you did, and that was exactly the same feeling I had about him. I'd prefer it if I didn't have to see him again, if that's all the same to you."

"Me neither. I'll probably phone him in a week or so, just to say we hit another dead end, but seriously, if you see him again, go the other direction as fast as possible."

10

Eric

I DIDN'T KNOW HOW Steve knew to call me. He said he had a feeling, but I could tell there was more to the story than he was saying. I'd always had an ability to connect with people, a little more than others could. My college girlfriend, before Lisa, was a hippie born too late. She told me it was because I was an empath. Of course, she said other things, like I was a crystal child, or Indigo Moon or something.

I didn't buy into the other stuff, but I thought she might be right about the empath part. I could sense when someone around me was upset or needed a shoulder to cry on. Since I couldn't make sense of why Steve had known I was in a place where I was considering taking pills to end it, I had to assume he was empathic as well.

The morning after I woke up and Steve was bustling around the small camper, cooking ham and eggs, I was filled with utter happiness that he was with me. That quickly turned to complete and total humiliation.

I'd never been so depressed that I'd considered suicide. No, I'd decided not to go through with it, but it had been premeditated, and I even let Flex and Mitch keep Puddles, so if I went through with it, she'd have someone to care for her.

At my lowest point, it felt like I had a room full of people standing around me, encouraging me to stop. I thought it must have been my mom, but all the energy in the room felt distinctly male but, I didn't know any dead men who cared enough to haunt me while I was considering suicide.

People like me couldn't live without others. I knew that about myself. I needed to be needed. I knew that sounded codependent, and I sometimes hated that about myself, but I'd long ago come to terms with it. I was what I was, and people needed to be an active part of me if I was going to be complete.

I'd been holding the pills walking around the small camper, thinking about what it would be like if I took them. What the consequences would be for Flex and Mitch, even my little dog had to be considered. I'd just decided I wasn't going to go through with it, and had put the pills down on the table, when Steve called.

I had no idea how, but I knew it was him before I even looked at my phone. If that didn't sound totally crazy, I'd have said someone whispered his name in my ear before the phone even rang, but I was in such a demented place; I would've believed anything at that point.

Steve's arrival met my every need. He basically took over, let me become a wet noodle, and held me through the night. I woke several times in a panic as nightmares washed over me. Each one was me being crushed in a cave-in. Nothing before that, just the rocks crashing down and killing me.

I'd wake up with his strong arms wrapped around me, and I'd feel alive again. I thought I had that dream three times through the night, each time waking to his strong presence. If Steve hadn't been here, I wasn't at all sure I'd have made it through the night. It was bad enough that I was dealing with depression, but add in the nightmares, and it was too much.

When I came into the kitchen, Steve was like a bright light in a dark storm. He didn't belittle me, force me to talk, or chastise me. He accepted me, saying that everyone had been there. It made it feel like it was quite normal that I was so distraught.

The morning walk was exactly what I needed. I looked over the vista before us, Steve's arms wrapped around me, and the world seemed right, like a piece of me had been askew and had now clicked back into place. When I turned around and saw his face, I knew then I would be okay. Even if he left, and I never saw him again, I would be okay.

It was a bit eerie that our destination was a cave that'd collapsed and killed a miner. My dreams had been of that very thing, but as I analyzed my feelings, it wasn't fear or pain I felt here... mostly, I felt serenity and acceptance.

As right as it felt to be in Steve's arms, that was how wrong it felt when we came upon the owner of the mine. Every hair stood up on the back of my neck before he even came into view. Just like last night, when I heard Steve's name, I seem to have heard someone warning me, "Danger!"

When the owner stepped in front of Steve, visions of the rocks falling on me, just like the dreams from the night before, filled my mind.

As Steve introduced us, and the man stared at me, not even trying to hide his creepiness. If Steve hadn't been with us, I knew deep in my soul, I wouldn't have survived that meeting.

When we got into the car to leave, I was shaken to my core. Not only had I faced my demise at my own hand, but I'd almost faced it at the hand of another. When Steve acknowledged that he'd felt the same thing, I knew I hadn't been imagining it.

I ended up falling asleep as we drove back to the motel. It was just before noon when we got back, and I thanked Steve, figuring he'd leave now that I was stable.

"Do you want me to leave?" Steve asked as I hugged him, clearly saying goodbye.

I shook my head. "I really don't, but I can't ask you to stay. You must think I'm a total nutcase at this point. Shouldn't you be running for the hills?" I looked out over where the park lay to our south. "Literally?" I said, pointing toward the mountains of Big Bend.

He chuckled. "I'll let you in on a little secret. I'm about as... um... different as they come. I don't think you're nuts. I think you're normal, and I'm happy I was able to help. Also, I don't want to head for the hills. I missed you and would really like to get to know you better, this time without one foot out the door."

"I'm not an easy man to date, Steve. I'm one of those weirdos who want relationships *and* friendships," I chuckled. "I guess you could say, I'm not the party, hookup with a different guy every week kind of man."

"I'm not looking for that either. I mean, I'm not proposing or anything, but I'd really like to date you, and I'd really like it if you'd consider working on the research with me again. I don't think I've ever enjoyed working alongside another historian as much as I have you."

"Is that cause we were having sex?"

Steve blushed. "Well, that's not really the first time that's happened to me either, but... well, it's never been this special," he said.

For the first time since meeting Dr. Steve Fowler, I saw vulnerability, and it struck me right in the middle of my chest.

I sighed and leaned back against his car, looking out over the vista behind Mitch's motel. "Let me get this out first. I may be the clingiest man I've ever known." I chuckled at the truth of that. "I'm needy as fuck, and even when I don't want to be, I tend to go there. Now that you've seen me at my worst, I feel embarrassed... well, mortified is a better word, but also connected. I'm afraid I'll push you too hard now, and Steve?" I looked at him standing next to me, and smiled. "I'm not going to do well with another rejection. So, for your sake and mine, I need to put some major skids on this."

Steve looked sad. "So, you don't want to be with me?"

I chuckled. "No, I want to be with you too much, and way too fast."

Steve smiled then. "No problem. Let's date like normal people, we'll keep things professional while you're volunteering, and we can go out to eat and stuff. No pressure either way."

"You're serious?" I asked. "Even after seeing me like I was last night, and after admitting I was a clingy, relationship guy, you're still interested in continuing with... well, with whatever this is?"

Steve came over and pulled me into his arms. "I'll do whatever I have to do as long as it means you'll stick around and not leave. I've never met someone who affects me like you do. I'd like to explore that and find out why."

I curled into his wonderful arms and felt safer, more needed, and more wanted than I'd felt in a very long time. Did that scare the shit out of me? You bet it did. However, just a few hours ago, I was considering ending it for good. If he was willing to open his life to me, even in the smallest way, I'd be a fool to reject it.

As I snuggled into Steve, I felt Puddles. I pulled back and laughed. "Hey, girl," I said, leaning over and petting her. "Did you have a good sleepover?" I asked, and she jumped up licking me on the mouth. I never had understood how that dog had such good aim.

Flex and Mitch appeared shortly after, along with Ace, Flex's dog, although he was too cool to hang out with us. I didn't have much experience with Jack Russells, but if Ace was any indication, they were very independent dogs.

"Feeling better?" Flex asked as he reached us.

"Much, thanks," I said, but Flex wasn't looking at me any longer. He was staring a hole through Steve.

"I don't believe we've met," he said. I could feel the protective suspicion coming off of him in waves.

"Guys, this is Dr. Steve Fowler. He's the one I told you I was working with in the park."

Flex didn't smile or say anything, and I was embarrassed that the guy I'd praised over and over to Steve seemed to be showing the exact opposite personality. I sighed inwardly, concerned this strange behavior was probably because he was suspicious of new people since being shot.

Mitch cleared his throat. "I'm Mitch, this is Flex. We're the owners of the motel."

That was enough to distract Flex from judging Steve.

"We do?" he asked, and Mitch laughed. "Well, *we* might as well own it, you work here as much as I do."

Flex completely forgot about Steve and pulled Mitch into an embrace, kissing him.

I chuckled, which caused the two to look at us again. This time, Flex didn't seem to have the same angry look. Just the giddy expression I'd become accustomed to seeing since he'd met Mitch.

"What are you two doing for lunch?" Mitch asked. "We're about to go to the ranch for Emma Jean's famous sandwiches. Care to join us?"

I smiled. "Emma Jean does make the best sandwiches. Hell, she makes the best everything. Steve, do you have time to go on an adventure?"

He smiled at me. "Sure, is this the ranch you were telling me about before?"

"Yep, Flex and his cousin run the place, but it's been in their family for generations."

I noticed Flex was getting the same expression he had before, both of curiosity but more protectiveness.

"Dr. Fowler is working for the Department of the Interior under a grant to survey the historical sites in the national park. I mentioned that your property runs next to the parks, and that your family has deep roots here as well."

Flex looked at Steve for a moment. "Can you give Eric and me a moment?"

I could tell Steve was repressing a smile. I, however, was getting pissed. Why was Flex acting like such an ass?

"I need to run to the grocery store to pick up supplies, why don't you all talk while I'm gone?" Steve turned to me then, and laid a very possessive kiss on me, pulled back, and winked. I didn't know if I was amused or frustrated, because Steve was clearly enjoying this too much.

We watched him get into his car and drive away, and I turned on Flex. "What the hell? You looked like you wanted to beat him to a pulp."

Flex stared at me a moment, then said, "When did you start dating guys?"

I felt myself blush. "Well, I've dated a few, I guess, before Lisa."

"And you never thought to tell me, your gay friend, before now?"

I sighed. "Flex, none of the guys I dated really meant anything to me. In fact, have I ever told you about any of the women I dated?"

He looked like he was deep in thought, and finally shook his head. "Besides Lisa, no."

"I honestly never thought it was a big deal. I'd have needed to be attached to them for me to bring them up to you."

Flex shook his head and looked at Mitch, who was looking very uncomfortable with the conversation. "Mitch, do you mind taking the dogs back in? I think I need to spend some time with my best friend... alone."

Mitch nodded, and looked over at me with sympathy. He picked Puddles up and called for Ace to follow him.

"Dude, you are dating some man, and all this time I thought you were straight as a damned arrow."

"I don't know why you're so upset. I haven't really dated anyone much, and really, I only date people I feel a connection with. I told you I thought I was pansexual before, so why are you surprised I'm dating a guy?"

"Well, you said that years ago, and because you mentioned it just as I was coming out to you, I figured you were saying it to be nice to me."

I laughed. "Flex, man, you are a piece of work. No, I was coming out to you at the same time. I like men and women, but attraction is weird for me. I don't usually feel attracted to someone until I get to know them."

Flex shook his head. "I'm confused. You were married to Lisa, now you're dating some doctor guy, and I'm your fucking best friend and never even knew you looked at men before."

Realizing for the first time what was going on, I pulled my buddy into a hug. When we pulled apart, I apologized. "Flex, sexuality has always confused me. I didn't mean to push you out. I thought because we'd discussed it, that you understood that I liked men and women. You never asked about my pansexuality, so I just figured you knew."

Flex led me over to the bench that everyone called the sunset bench, and we both sat down. "I'm sorry I never really asked much about your sex life. I just figured when you dated Lisa, you'd accepted that you were straight," he chuckled. "So, are you two like *together*, together?"

"Well, we're just discovering that, but if you're asking if we've had sex, yeah, and before you ask, it was amazing."

Flex laughed. "Is he better than the bitch you married?"

I turned to him, shocked, then laughed at the disgusted expression on his face.

"Lisa wasn't that bad. She was just the wrong one for me."

Flex sputtered. "Lisa was a tool from hell."

I looked at him for a moment. "If you felt that way, why didn't you ever say anything?"

"Because, dude, you were so over the moon for her, I knew if I did, you'd tell her, and she'd force you to never speak to me again."

I leaned back against the bench. "You're right. If she had any inclination you didn't like her, she'd have done everything to get between us."

Flex put his arm around me and pulled me into his side. "Eric, you're my best friend on the planet. I love you like a brother. I won't ever come between you and someone you love, but Lisa wasn't a good person. The only person she ever loved was herself."

We sat like that for a moment, before he finally added, "Are you sure about this Steve guy? I know you're vulnerable right now, and I almost came out to the camper last night, but every time I got up to go, something held me back, like you needed your space to figure out whatever was going on. If this guy is good to you, I'll be his best advocate, but I don't think I can watch you with another Lisa, especially right now. That would screw you up too much."

I sighed and leaned into my friend even more. "He isn't Lisa. To be honest, I don't know what kind of person he is yet. But, I do know he's got a good soul, and last night, I really did need him."

I didn't want to admit to Flex that I had been as far deep in depression as I was last night. If he knew I had been considering what I had and didn't turn to him, it would hurt him. Instead, I said, "I was in the darkest place I've ever been last night, Flex. Too much of my world has been turned upside down, and something brought him here. I can't explain it, but I can say he filled the holes that needed filling."

Flex sat stoically for a moment before he pulled me back into a side hug and burst out laughing. "He filled your holes, huh?"

"Dude, you are so crass," I said, and laughed with him. "Well, maybe I was the one filling his, but not last night."

Flex was about to roll off the bench with laughter when Mitch came up behind us. "What's so funny?" he asked.

"Eric's found a man who fills his holes," Flex said, bursting into another fit of laughter.

I elbowed him in the ribs and stood up. "You're an ass," I said, grinning. As Flex continued laughing, I came up behind him and put my hand on his shoulder. "I'm sorry I didn't communicate better."

Flex wiped at a tear that had escaped his eyes during his laughing fit and patted my hand. "It's okay. I'm glad you're bringing him to the ranch. Emma Jean will give him a once-over, and if she approves of him, he'll have my blessing."

"Like he needs your blessing," Mitch said, and I chuckled.

"Thanks, Mitch," I said, and turned to go toward the camper. "Do I need to bring Puddles over to the camper before we leave?"

"No," Mitch replied. "Ace and she are curled up on his big bed in the kitchen. They'll be fine together until we get back."

By the time I'd gone into the camper and washed my face, getting all the dust off from our walk, Steve had returned.

"You and your friend okay?" he asked.

"Yeah, we're fine."

"I take it he didn't know you like guys."

I smiled. "No, I sort of neglected to explain that clearly."

"Is he jealous?" Steve asked apprehensively.

I laughed. "No, Flex is like a brother, and he's crazy in love with Mitch. Like grossly, disgustingly, get a room, please, in love with Mitch."

Steve smiled. "Well, if I'm the first guy they've seen you with, this might be interesting."

"It'll be easy... well, relatively easy. Emma Jean is a hard nut to crack, but if she likes you, it'll all be downhill from there."

11

Steve

THE RIDE TO THE ranch was light and fun. Eric told me about growing up here during the summers, and how Flex, Eddie, and he would run the property like wild animals. Eric decided to drive since he knew the way, and I didn't have to be back at the RV anytime soon, so I was happy to sit back, enjoy the view, and hear him talk about his friends.

Pulling onto the ranch, I immediately felt nauseated, and broke out into a cold sweat.

Eric looked over at me and was instantly concerned. "Are you okay?" he asked.

"I think so," I said, but I knew I wasn't.

When he parked, he looked over at me. "You don't look good, Steve. Why don't we go inside and get Emma Jean to give you a wet towel or something?"

I nodded and let him help me out of the car. Flex and Mitch had pulled up beside us, and seeing that I was having trouble, came over to help.

I noticed their concern, but the truth was, I'd never been overtaken with this level of nausea before, not this fast, so I couldn't do anything other than let them help me into the house.

The door opened, and I had just enough time to see an older woman and man standing in the doorway, before the world went completely black.

I had no idea how long I was out, but when I woke up, I was lying on a sofa in someone's living room. I looked over and saw a concerned Eric sitting next to me. "What happened?" I asked.

He shook his head. "You sort of went into a trance," he said. "Are you okay? When you fell, you might've bumped your head."

I reached up to feel the top of my head, but it didn't hurt. My pride, however, was seriously dented.

"What kind of trance?" I asked.

That was when I noticed the room was full of people. I sat up, feeling my face blush.

I'd never gone into a trance before, but my granny had warned me it was possible and not uncommon. "Only when it's really important," she'd told me.

I was trying to figure out how to minimize what had happened. I didn't want to suddenly become the pariah I'd always avoided being.

"I must have a cold or food poisoning, or something."

An older woman, one I recognized from before I passed out, came over. "Or something. More likely, you have the sight."

"Um... the sight?" I was trying to act like I didn't know what she was talking about. I really needed to get out of here.

"Do you remember what you told us after you went into a trance?" Eric asked.

I shook my head. I didn't remember anything.

"You kept repeating it until we wrote it down."

"I don't... I'm sorry, I don't remember."

The woman lifted the piece of paper and read:

"Three brothers died at the hands of three others.The past is past, but now it's repeated,The tables have turned; two have lived and two have died. Do not rest yet, the third brother is still at risk. Between enemy brothers, one will die.Only love can conquer the darkness. He will need his both his lover's and his family's love to survive."

I shook my head. "I'm sorry, Eric, I should probably go. I must be coming down with something."

The woman ignored me, and asked, "Have you ever done this before?"

I shook my head, thankful I didn't have to lie.

"Have you ever seen spirits before?" she asked, and I froze.

"I'm sorry this is getting too strange. I need some air." I was about to run away, if only I could get up and out the door.

Flex, Eric's friend, stood up and came to the couch. "I began having dreams a few months before I was shot. A giant snake winding its way toward me, I saw how I was going to be shot, and that Mitch, my boyfriend, would save me."

Another man I hadn't met stood then, and said, "I began seeing a ghost by the name of Diamondback Jack right before my boyfriend, Alex, came to us on the ranch. He and Alex looked so much alike, I thought he was the same person. I even accused Alex of showing up on the ranch for malicious reasons. I know what you're feeling right now is freaking you out, but don't worry, it isn't the first time freaky things have happened here."

Eric looked around at the group. "Why didn't y'all tell me about this stuff?"

They all shook their heads. "We're sorry, Eric, it was a little too weird to talk about, and you weren't here."

I struggled up onto the couch, still wanting to run, but intrigued and concerned by this family. I immediately became paranoid that this was a trap to get me to admit that I saw spirits, so they could discredit me, but how would they know me? Unless, Eric was part of the trap.

The moment the thought sank into my head, I began to panic. I managed to get up and run out of the house, but the moment the door closed behind me, I was standing face to face with my ghost, standing between two others.

Obviously, I wasn't the only one who could see them this time. Eric gasped behind me as he came out the door. "What the hell is this?" Eric asked, and I unconsciously reached over and put my arm around him.

"They are brothers, and I'm guessing they're your ancestors?" I asked, turning toward the men who looked very similar to the spirits who stood before us.

When the entire group was outside on the porch with me, Flex looked over and nodded. "We've never seen them this clearly, though."

"That's probably because of me," I sighed. I was about to admit something I'd never admitted since I was a child and told my parents. "Can we go back inside? I don't think these three are going to let me leave until we talk."

The others went in first, and I watched the spirits, each with a determined look on their face. I nodded, understanding what these three were expecting from me, and with dread that reached into the bottom of my soul, I turned to follow the others inside.

12

Eric

MY WORLD WAS SPINNING. I'd never believed in ghosts, well, not in the sense that they'd come out and stand in front of you. I almost felt like I'd been thrust into a comedy show, and at any moment, a cameraman or woman would pop out and ask me about my experience.

But, I'd seen them with my own eyes, the three brooding and very unhappy men dressed like they were just done filming a Western.

I wasn't really freaking out because of the ghosts... mostly I was concerned because one of them looked just like me. At one point, my twin ghost turned to me, like he knew I was freaking out, and I could feel him trying to soothe me, although I had no idea what he was saying.

As I walked back into the house, I checked my emotional response. Fear? No, I wasn't afraid. Confused, overwhelmed, skeptical? Yes, but not afraid.

Flex pointed Steve to the chair where Jimmy usually sat, because it was the focus of the rest of the room. Steve stared at me until I turned to meet his gaze, then he turned toward the others.

"I've never told anyone besides my family what I'm about to tell you. Before I do, I need all of you in this room to promise... no, I need you to swear, you'll never tell anyone what I'm about to say."

When we all nodded, he sighed. "I wish I could make you all sign non-disclosures, but your ancestral specters out there aren't going to allow me to do anything, until I come clean."

He looked around the room, sighed again, and looked at Emma Jean.

"You're right, I've got what my grandmother called the sight. I've been able to see those who have passed on... who are deceased, ever since I can remember. Most of the time, they ignore me, but occasionally, like these three here, they're more substantial, and even demanding."

"Did you see them before you came here?" Flex asked.

Steve shook his head. "No... well, yes." He looked at me and then away. "I began seeing the one who looks like Eric the morning I met him. He was friendly, and led me up from where

I was staying along a creek bank and toward a watering hole. I've seen him off and on since that day."

"Wait a minute, is he the one you were talking to when I came up on you at the mine?"

Steve looked at me and nodded. "When I first saw you on the trail, I thought maybe you were him. You both looked so much alike it took me a moment to see that you were... um... well, alive. Then when I walked past you, I sat up by the entrance, and the... um... well, he came and sat next to me." Steve smiled at me then. "I was sort of freaking out because when you sat next to me, he was on one side and you the other. I'd never experienced that before... it was like I was sitting between twins."

"How did you know we weren't brothers, or that he hadn't died recently?" I asked, and he shrugged.

"I knew he'd been dead for a while. You can tell, some spirits have a... well, a weathered soul." Steve shook his head. "This is all hard to explain. I've never talked about it before, so it's confusing to try to express what it's like or what they're like."

"Tell us about the trance," Emma Jean said then.

"I haven't experienced that before. I felt sick as we pulled into the driveway, then when I got to the house, I passed out. I don't remember being in a trance or telling you the stuff you wrote down."

"So, why or how do you think it happened?"

Steve looked out the window, and seeing the three men still there, said, "I'm guessing one of them possessed me."

I drew in a breath. "That doesn't sound safe or fair. Why would they?"

"I don't think they usually can, actually. I must be somehow linked with them as well. Unlike what you see in the movies, I believe spirits are confined to the laws of physics, not unlike we are. Theirs seem to be even more rigid, though, probably because they aren't technically supposed to still be in this dimension. From what I've learned over the years, possession usually only occurs when someone is a blood relative, and even then, it's really uncommon."

"Why did it make you sick?" asked Alex, Eddie's boyfriend, who up until then had remained quiet.

Steve shrugged. "I really don't know. Maybe it was because a foreign object was inside me. Maybe it was because I hadn't agreed to it... I really don't know enough to tell you why." He sat for a moment. "I'm guessing what was said must've been important, or I doubt they'd have put me at risk. I get from these men that they are good, light-based spirits. I don't feel any darkness from them."

This seemed to satisfy everyone.

Steve looked exhausted, both emotionally and physically. I was about to go to him when Emma Jean stepped up first.

"Come with me," she said, helping him out of the chair. "You look like you could use a good meal and a moment to get yourself together."

She escorted him into the kitchen, away from the rest of us. I was about to follow when Flex caught me. Both he and Eddie led me outside. They sat in the swing, and I sat in the chair across from it.

I looked over to where the three spirits had stood earlier, but they were gone, which was a relief.

"How well do you know this guy?" Eddie asked.

"I don't know him very well… well, not personally at least. I've known *about* him for a long time. Hell, I even had his book in one of my graduate classes, but I met him for the first time a few weeks ago."

Each of us sat quietly thinking.

"We have to believe him," Eddie said. "Hell, I certainly recognized Jack."

"Yeah, the older brother, we have a picture of him too," Flex said. "He may look like me, but he's Mitch's ancestor."

"That's a good point. I look like one of them, but I'm not related to you all."

"Well, we don't know that for sure, Eric." Flex said, "Have you traced your family tree all the way back? It's possible we're related."

I shrugged. "I guess. My mom's family is from West Texas. They even owned oil rights somewhere near Pecos, but I have no idea how we'd be connected."

"How's Steve connected?" Flex asked. "I think that's the biggest dilemma. I mean, we've seen some weird stuff lately, but nothing this *in your face*. I should probably trust him, since our ancestors clearly do, but I can't help but be skeptical. How do we know he isn't after something else?"

Eddie chuckled. "Are you sure you're not just mad that Eric has a boyfriend that you didn't know about?"

Flex looked at his cousin and flipped him off. "Okay, so maybe that's part of it. I'm still overwhelmed by you being gay or bi, or whatever, but…"

Flex looked at Eddie. "How do you know about it?"

Eddie chuckled. "Well, first, I thought Eric was going to come unglued when the man passed out, and that's not just concern written on his face, it's attachment. I happen to recognize that look. Also, when the man was in a trance, I could feel Jack and his lover standing next to Alex and me. I could also feel the love between you and Mitch. But, and this is a little vaguer, I could tell there was something happening with Eric and him."

I shook my head. "To be honest, guys, I've felt drawn to Steve from the moment we met. Maybe not sexually, not at first, that came later for me, but I was attracted to him, like I've never felt for anyone else before." I leaned back and sighed. "Last night, I was in a really dark place, *really* dark, and Steve just knew I needed him. I hadn't talked to him since we parted ways a few weeks back, but I heard someone whisper his name mere seconds before he called."

I didn't add anything else, but I didn't really need to. The look on Flex and Eddie's faces told me they understood just how dark things had been.

"You should've told us," Flex said, and I shook my head.

"Guys, I'm alone, like never before. My dad and brother have pretty much pushed me out. You're both in healthy, happy relationships. I didn't want to be a burden."

"That's fucking shit," Eddie said. "Dude, I was the same just a little while ago. My world was crashing around me. The only difference was I had two boys to think about, but you know I understand. You're our family, Eric. You've *always* been family. Don't *ever* push us away again. When you need us, we're here."

"And I'll be pissed as hell if you ever go down the rabbit hole again without reaching out for help," Flex said, and from the look on his face, I knew he was being real.

"I love you guys, thanks, and I... well, I'll try, okay?"

Eddie and Flex pulled me up out of the chair and hugged me. "We are brothers, you know that, right?" Flex said, when we pulled apart. "We're the three brothers the prophesy was talking about. Two have survived, that's Effie..." Flex switched to his nickname for his cousin, "...and me. We survived, and I'm afraid that means it's your turn, Eric. You're probably at risk. What did he say? '*Only love can conquer the darkness. He will need both his lover's and his family's love to survive.*' That means you'll need us to survive, Eric, so you can't go running off being the lone wolf any longer."

I smiled. I tried not to think about the other parts where *one brother must die*, or the part that got my heart pumping the most, that *I'd need my lover*. I still hadn't worked that out in my mind yet, but it sounded ominous on the one hand, and extremely hopeful on the other. Was Steve my lover?

I shook my head to get past those thoughts. I needed to keep things out of the instant romance that I seemed to yearn for if we had a chance of making it. Ghosts, paranormal trances, or not... I needed to keep a clear head.

13

Steve

I THOUGHT I'D BE more freaked out than I was, but after the older woman pulled me into the kitchen and began plying me with food, I searched my reactions and found, surprisingly, I felt relieved. The secret that had lived inside of me for so long, the one my parents were so afraid of, that *I* was afraid of, was out, and there was nothing I could do now but ride the roller coaster and see where it stopped.

It didn't go without my noticing that Eric was himself a historian, who knew my work. The paranoia came back again. Now that he knew, he could easily discredit me in my field. This family's ranch was right next to Big Bend, and their gossip could undo my credibility. Something... something I couldn't quite explain, made me feel they wouldn't. Believing it, though, didn't prevent it from happening. I wasn't a teenager with the expectation that people would honor their promise not to tell. People, in my experience, just weren't that good.

"So, you said we're the first you've told this to. Why is that?" the old woman asked.

I shook my head and sighed. "The only thing I know about it is what my grandmother told me before she died. I used to stay with her, and she'd snuggle up with me and tell me stories about seeing otherworldly entities. She said I had a gift, and it was called the second sight. She told me I should keep it very quiet, because people didn't understand, not even tell my parents about it. She died when I was still little, so unfortunately, after she was gone, I didn't have anyone to confide in. Well, she stuck around a long time, but we weren't able to talk like we used to. Anyway, I did as she recommended, and kept the secret to myself, until I began being harassed by a kid who died in our school. The poor kid probably just wanted someone to lean on, but the pressure of dealing with a kid my own age, that I'd sort of known in life was too much for me at the time."

I exhaled and took a drink of tea the woman had put in front of me along with a sandwich. "I forgot my grandmother's advice and told my parents I'd been seeing the ghost of the kid who drowned in my school's pool. Of course, my mom freaked out. She rushed me to a psychiatrist who diagnosed me as schizophrenic and began medicating me." I heard the bitter chuckle come out, but I couldn't stop it. "The medication was awful. It made me tired and lethargic, almost like trying to live underwater. I kept seeing the kid and other ghosts. The meds, of course, didn't work, because I didn't have a mental disorder. I had a sixth sense. After that, I pretended as though I'd made it up, and the psychiatrist stopped the meds, and that was the last time I ever told anyone."

Eric came up behind me and wrapped his arms around me. "That's one of the saddest stories I've ever heard," he said. "No wonder you looked like you were about to run away earlier."

I tensed when he embraced me, but damn if it didn't feel good to have his arms around me. I felt so vulnerable at the moment, relieved, but exposed.

"You don't have to worry about any of us," the woman said, and winked at Eric. "Your secret is safe with us. We've seen plenty around here, and people would think we're nuts too, if it got out."

I chuckled and let Eric hold me from behind until the woman left the kitchen.

"So, you don't want to run away now that you know I'm whatever I am?" I asked.

Eric smiled as he came around and sat down next to me. "No more than you wanted to run away this morning when I told you I was a clingy boyfriend."

I leaned over and kissed him. "No offense, but I would rather not be around company at the moment. Do you mind if we go spend some time alone?" I asked.

"No, I don't mind at all… I doubt after all this anyone would mind too much."

Before we left, Flex made us promise to come back before the weekend to discuss what I'd said during my trance. "If Eric is in trouble or isn't safe, we need to analyze it and try to prepare for it," he said.

I agreed, but would give myself a couple days to come to terms with being out of the ghost-seeing closet.

Eric didn't ask questions, which shocked me. I figured if I'd been in his situation, I'd have had a million questions, and I knew my personality would've kept me from being quiet.

I accepted his gift of silence, though, and let the subject ruminate for the first day and night.

We followed his friends back to the motel, and he picked up his dog Puddles from them before going back to his camper. The dog was seriously unhappy about sleeping on the floor, because I was there, but two men and a dog just didn't fit in that bed. We seemed to have made a pact though. When I had a lap open, she was welcome to it.

I'd never had a dog, and having Puddles snuggle against me was sweet, if a bit weird.

I certainly saw the connection between the dog and her owner, though. Both were extremely cuddly, and both shared the same sweet, calming personality.

I needed to get back to my RV the next day. I only had a pass to be in my current spot for a few days, so I needed to move it before going back to the ranch to face the music of my confession. Remarkably, I wasn't dreading it as much as I probably should be. Maybe that was because Eric was being so great about it.

When I told him I needed to move the RV, he smiled. "Would you be totally against staying at the ranch? They have an RV park with full hookups."

I groaned a bit, and he laughed out loud. "Is it because you don't want to talk about... stuff?"

"Yes, I'm uncomfortable about what happened, but mostly it's because your friend Flex doesn't seem to like me."

"Flex likes you fine. This isn't your fault, it's mine. I told him years ago that I'm pansexual, and he didn't really take it in. He thought I was just saying it to be supportive of him, so when I showed up snuggled into you, it sort of freaked him out."

"Isn't pansexual like you're bisexual, but attracted more to personality than sex?"

I chuckled. "Close, it's more about relationships than gender. I can fall in love with either men or women, as long as we have a relationship to base it on." And, if we're going to be technical, I think I'm what they refer to as panromantic demisexual. But, that's usually too much to explain so I just tell anyone who cares enough to ask, that I'm pansexual.

I pulled him close, tucking his head under my chin. "That's what you were trying to tell me earlier. You're an all-in sort of guy, at least when it comes to relationships."

"Yeah," he sighed then continued, "I don't see a difference between enjoying being with you and wanting to be *with* you. It's all connected for me, which freaks most people out. It feels like I'm codependent or clingy, or trying to move things along too fast, but I'd be just the same with a friend."

"So why didn't you connect romantically with Eddie or Flex?"

He smiled. "I didn't know Eddie was bisexual, or I might have considered it, but to be honest, I doubt I would've. We're like brothers. We've been that way since we met in school. I'm closer to Flex than Eddie, and after Eddie's mom got between him and Flex, and, of course, my ex came in between all of us, I sort of lost track of Eddie. Now that I'm back here, though, he's family. I think I forgot that... which is why I was in such a bad place when you found me."

I cuddled with him and kissed his head. "You can stop worrying about that now. I saw you, and I still feel the same about you."

Eric looked up at me. "I still feel the same about you too." He crawled up on top of me then and slipped my shirt off, kissing my neck while his hands explored my body. When we were both naked, Eric straddled me and with a shy expression, said, "So, I think I'd like to try being a bottom now, if you're willing."

"Really?" I asked, feeling extremely excited all of a sudden. I'd been thinking about that cute ass of his for as long as I'd known him.

Eric shrugged. "Yeah, but I'm nervous about it."

"We can take it easy. If at any time you don't like it, you can tell me, and I'll stop."

He nodded, then got a naughty look on his face, and began rocking his taint up and down my already super-hard cock.

"Fuck, Eric," I said, and arched back, enjoying the sensation of him riding me.

I flipped him onto his back, causing him to laugh, then I moved down his body, taking his cock in my mouth.

"Mmm," Eric moaned, and I realized how much I'd missed hearing that sound coming from him.

I deep-throated him and swallowed, something he really loved, and he arched against me and began bucking into my mouth.

"Fuck, I've missed this," he cried, and I let him mouth fuck me to the point of ejaculation, then pulled off, edging him.

"Oh, that's mean," he said, and I chuckled.

"You won't mind in a moment," I said, and took his cock back into my mouth.

I edged him again, then went over to my bag and took out the lube and a condom I'd stored there.

When I crawled back onto the bed, I looked Eric in the eye. "This will feel a bit strange since it's your first time, but just tell me how you're doing. I can stop at any time."

Eric blushed. "Um, well, I've been practicing some."

"Really?" I asked, amused.

His shy smile melted my heart. "I wanted to know how it felt, and... well, you seem to enjoy it so much."

I laughed and leaned over to kiss him. "God, you are so sweet. I can't believe I was able to stay away for so long. You tie me in all kinds of wonderful knots."

I could tell Eric didn't know if that was a compliment or not, so I kissed him. Like the Cher song said, *It's there in his kiss,* and in this case, I could show him better than tell him how I felt.

I lubed his ass, and he squirmed with pleasure. I took his cock back into my mouth and sucked as I prepped him.

When I penetrated him with my finger, I looked up at him, making sure he was still into this. His face was flushed with pure pleasure. I sucked harder as I probed him, searching for and finding his prostate. When I did, he arched against me.

"Fuck..." he said. "Damn, what is...?"

It took everything in me not to stop sucking him and laugh. This must've been the first time anyone had probed his prostate in a sexual way.

I took him deep into my throat, swallowing again just as I slipped my second finger in.

Eric began bucking against me. "Yes... oh, fuck... yeah..."

When I slipped my third finger in, he sucked in a breath. "Too much?" I asked, and he quickly shook his head.

"Fuck no, it hurts and feels amazing all at the same..."

I must've hit his prostate again because he stopped midsentence and drew in a breath, arching his back into the bed.

I chuckled, knowing how amazing it felt.

After scissoring him, ensuring he was as loose as I could get him, I slipped the condom on, lubed up, and pushed my head up to his hole.

Eric was staring at me now, his face awash with emotions.

I massaged his opening with my cockhead, watching him as the pleasure of that overtook him.

When I finally pressed into him, he sucked in a breath and tensed.

"Breathe, and now press down against me, that'll release the tension."

He did as I asked, and I saw when the ecstasy overtook the pain.

"I'll go slow. You concentrate on pushing down."

When I was halfway inside him, I saw his body give way and the pleasure overtake him.

"Fuck, that's amazing." His voice rose as my cock slid all the way in. "Fuck, god... yes, that's a... that's..."

When I pulled back and slowly pushed into him again, words left him, and he squinted his eyes, but in a way that I could tell he was enjoying the intensity.

"God, you feel so good, Eric, so tight and warm."

I pushed into him, then rolled back and into him again, while his body rocked with me in time to my thrusts.

I slowly picked up speed, enjoying the tight feel of him on my cock.

When he looked up at me, a connection linked us as I pushed into him. When I drew back and moved into him this time, he leaned up, and I met him halfway, kissing him and feeling the connection grow as we made love.

When he lay back down, I could tell he wanted more, so I thrust into him harder, and he moaned my name.

"Steve, fuck yeah, that feels so good. Fuck me!" he exclaimed.

I thrust harder and harder, and he rode me, meeting each thrust with his own.

He began to jack himself off, and I knew he was close. I shifted my angle, ensuring my cock would strike his prostate.

He immediately called out. "Fuck, yes, fuck, fuck!"

When I thrust hard into his prostate this time, he blew all over his chest and stomach, gorgeous strands of white cum coating him.

I pulled out while he was still in the throes of ecstasy, then I ripped the condom off my dick, and immediately shot all over his stomach, mixing my cum with his.

I fell down next to him, totally spent. "Fuck, that was amazing," I said, then looked over at him.

"Are you okay?" I asked.

He nodded, but I could tell he was still too overcome for words.

Eric looked at me seriously. "That's probably the most intense sexual thing I've ever done in my entire life."

"Intense good or intense bad?"

"Intense *amazing*," he said with a smile. "It's scary as hell, though. I don't think I could do that with just anyone."

I smiled, leaned over, and kissed him. "Am I a possessive caveman if I don't want you to be able to?"

"Maybe, but apparently, I have a thing for cavemen. Who knew?"

I made a pretty good rendition of a caveman grunt, and kissed him. "You sure make me crazy, Eric Anderson. I'm not sure I've ever felt so much for another guy before. Thanks for letting me be your first."

He smiled and rolled over, then cuddled up against me. We lay like that, dozing off and on until Puddles complained that she needed to go out.

After we both showered, Eric called over to the motel and asked if I could pull my RV into one of the ranch's RV spots for the next few days. Apparently, it was quickly agreed. I guessed it was a good thing, since I needed to talk to his friend Flex anyway. I liked Eric, and I'd prefer not to have his best friend driving a wedge between us.

Eric rode with me to pick up the RV, Puddles happily riding in his lap. The little dog was cute, staring out over the landscape as we drove along.

Eric put her on her leash once we got to the RV and let her do her business. I'd warned him before she got out that I'd seen coyotes every day since I moved to this spot. Little poodles and coyotes didn't mix well.

I went into the RV while they were walking, and began pulling the slides in, preparing to transfer it to the ranch. I felt the angry glare before I looked out the window. When I saw it was Mr. Brice, I felt both sick and intensely protective. I rushed out of the RV, grabbing a baseball bat as I went.

I saw Eric pick up Puddles and rush toward me, alarm written on his face. "What's wrong?" he asked when he got to me.

I was looking around frantically, but I already knew I hadn't seen Mr. Brice, it was another fucking ghost.

"I'm sorry, I thought I saw someone."

Eric squinted his eyes. "You did see someone, but you're not telling me."

I sighed and looked over at him. "I did, but I think it was... otherworldly. I'm sorry, I didn't mean to lie. I'm just not used to being honest about this."

He shook it off. "What did you see?"

"I thought I saw Mr. Brice, but when I got out here, he was gone. I think it was someone else, someone from before."

"Was he dangerous?"

I nodded, and swallowed the lump in my throat. "Yeah, he wasn't a good guy."

"The prophesy you mentioned that night said I had to be careful, or the brother had to be careful. Do you think he might be what I need to avoid?"

I shook my head. "No, I think you were being warned about the real Mr. Brice. This was an apparition, and he can't hurt you, but the one who looks like him and is still alive, I believe *he's* the one who's dangerous."

Eric came inside with me then and I could tell he was shaken. I wish I could've made him feel better, but on the other hand, I preferred him upset and safe, than naïve and vulnerable.

I finished putting the RV together, then attached my car to the back, and we set off toward the ranch.

"Do you think you'll see him again?" Eric asked.

"That I don't know. Spirits come and go as they choose. There's usually no rhyme or reason to their appearances."

"What made you so upset when you saw him, besides obviously thinking it was that horrible man come to cut me into pieces?" Eric shuddered.

I reached over and patted his arm. "I could feel his anger and what felt like jealousy. The spirit almost felt like he wanted me to know you belonged to him. That's all I got before I rushed out the door. He was gone when I got there."

"Like he *owned* me?" He stared out the window as the countryside moved around us. "Like that ass looked at me before."

I nodded. "I need to do some more research on him, and your family for that matter. Until we understand more about how we're all linked, I'm afraid we're at a loss. I can tell you how I felt when he was in front of me, but I have absolutely no idea why."

"Let's talk to Flex and Eddie about it too. They might have some insight into it all, especially since they've been dealing with this longer than we have."

I wasn't looking forward to that, but oh well, so far no one had called the police on me, or threatened to have me committed. In my mind that was something to celebrate.

14

Eric

EDDIE MET US AT the lodge and showed Steve the best place to park, so we had privacy from the house and incoming guests. The RV park was big for this part of Texas. Mitch only had a dozen sites or so, but there were fifty full hookups here at the ranch.

One of the film crews had also left a fence that went all the way around the RV park, so Puddles could come and go without being eaten or running away. Unfortunately, there really wasn't much of a view, especially considering what the place looked like where Steve had been camping before, but what it lacked in vistas, it made up for in privacy and convenience.

I could tell Eddie liked Steve. They chatted while Steve put all the connections together. I put Puddles on her leash when it was clear they wouldn't need me and walked her toward the house.

Emma Jean and Jimmy were sitting on the front porch, drinking what looked to me like lemonade.

"Hidy, Mrs. Emma Jean and Mr. Jimmy," I said, making them both smile.

"Son, you know you can just call us by our names now. You aren't a kid any longer."

I chuckled. "I'm not sure I have the nerve, Mrs. Emma Jean," I admitted, causing her to laugh again.

"Well, you hang out here long enough, and you'll feel more like we're just part of the family," she said as she winked.

"Which, of course, you are. You know that, right?" Jimmy chimed in.

"I do and thank you both for reminding me."

I sat down on the rocking chair across from them. Emma Jean went into the house, and came out with a glass of lemonade, handing it to me without asking whether I wanted any or not. I smiled. This was just how things were. If they were enjoying something, their guests would too. No questions asked.

"So, is that man of yours getting settled in?" Jimmy asked.

"He ain't my man," I quickly clarified. "We've only just met and are in the super new phase of whatever this is."

Both the older folks looked at me and smiled. Yeah, I wasn't fooling anyone, except maybe myself.

"He seems to be a nice fella, at least from what we could tell," Jimmy remarked, and took a long drink of his lemonade.

I wanted to ask how they could tell, but there was no need. Even with the commotion that happened with the first visit, Emma Jean and Jimmy were the best judges of character I knew. If they said he was a good guy, he was a good guy.

"Seems like he comes with some baggage," Emma Jean finally said. "Y'all talk about that anymore?"

I shook my head. "No, I knew we were going to be talking about it tonight, so I decided to give him a break until now. I like him, maybe more than I should, so I'd rather not chase him away, just yet."

I chuckled inwardly, but truth be told, everyone except maybe Flex and Eddie had left me eventually. I couldn't help but believe it was just a matter of time before Steve would leave—this time for good.

"Well, that was mighty honorable of you," Jimmy said. He looked over at his wife, winked, and said, "Some folks gotta talk a thing to death, makin' it unbearable to breathe sometimes."

Emma Jean smirked at him, ribbed him really good, then kissed his old, weathered cheek. "Some folks need to learn how to open their mouths and communicate from time to time, without their wives having to prod stuff out of 'em."

"And you're a figurin' you'll be able to teach new tricks to a seventy-year-old dog like me?"

She shook her head. "No, I'm a figurin' I'm stuck with what I got. You might be able to teach an old dog a new trick or two, but you can't teach a stubborn old goat a bloomin' thing."

Jimmy leaned back in the swing and laughed loud and full.

"I guess you're right about that," he said, and hugged Emma Jean tight. She nestled in, and I sighed. I wanted exactly what these two had. Someone to grow old with and love completely and utterly no matter how annoyed they made me... or, more likely, I made them.

Emma Jean pushed herself up. "Eric, son, why don't you come on into the kitchen with me? You can peel some potatoes while I get the roast on. I always liked it when you helped me in the kitchen."

I smiled. I'd always loved cooking, and Emma Jean would chase everyone but me out of the kitchen when we were teenagers. I always figured it was because she knew I'd lost my mom and needed a woman to talk to, but it was our tradition, and I was excited to get back to it.

I sat at the old peninsula and peeled potatoes like I had so many years ago. Just like when I was young, Emma Jean talked about all the things going on around the ranch. This time, it wasn't about the hands, or Eddie's and Flex's grandparents, it was about my friends.

She talked about how scared they all were when Alex, Eddie's boyfriend, was abducted, or how he'd seen Diamondback Jack in his dreams, then in real life. She talked about all the things that'd happened since Flex and I had shown up when he was thinking about selling the ranch, and how Eddie's boys had changed her life for the better.

I knew this tactic. I understood now, like I had even then, that Emma Jean was making me feel safe and comfortable, talking about things she knew would eventually lead me to spill my guts. It worked now just like it had then.

"I really don't understand all that's going on, Emma Jean. It seems like a strange fairy tale to me. Is that bad?" I asked.

She chuckled. "No child, it's normal. Most of us don't deal with ghosts, or dreams of being struck by giant snakes. Most of us sail through life, blissfully ignorant."

I finished the last potato, and handed them over to Emma Jean, who began washing and then cutting them up for the roast.

I didn't really know what to say next, so we sat in silence for a few minutes.

"Tell me about this guy. What do you know about him?" she asked.

I went over the same things I'd told Flex. He was a well-known and respected archeologist. That I'd admired his work for years. He was a prodigy who had graduated early, and had his Ph.D. before most of us were done with our bachelor's.

"What's he like?" she asked.

"Kind," I answered, before I even thought about it. "He's quiet, reserved, always up in his head about things, but always attentive and respectful. I'd say he's an introvert, but then again, he seems to do well with people, even the first time he meets them."

"Would you say he's prone to tall tales, or flights of fancy?"

I chuckled at the old phrase but shook my head. "Emma Jean," I paused to feel what it felt like to say her name without the formal title of Mrs. "no, of course not, he's a well-respected scientist. If anything, he's a hard ass when it comes to research. I volunteered with him for a couple weeks, and if I made an assumption without evidence to back it up, he put me back onto the research trail until I could *prove* my assumption, or at least support it."

"Do you think he's making up the spirit thing?"

I'd guessed this was where she was going, so I shook my head. "He has nothing to gain from making it up, and he was truly out cold when he went into that trance."

I waited until she looked me in the eye, then I added, "when he woke up I saw terror on his face." I shook my head. "I once saw a gang member pull a gun on a student in my old school. The expression that poor kid had before the gang member ran away was the same look I saw on Steve's face. You can't fake that."

She nodded before walking over to me. "I know his grandmother called it a gift, but, baby, it probably isn't. I'd say it's more of a curse, for someone like him especially. Flex and Eddie's grandmother used to talk about how people in this family had the gift of second sight. I ignored it as fanciful thinking, and having grown up strict Catholic, I'd been taught anything like that was evil. I made the mistake of saying something like that to Flex, and it was almost to my own peril."

She wiped her hands on a towel before turning to me. "Flex dreamed a giant snake was going around the homestead setting fire to outbuildings and even the house. I put him off at first, but before I could completely discount him, I remembered all the talks his grandmother gave, and how we had to listen to the warnings. I told Jimmy about it, and he turned the cameras on, but the most important thing, we borrowed dogs from our neighbor down the road. If it hadn't been for the dogs, that snake would've burned the house down, and more likely than not, with us in it. I won't pretend that I understand it, but if this man's seeing trouble, you'd better pay attention, Eric, and not just for your sakes. With both Flex and Mitch, and Eddie and Alex, they weren't the only people at risk. Each time, all of us were in danger. If you're being targeted, all of our safety could rely on this man's abilities."

She turned back toward the roast, adding carrots and potatoes, before adding seasoning and sticking it in the oven. "Just don't kick a gift horse in the mouth," she said and, after washing her hands, went to the refrigerator, pulled out a piece of pie, grabbed two spoons, and brought it over for us to share—another tradition we'd developed together.

As we ate in silence, I thought about what she'd said. Could Steve be the key to our safety? After the last few days, I figured anything was possible.

I was relieved that dinner was the usual chaos that I'd come to love about being here. Eddie's boys thankfully hadn't been around during Steve's first visit, so they were clearly reticent to find a stranger at their table, but they warmed up to him quickly enough, especially when he began talking about his adventures in Florida, looking for mound builder sites among the alligators and snakes.

Flex seemed content, although I knew it was mostly put on. I inwardly thanked him for not hounding Steve before he'd had a moment just to relax and get to know everyone.

Steve and Alex seemed to monopolize the conversation. Alex was intrigued by Steve's knowledge of North American's native people and had more than a few questions for him. Unfortunately, before Emma Jean pulled out dessert, Alex was worn out, still recovering from his wounds after being beaten half to death by a couple of drug dealers.

"Save me pie, or else I'll be really mad," he said as he messed up the boys' hair, wishing us all good night. I heard the ATV they'd arrived in start up as Eddie drove Alex back to their side of the duplex.

When Eddie got back, Emma Jean brought out the pie and set it on the old buffet. She put a piece aside for Alex, as he'd requested, then served each of us. I didn't say anything about the fact that Emma Jean and I had shared a piece earlier, and when I brought my plate up, she winked at me conspiratorially.

After we'd eaten our fill, Eddie sent the boys back home to brush their teeth and get ready for bed. "Make sure you check on Alex too, just in case he needs something before you two tuck in. I'll be over later to check on you, okay?" he said, and the boys made their rounds kissing and hugging everyone.

"They seem to be doing well," I told Eddie as they ran off.

"They're as freaked out as the rest of us over Alex being hurt, but I think having him with us has helped some with that."

"They've gotten really attached."

Eddie smiled. "It's hard not to get attached to Alex, but yeah, it's been fun how quickly they've embraced him as part of the family, especially now they are going to be a *real* part of his family."

Eddie smiled, beaming with a hint of pink in his cheeks. It was clear just how much Alex meant to him. He had proposed to Alex just a few days ago and when he'd agreed, I thought Eddie might just float away. He walked around with a huge smile on his face all the time now.

We all cleaned our plates and handed them over to Emma Jean, who began taking them into the kitchen. When Flex stood up to help her, she waved him back. "I'm going to put these in water to soak, then we all need to go sit on the porch and talk. Some things are more important than dinner dishes," she said. The rest of us followed Jimmy out to the long porch.

I always loved how the porch had so much space. When we were kids, it was packed with people all talking at once, but now, it felt just as comfortable filled with this little group of friends.

When Emma Jean came out to join us, sitting next to Jimmy on the big swing, she began the conversation by pulling out the paper she'd written the prophecy on.

"Three brothers died at the hands of three others.The past is past, but now it's repeated,The tables have turned; two have lived and two have died. Do not rest yet, the third brother is still at risk. Between enemy brothers, one will die.Only love can conquer the darkness. He will need both his lover's and his family's love to survive."

After she read it, she pulled her glasses off. "So, what does it mean?"

"The first part's obvious," Flex said. "Three brothers died at the hands of three others. We know what happened to Levy and Jack, but we don't know what happened to Sampson, but I think this pretty much tells us he didn't make it."

Eddie nodded. "The past is the past, but now it's repeated. I think that's what it says. We're reliving their lives, or at least the challenges the brothers faced when they were alive."

Flex continued. "I was shot, but didn't die, thanks to Mitch. Alex was captured and beaten, but he survived too, unlike Jack."

"What I don't get..." Eddie said, "...is why Alex was hurt. He's not one of us. I mean, he's my heart..." he quickly glanced over and winked at Alex, "...and he's descended from Jack, of course, but he's not one of *us* three," he said, gesturing between the three of us.

"And…" Flex added, "Neither Effie nor I are descended from the brothers, if that's the connection."

"What do I have to do with any of this?" I asked. "As far as I can tell, I'm not related to *any* of you."

Steve smiled. "You are all thinking linearly. The spiritual realm seldom works that way. It would make sense in our world if all three brothers had descendants who represented them in this new crisis, but in reality, it's the spirit, or the soul that counts. Flex, you represent the older brother. You're linked to him through Mitch, but also probably in other ways. Alex is descended from Jack, but Eddie, you probably represent someone Jack loved and lost."

Both men nodded.

"Yes," Eddie responded. "We now know I represent Jack's love interest. He was one of the ranch owner's children, although we don't know much about him."

"And Mitch definitely plays a role in this," Flex added. "His great-great-great-grandmother was the daughter of the same ranch owner. We know she married Levy and we can assume Jack's lover was also her brother. We don't know if Levy had a male lover, though."

"Well, about that…" Flex said with a smile. "I had a dream that seemed to be from Levy's point of view. I blew it off then, but, trust me, he definitely had a thing for men."

"I think you're right, Flex." Steve quickly added, "I can feel that all three men loved other men, and they were somehow associated with this ranch... although not the home, I don't think. When was this house built?"

"Imma guessin' the first part of the house was built in the early nineteen hundreds," Jimmy answered.

"Is there another homestead, probably smaller and maybe adobe?" Steve asked, and everyone turned shocked eyes on him.

"Yes, down by the river. It was the original homestead," Eddie answered.

Steve just nodded. "I think Mitch's ancestor was in love with one of the brothers. I'm not sure why he ended up married to the sister, but that's what I'm feeling."

"Do you see them now?" Eddie asked.

Steve shook his head. "I don't see anyone now. At least, not anyone who's passed on. Sometimes the place itself reveals secrets." He chuckled. "That's usually how I do what I do. I can feel something or know something, and then I can do research to prove it. Well, sometimes, I think of it as professional cheating, but with ethics."

I looked around the group, and I knew they were clueless as to what he was talking about. I was the only one grinning, but I knew his work, and understood the secret to his success now.

"Steve, where do you and I fit in?" I asked, hoping to take some of the pressure off him, and understand why we were involved.

Steve looked perplexed. "That's not clear. I can feel us here, and I know that one of the brothers was closely linked to you, but that's about all I can see or feel. I think you and I are both going to have to do some genealogy homework to figure this out."

Emma Jean looked back down at her notes.

"Do not rest yet, the third brother is still at risk. Between enemy brothers, one will die.Only love can conquer the darkness. He will need both his lover's and his family's love to survive."

"I think it's a warning more than anything else," Steve continued. "It would seem now that the two of you are safe," he said, looking toward Flex and Eddie. "You probably feel like you're able to let your guard down, but this is telling you that you can't. If Eric is the third brother, he's at risk."

Steve stood up and walked toward the opening of the porch. When he turned around, he said to me, "Do you remember when we were standing on the ridge above the Little Bird Mine?" I nodded. "I saw the brother there, the one that looked like you. It felt like he was the person killed in the mine—the one buried there."

His eyes shifted back and forth, and he put his hand on the railing, almost like he was about to lose his balance.

"When the other two brothers were killed, he was the most at risk. He didn't know who'd killed the others, just that they'd been killed. This morning, before I drove Eric and myself over here, I saw a figure, someone who looked like a man I worked for before I came to work at the park." Steve looked up at us.

I could see he was warring with himself whether to say any more, so I stepped in, "There was a man we met after we went up to the Little Bird Mine. Like Steve said, he was the owner of the property, and as far as we know, he's a direct descendent of the original owners. The man was definitely a threat to me. Both Steve and I felt it.

Then, this morning, I saw Steve running out of the RV with a baseball bat, and when I got back to him, he said he'd seen the guy, or someone who'd looked like the guy, staring menacingly at him."

"So, you think this man might have been associated with the other brother?" Emma Jean asked.

Steve shrugged. "Until I do some more research, there's no way to know for certain. What I do know is neither the man, nor the ghost who looked like him, were friendly."

A gentle breeze blew across us, and Steve looked up. I knew he was looking at someone none of us could see. Steve looked at me, and we quietly acknowledged it.

"We have enough leads to go on. I'll go into Alpine tomorrow and begin going through old newspapers from that time," I said.

Mitch, who'd been quiet up until that point, said, "I've got articles from when my ancestor passed away. I can give you an estimated timeframe, so you have a better grasp on which papers to look through."

Steve acknowledged us both, then said, "I've already done a lot of research on the Little Bird Mine. I'll go through it to see if there's anything I might have missed. I already asked for death certificates of who might have been killed at the time, but the county assured me they didn't have records of who it was."

"The three brothers were stationed at Fort Davis before moving here." Mitch said. "If you could track down the names of my ancestor and his brother, Jack, maybe you could identify what happened to Sampson, the third brother."

Steve was smiling. "I think I should hire you all to help with research."

We all smiled, but no one responded. Of the people here, I was the only one who had any interest in research, unless someone was hiding their desire and skill from us.

15

Steve

THE NEXT DAY ERIC and I walked over to the main house where Emma Jean was putting out breakfast. "I haven't cooked this much since Alex's film crew left," she said, smiling. "But, since everyone seems to be working together to figure all this out, I feel we all need a good start to our day."

Alex, Eddie, Flex and Mitch sat across from us, and we all caught Alex up on the conversation he missed the night before. "I have information on Jack that my family looked up while preparing for the movie we did here. If that would help, I can have my assistant email that to you as well."

I smiled. "I appreciate everyone's help with this. To be honest, I'm not used to having help. Usually, I'm alone with my research processes, and I'll admit it's sort of nice. Would you all mind telling me everything that's happened, in detail and through your timeline? I think that'll help me understand this more than anything else."

Flex sighed. "I inherited the ranch from my grandparents a few years ago. I didn't get access to the property, however, for five years," he looked over at his cousin and sighed again. "There was a long, drawn-out legal battle, and I had intended to sell the place. Memories of the legal fight overshadowed the love I'd had for this area. When I came for a visit, however, I fell back in love and decided that I'd be keeping the property. It seems to me, at least, that's when the problems began."

Mitch put his hand over Flex's, and added, "Well, I played a part in that too. In fact, it began when Eric and Flex came to stay at the motel. One of my RV owners didn't like Flex, because she assumed he and Eric were lovers. She created a stink, and when I found out she was lying to me, I kicked her out of the campground. Long story short, she and her friends sued me, but lost in court. There was a preacher in town, the particularly nasty kind, only focusing on the parts of the Bible he could use against other people. Since he was one of the men killed..." Mitch looked over at Alex and hesitated. Alex nodded him on and seeing he wasn't upsetting Alex, he continued, "Now we are fairly certain he came out to the ranch one night after my court case and shot Flex."

"If it hadn't been for Mitch, I'd have died that night," Flex took up the story. "Mitch ended up shooting him before he could finish me off." The two men looked at each other for several long moments, and I could feel their love and appreciation for one another from across the table.

"You said there were dreams of a snake. How do they fit in?" I asked.

Flex told me the story of how he'd been given a vision of the place being burned down.

"Is that also the dream where he shot you?" I asked.

"No, that one came later," Flex said. "In the dream with the snake, it was slithering toward me, and when I turned, it struck. I couldn't tell in the dream what happened. It seemed like lightning struck the snake, but it saved me. In real life, it worked out that the snake was the man who shot me in the back when I turned away, and Mitch shot him before he could finish me off."

"But, you didn't see a ghost, or anything like that?"

Flex shook his head, "No, not like we saw the three bothers that day. I saw an image of Levy in my head a couple of times, even the day I was shot."

I turned to Eddie. "In your story, I understood you did see a ghost, your ancestor, Jack?"

"My ancestor," Alex corrected.

Eddie winked at Alex, then they told me the story of seeing Jack, and how Eddie had mistaken Alex for him, and the entire process of their reconciliation.

"Anyway," Eddie said. "My experience was different from Flex's. Jack came and went freely. I saw him often, and even talked to him. Mostly, it was him warning me, or preparing me for Alex's arrival on the ranch, but it was like you and me talking right now."

"I don't even have that," I admitted. "I can never really hear them, not like I'm hearing y'all now. Sometimes I know what they're saying, but it's not hearing per se. So, why was Jack manifesting himself to you so clearly?" I asked.

"Well, I think it was to keep me from running Alex off." Eddie chuckled. "Mostly, though, it was to warn us. The man who'd shot Flex was still lurking around, and my ex's new husband was a real piece of work. Drug dealer in Houston who apparently trafficked through these parts, and worked with a cartel in Juarez, Mexico. Jack seemed to be warning us to keep away from them."

"Do you know why Jack was on the property?" I asked.

Everyone looked at Jimmy, who'd been sitting silently through the entire discussion. "What, y'all want me to tell this part?"

The group laughed, and Jimmy cleared his throat and I knew we were in for a tale.

When he'd finished talking, I sat quietly considering everything. "So, Jack was hired by one of the former owners of this property to protect it from bandit brothers. Are we assuming these are the same brothers who had killed Mitch's ancestor in Alamito?"

"Minus the one that was killed in that raid," Mitch added.

"Where is this gold mine he was protecting?" I asked.

"It's not far.," Eddie said, "It's located in what our grandmother used to call the volcano."

"I'm assuming it's no longer a viable mine?"

The two cousins shrugged. "It really hasn't been mined since Jack, at least not that we know of," Eddie said.

"Jack did extract enough gold from it to start our family on its way toward prosperity," Alex added, "so there's gold down there, or at least, there was."

"Why didn't your family pursue it further?" I asked, looking at Flex.

"I don't think anyone really knows. I'm guessing they were so frustrated with the mine and the trouble it had brought to the ranch that they just wanted it to go away. It never produced enough gold to be worth much. I think it was more of a nuisance than anything else."

I nodded, letting everything settle into my mind. "Have you all seen anything else around here that could be paranormal?"

"I saw Jack's lover, the one that looked like a tall version of me," Eddie said. "That was after I found a little sculpture Jack did of him in the cave that opened up next to the mine. I was wrapping the figurine when Jack appeared in my living room." Eddie chuckled. "Jack just came and hung out while I wrapped it, like we were old friends or something. We talked about him and his lover, and how he'd made the little sculpture for him when they were forced apart by a visit from Jack's son.

He was very conversational. I still think Jack was lonely. He'd fallen hard for this guy, he'd talked about loving others he'd lost, and how he didn't think he'd be able to love again, then... well, we all know they ended up together. I think he meant to come warn me about the men who were wandering around the cave and mine. Those are the men who eventually kidnapped Alex. What's strangest, I think, is that after Jack disappeared, I felt... you know, now that I think about it, I could feel the spirits before I saw them. Well, I felt someone else and turned, thinking it'd be Jack. Of course, it wasn't, it was the one who looked like me. Unlike Jack, who was talkative from the minute I met him, this one just smiled and winked at me, then he was gone."

The entire group were fixated on Eddie. "You never told us this," Flex said.

Eddie shrugged. "It felt private. Like I was somehow involved with their personal love lives. I did tell you I'd been warned though, just not all the details of how."

Alex reached over and took Eddie's hand into his own. "I love that story, honey. Do you think they're back together?"

Even though Eddie shrugged, I nodded. "Yeah, they are. I can feel that now you've told me the story. Something changed just recently, I think, and they are together."

I looked over at Flex and Mitch. "Yours, they're together too."

They looked at me strangely. "Ours?" they asked in unison.

I nodded. "We need to work it out, but like I said before, I think there's another lover involved." I thought for a moment and then added, "I think he's one of the kids born here on the ranch."

"Wait," Mitch said excitedly. "There *was* another brother. There was some outlaw preacher who ended up killing a man who worked in the saloon, saying he was an abomination. I remember now. The man who I later discovered my ancestor had killed. That's how Levi became a lawman. The preacher was one of the brothers who were wanted by the Texas Rangers. There was even a reward. Do you think my ancestor, Levy was lovers with one of the ranch brothers?"

I nodded. "I'm sure of it. If you have more information on him, send that to me as well. I'm thinking the more pieces of this puzzle we can put together, the quicker we can figure out what the warning might mean."

I was enjoying the mystery part of all this, putting pieces together, having support from new friends. Yeah, I was already beginning to think of this group of people as friends, which was odd since I'd pushed people away all my life. Now, here I was with a group of people who knew a secret about me that could destroy my career, and I was thinking of them as friends.

I felt myself floating, until I looked at Eric. "This is more than just history, though, isn't it?" I asked the room in general before I thought about it.

The room fell silent, and they all turned toward me.

I cleared my throat. "Flex, Alex, you were both nearly killed. Alex, you're still recovering. I've always researched and dealt with historical research for the purpose of academics, never because lives have depended on it, not in a forensic way. But, if recent history is any indication, both Eric and possibly even myself, are at risk."

Eric reached over and took my hand. "The difference is, you and I know the enemy, or at least know who the enemy might be. Up until now, it seems everything was in the dark."

"You also have your gift," Emma Jean added. "Neither Flex nor Mitch had access to the spiritual world, not to the level you do. You should use your gift to keep you and Eric safe. If the spirits can help guide you, don't hesitate to use them."

I nodded, but the thought of actually using my sight to do more than just gather insights about ancient cultures was something I'd never done.

"That scares you, doesn't it?" Eric asked.

"Yeah, I've never actually used it. Not in that way. The one we think is Sampson, like I told you, he's visited me, but never warned me... well, maybe he did, maybe on the rise above the Little Bird Mine. This is all new for me too. I might have seen spirits all my life, but my normal reaction is to ignore them, or pay as little heed to them as I can."

I felt the empathy as the room continued to sit in silence. I didn't know what to say. Maybe if I'd been stronger, or felt more secure with what I could see, I would've been able to alleviate their concerns and convince them I could use my gift to keep everyone safe, but I didn't have that ability.

"You'll know what to do when it's time," Emma Jean said, and stood up to begin clearing the breakfast dishes. We all stood to help her, and she waved us away. "You all go on and get to work putting the puzzle pieces together. I'll see you back here tonight for dinner. In fact, for the next few nights, why don't you all plan to be back here at dinner time, so we can share what you've learned? I'll enjoy having everyone under the same roof for a change, and it'll do Eddie's boys a ton of good to have a big family gathering like we used to."

Eddie smiled at her, and she winked back at him. "Okay, off with you all now. I'm gonna make chicken pot pie, and that takes some doing, so I prefer you all be out from under my feet."

I got the email from Mitch soon after he and Flex got back to the motel. I gave the timeframe for the research to Eric, who had me print a copy of the articles, then took them with him to the library in Alpine.

I needed to spend a couple hours on my grant project, then hopefully I'd have more information from Eric's research to get a good start on looking up the brothers.

I'd already decided I wanted to create a family tree that traced the lineage of the brothers, and relationships they'd had. I had a feeling, the devil, you might call it, was in the details.

I found it almost impossible to concentrate on my grant work, so I finally gave up and began writing up the family tree. I wrote the brothers first, then I used data from Alex's family, the most complete data down to today.

Jack's daughter never married, so I assumed the bloodline stopped there. He did, however, have several cousins that branched off. Most lived in Mexico, however, so they probably didn't influence either Eric or me.

I then began exploring Mitch's family tree. When I phoned him, he was able to tell me his grandfather's name, which got me through his entire line back to Levy.

I got as far as I could without digging deeper, and after navigating various documents, I saved my data and opened up the research I was doing for the parks. I let my mind wander as I searched papers and articles written back as far as I could find. Research was cathartic for me. I was lost in my research, only to look up and find an entire day had passed me by. When Eric returned to the RV, disappointed with his lack of success, I'd managed to focus on my job for over four hours.

Eric updated me on what he'd been doing. "I found the articles Mitch sent, but besides that, we seem to have hit a dead end. There's absolutely nothing in the papers of that time about the Little Bird Mine, except what you already had. Some poor man was buried alive while the mine was being raided. The article spoke about who the raiders were, and later I found reference to their trial and hanging, but I never found any reference to the brother."

"Same as me," I agreed. "He seemed insignificant to the story. I asked Mr. Brice if he had family records of who worked in the mine before it collapsed, but he didn't know of anything either."

Just mentioning the name caused Eric to shudder. "I'd prefer if we could do this without including him."

I hugged him and agreed. "We can assume the brother is the one down there, but we need evidence to prove it. We can spend some time on that tomorrow."

I thought for a moment, then smiled. "Wanna take a day trip over to Fort Davis? I'm sure we could dig up quite a lot of information about the brothers there.

Neither Eric nor I had gotten much sleep the night before, as we lay awake discussing the different ways we could research the last brother. So, we both decided to take Puddles for a quick walk, and then crash until we had to go over to the main house for dinner.

That night, everyone was full of talk about what they'd found during the day. Mitch started off by telling us what he'd found. "As we all know, my great-great-great-grandfather became a federal judge and had two daughters. One died young, the other married and had three kids, one of whom was my grandmother. I couldn't find anything in our family history that explained what happened to the other two siblings. My great-grandmother only had one child before she died of tuberculosis, and that was my grandfather."

I nodded. "I found basically the same thing. Your grandfather's aunt and uncle disappeared off the census rolls as well, so until I have more time to go through records I won't know where they ended up, or if they had children.

Alex chimed in next. "So, I had my father go through his records about my aunts and uncles. Most of my family migrated back to Mexico. I chased those leads, and some of them seem to have migrated back to the US, but that's been within the past fifty years. They're also scattered all over the states, and none seem to have settled back in Texas."

"So, that's a dead end as well?" I asked.

"Not necessarily," Alex continued. "It appears Jack's daughter is more of an enigma than we thought. She never married, though we already knew that, but my fourth-great-grandmother, Jack's ex-wife, and their daughter lived together until she died. They lived on the Juarez side of the international line. She was from a fairly well-off family, and probably because her parents died shortly after she and Jack split, she inherited the land and home. Anyway, Papa traced who inherited the property in Juarez, and it appears it was a man by the name of Clifford Cox, which is strange, since it isn't a typical Latin name. Cox sold the property shortly after Jack's daughter passed away, and Papa lost track of him from there."

"That's promising," I said. "So, it's possible your way back great aunt had a baby out of wedlock."

"Very. There are no records in the church they went to, but it's also possible the church refused to christen a child born out of wedlock. That would've been pretty much how the church operated at that time."

"Would there be birth records anywhere else? Or maybe death records?"

Alex shrugged. "Papa is trying to find more information now. If we could find out where Cox moved to after he left Juarez, it might help."

"That's good. We have some leads then," I said, unable to stop myself from grinning.

"We're going to take a day trip to Fort Davis too," Eric said cheerfully. "Maybe we can find Sampson and trace his information as well. Maybe he had a kid or two that we're missing."

I shook my head. "I don't think so. It doesn't *feel* like he had children, but like I said before, I don't always get it right. I could be wrong."

16

Eric

S TEVE CONNECTED WITH ONE of his contacts at the Friends of Fort Davis, who had access to most of the information regarding commissioned officers that operated at the fort. We drove over early Saturday morning, leaving Puddles with Flex and Mitch, as the fort didn't allow pets on its premises.

As we surfed through the non-electronic files, we finally found Levy, who was the highest-ranking officer of the three brothers. Shortly after that, we found Jack's name. Unfortunately, we were really having difficulty finding any reference to Sampson, until the man who managed the archives showed up to talk with us.

When we told the old archivist what we were looking for, he laughed. "They are the most well-known officers during the time they were here. It was unusual that all three brothers were stationed in the same fort so far away from civilization."

He went over to another set of records, looked through them and pulled out a photograph. In the photo were three men, their names neatly typed underneath. Levy Seawell, Sampson Seawell, and Jack Seawell Zitlal.

"I'll be damned," I said, and stared at the picture. "It's grainy, but damn, he does look a lot like me."

The archivist looked at the photo, and smiled. "I'm guessing he is an ancestor?"

I shrugged. "That's what we're trying to figure out. Do you have any way of knowing what happened to the three men after they were discharged?"

"You can see if they were receiving a pension after they were discharged, but I wouldn't hold my breath. Unless they lived past eighteen ninety, or even better nineteen hundred and seven, when the pension act was changed, they probably didn't get anything after they were discharged, meaning the US government didn't keep track of them.

"I'll look through the archives and see if there's any mention of where the men went, but I doubt I'll find anything. Meanwhile, if you two want to go to the courthouse, you can look at the marriage rolls. I know Jack was married while at the fort, because we have records of when he and his family were here. I'm not sure about Levy or Sampson though. You'll have to do some research on that, I'm afraid."

We left the archives and went to the courthouse before it closed. We found mention of Jack and his marriage to a Maria Barbier, along with the birth certificates of their two children. We made copies of everything, figuring if nothing else, Alex might want them. Finding nothing else, we left and headed back toward the ranch.

With the exception of spending an enjoyable day with Steve, we didn't accomplish much more than getting a picture of the brothers together. When we got back, neither of us were in the mood for company, so we ate protein bars and hung out in the RV.

"What did you think of our excursion?" I asked.

"It was semi-productive. I like that part of Texas anyway, the Davis Mountains are pretty."

"I agree," I said, and came over to where Steve was sitting. When I leaned over and kissed him, he smiled under my lips. "Someone feeling frisky?" he asked, and I chuckled.

"Maybe... would you be interested if I was?"

Steve all but picked me up and tossed me onto the bed. We made love before falling into a dreamless sleep.

The next week went by quickly. I buried myself in research for the lineage project, which included signing up for one of those online ancestry services. I even called my father to ask what he knew, but he didn't answer and never called me back. I knew it was a long shot with him. He and my brother had completely shut me out, but I didn't let that get to me. I had a nice little family here at the ranch, and I didn't need to go chasing people who didn't care about me.

Steve was buried with grant work, saying he'd gotten behind the week before. He had to visit a couple more sites in the park, and elected to go on his own, which hurt my feelings a bit. When he confessed he needed to *feel them*, I understood. If I went, I'd be a distraction... Secretly, I did like the fact that I distracted him enough that he had to leave me behind.

I spent the morning in the Alpine Library going back through the papers looking for Sampson's name, and still had no luck. I left just a little after noon, grabbed a bite to eat at a little diner in town, and walked over to the courthouse.

I'd had some luck with the name Sampson Seawell. The Brewster County Courthouse had a mining document in their online files from nineteen fifty-five that mentioned the name. I didn't think much about it, though, since even if he'd lived into old age, he wouldn't have been alive in nineteen fifty-five. I was hitting roadblocks, so I decided I'd delve deeper into the documents to see if maybe the nineteen fifty-five Sampson was a descendant of the Sampson Seawell I was searching for.

The clerk led me into a room, put me in front of a huge book from nineteen fifty-five, and showed me where the documents were. I was flipping through them, rather bored, to be honest, when Sampson's name showed up. I looked it over, and almost jumped out of my chair when I saw that it was *exactly* what we were looking for.

The paperwork was for the opening of a uranium mine in Altuda, a ghost town north of Alamito, but still in Brewster County.

The mine was owned by the same family who owned the Little Bird Mine, although distantly. The family had to document past mining efforts in the county, so they'd submitted information from Little Bird. The documents showed that Little Bird had collapsed during a raid on the mine. The bandits had tried to steal dynamite, but someone had tripped a wire that ignited the explosives, causing the mine to collapse.

There was one casualty, but the document didn't show who had passed. It was in the list of miners where Sampson's name had shown up. Now, I had something I could research. I just needed to narrow down the names of each individual who was there with Sampson. If he was still alive after the mine collapsed, he wasn't our guy. If he was the only one I couldn't find, though, evidence certainly pointed in his direction.

I went back to the library, opened my computer, and began searching the names on the list from the Little Bird Mine. It only took a couple hours, and I was done. I'd eliminated every miner except Sampson. I couldn't find anything about him before or after the mine collapsed, but for our purposes, that was enough evidence to support our theory.

"I see you're looking up the Little Bird Mine," a voice said behind me.

The hairs on the back of my neck instantly stood on end. I knew who was behind me before I even turned around.

"Yes, I am," I said, pasting a fake smile on my face. "Mr. Brice, it's a pleasure to see you, and maybe a little timely."

"Do you have information about my mine?" he asked, his eyes boring into me.

"Actually, I think I may know who's buried in your mine."

Brice seemed to be startled by this. I couldn't be sure, but it appeared like a look of apprehension crossed his face. That was odd, of course, but it was a relief from his creepy staring.

"I found a list of the miners who'd worked for Little Bird, in a recording made by relatives of yours for a mine they were opening in nineteen fifty-five. I've gone through the list of miners, and the only one I can't account for is a Sampson Seawell. Does that ring a bell for you?"

Again, his face held a confusing expression. I couldn't be sure, but it almost looked like the man was angry.

"No, the name doesn't ring a bell," he said, his answer short.

"I didn't think it would, it was a long time ago. Oh, well, I'll keep looking and see if I can figure out who this character was."

I looked up to see the creepy expression had returned. "Why don't you come to my place, and we can… go through my family's records. You might find something there," he said.

"I can ask Steve if he'd like to meet you," I said, causing the creepy expression to turn back to angry.

"Dr. Fowler has already been through our documents."

"Well, he would know what to look for," I said, and started to rise and hopefully make my escape.

"I'd like to take you to dinner," he said.

"That... well, that'd be a little weird," I said, before I could stop myself, and the man laughed.

"What, are you going to tell me you aren't attracted to men?"

I shrugged. "I'm currently attracted to one man in particular. I'm sorry, Mr. Brice..."

"Well, I'm sure if you'd give me a chance, you'd like what I have to offer more than a broken-down old scientist."

"You are confident, and I have no doubt, you do fine with the men or women, whichever you prefer, but I'm sorry, I'm not interested."

I started to walk away, but he grabbed my arm, his strong grip digging into my skin. I knew I'd have a bruise there the next day, though I'd be damned if I'd show this bully, I was afraid of him.

I looked down at his hand on my arm and back up at him. "Sir, I would highly recommend you release me at once, unless you want to explain to the sheriff why you thought you had a right to put your hands on me."

His look was sly, until I mentioned the sheriff, then it turned to mutinous. "I'm not a faggot anyway," he said, and shoved me, slamming my hand into the side of the table.

"Fuck," I said, causing the librarian to stand up behind her desk and look our way. "You need to leave now!" I said, loud enough that she could hear me.

He looked over my shoulder at the librarian before hocking a loogie at my feet.

If my hand didn't hurt from being thrown into the table, I would've thought the act was humorous. It was something you'd have seen happen in an old Western. Of course, I couldn't remember any Westerns featuring a jackass who was angry because another cowboy had turned down his advances.

I walked toward the librarian, stopped, then told her he'd threatened me and spat on the floor. By the time I'd finished speaking, however, the asshole had walked out of the library.

"Do you want me to walk with you to your car?" she asked, and I shook my head. "No, I think he's done what he's going to do."

"Why did he attack you?" she asked, and I shrugged.

"He asked me out to dinner, and I said no."

The woman smiled. "Couldn't take no for an answer?"

"Apparently," I admitted and felt a little better about it all.

"Well, that hand of yours is beginning to swell," she said, looking down at my hand. She must have seen it hit the table when he shoved me.

"I don't think he did it hard enough to break it, but I'm going to have quite a bruise," I admitted.

She nodded. "I'll have to report this to the sheriff. It's required for any incident in the library, so I'm guessing he'll be calling you, unless you just wanna run over there and let them know."

I could tell that was what she'd prefer, guessing there would be quite a hurrah if I didn't.

"No problem, it's just around the corner. If you'll call and tell them I'm on my way, I'll give a statement and then be done with it."

She nodded, clearly pleased I wasn't going to cause her much trouble.

When I got outside, the SOB was nowhere to be seen. I was relieved, since I wasn't too anxious to see him again anytime soon. I considered leaving the car parked at the library and walking, then thought better of it. I didn't want to have another encounter with him if I could avoid it.

When I got to the Sheriff's Office, the sheriff was waiting for me.

"So, you had a run-in with our own Howard Brice, I see?"

"Unfortunately," I said. "It wasn't really that big of a deal, but the librarian looked like she'd prefer that I handle it myself, instead of dragging the library into it."

He smiled. "Missy Jane isn't too fond of paperwork, so I've no doubt you're telling me the truth."

I gave my statement, including the part where he yelled that he wasn't a faggot.

The sheriff chuckled. "Well, for someone who don't like men, he sure sounded disappointed."

"Apparently," I said, and smiled. "Anyway, I don't need to press charges or anything, mostly I'd like him to leave me the hell alone. And just so you know, Sheriff, I'm dating a man who worked for him a few months before we met. I've even been helping to research the mine for him, so he might bring that up if you talk to him."

"Where're you staying, young man?" the sheriff asked. When I told him Flex Henry's ranch, he looked up at me oddly. "Why are you staying there?" he asked.

"Flex, Eddie, and I have been friends since we were kids. I used to stay there in the summers when their grandparents were still alive. I'm in between jobs, so it just makes sense to hang out with them."

"Those boys have had a heap of trouble the past couple of years. I'm sorry it seems you are dealing with our town bully yourself. Unfortunately, I'd have told you to keep off Howard's bad side. The boy's been nothing but trouble since he was a kid. Now that his dad has passed and he's inherited the estate, he's become an even nastier bully."

"It ain't like I went looking for trouble, Sheriff. He came looking for me. Other than meeting him at his mine while hiking around it with Steve, and then again today, I'd never met or heard of him before."

"I have no doubt of it, Mr. Anderson. Just know he seldom lets a perceived slight go. I'll go talk to him and make it clear you aren't to be disturbed, but for the next little bit, I'd keep my eyes open for him. If he comes around again, you let me know."

I nodded my agreement. "I'll keep that in mind, but when I mentioned you to him, he seemed concerned. I'm gonna guess if you plan to speak to him about this, that'll do more to keep him off my tail than filing charges. I get a feeling he doesn't want too much of your attention, if you know what I mean."

The sheriff laughed. "Well, you are perceptive. No, he's on a pretty short leash. Like I said, he's had some trouble with us before, so I doubt the judge'll be too happy to see him back in court."

I nodded. "That's good news for me. Anyway, I'm off. I found most of what I was looking for at the library, so won't need to be in town again, at least not by myself. Maybe that'll give him enough time to cool off before I run into him again."

The sheriff nodded, but looked skeptical.

Oh well, I thought. There wasn't much I could do about it at this point. The world was full of assholes. At least I knew him being a local wouldn't prejudice the local law enforcement against me. To be honest, that was my biggest concern about making a statement.

By the time I got back to the ranch, my hand was hurting, and I knew I probably should put ice on it. I'd broken my hand when I was a kid, so I knew it wasn't broken, but it most assuredly was sprained. When I went into the kitchen where Emma Jean was fixing dinner and asked for ice, she saw my swollen hand and asked what happened.

"I got into it with an overly amorous asshole in town," I answered, which caused her expression to turn more inquisitive. I put the Ziploc of ice over my hand and explained what happened.

"Do you know Howard Brice?" I asked, and she shook her head.

"No, not really. I've only met him a couple times," she said.

"But you know of him?"

She nodded. "In fact, he came by here when Flex had just taken over the property and was asking questions. He was acting like he was interested in buying the place."

"Hmm, well, considering how he acted today, we probably need to tell everyone. I'd normally ignore it, but with our recent warning, I'd say we'd better not discount any potential danger."

"That's wise, Eric," she said, and went back to her cooking. "Is Steve back at the RV?" she asked.

"No, he's out surveying or visiting sites in the park. I didn't really ask him details, since I knew I wouldn't be able to go with him today. I wanted to do some research at the library, which is why I was in town."

"Did you find anything?" she asked, and I remembered the good news.

"Oh, with all the commotion, I almost forgot my good news. Yeah, I've figured out what happened to the final brother, or at least I'm pretty sure I've figured it out. Sampson Seawell, the middle brother, went to work in the Little Bird Mine after Levy and Jack were killed. He worked there until the mine collapsed on him. I have evidence to conclude it was him that was buried in the mine."

"Oh, that's good news," she said. "Sad news, but good news."

I nodded. "It confirms what Steve said he felt. Anyway, I'll bring all the paperwork with me tonight when we come for dinner and will share it with the everyone. Now that we have confirmation it's Sampson in the mine, we can focus on whether the collapse was an accident or on purpose."

Emma Jean smiled. "It helps to have two history experts on the case. All this would be very interesting in and of itself, if we weren't afraid you and Steve were in danger. Maybe once this is all said and done, you can write a book about what you've learned."

When I met her expression, she smiled and winked at me. Emma Jean and I used to talk about my aspirations for when I became an adult. I'd told her I was going to write books about history and about Flex and Eddie's family. I'd actually forgotten those conversations, but now we were talking about it, I couldn't help but smile.

"You think you're sneaky slipping those suggestions in, Mrs. Emma Jean, but I'm onto you."

"Ain't nothing to be on about, I'm just reminding you what you said you wanted to do before you grew up and got whisked away up north."

I chuckled. "I'll think about it. For now, I think we'd better keep our eye on the ball and see how it all turns out."

She nodded and sent me on my way. The ice was helping my hand, and by the time I got back to the RV, most of the swelling had gone down. Since I couldn't really use my hand to type right now, I decided to take Puddles on a nice long walk around the ranch. I'd yet to do much hiking since I'd landed here. I used to love hiking through the hills and valleys of the ranch. Today's sky was slightly overcast, so it wasn't as hot as usual. It was a perfect day to hike.

I grabbed a bottle of water, tucked it into my backpack, along with a portable dog waterer, then Puddles and I took off. Puddles dashed around me, wanting to smell everything as we walked. Not for the first time, I felt ashamed I hadn't done a better job training the little animal how to walk properly on a leash.

We'd only gone a short piece before the ranch dogs that Flex or Eddie had taken in when things had gotten scary with someone attacking Flex showed up. "Hi boys," I said, petting them all before we all continued on our way. I considered letting Puddles off the lead, but I was still too afraid she'd be struck by a snake, or more likely, eaten by a coyote. Those damned things had no fear and a distinctive taste for poodles, so I decided to endure her continued wrapping me in the lead, just to be safe.

We hiked about a mile or so before we came to the area Flex and Eddie's grandma used to call the volcano. When we were kids, Eddie, Flex and I would race to the top. I lost every time, because I was never as competitive as the cousins were. When I came to the place we used to climb, I found a nice boulder that was flat on top. We all used to sit on the top of this boulder when we were done climbing, and pick on each other about who was the best.

I poured water for the dogs and took a long drink of my own, then lay back on the boulder, enjoying the warmth of it. The dogs all lay down on the ground around me, so I tied Puddle's lead onto my belt loop and let my mind drift.

I must have fallen asleep.

At first, the dream was sweet. I saw myself in old western-style clothes, wandering around the countryside on a horse not un-like the one Eddie seemed to prefer. I rode alone over the hills and gullies. Bighorn sheep danced along the side of a steep cliff, and I slipped off the horse and sat down, looking over the vistas.

I was so relaxed, enjoying the scenery and the serenity, when I realized I wasn't alone. There was no alarm, rather curiosity, as I turned and saw Howard Brice. Well, a version of him anyway. This version was more muscular, better filled out, like he'd been trying to become a bodybuilder or something. I wasn't con-cerned about his presence, in fact, I was happy to see him. He sat next to me, ran his hand down my crotch, and leaned over to kiss my neck.

I purred into his touch. I'd waited a long time for him, wanting, watching, and waiting for him to make a move. His kisses sent fire through my body, and the longing for him was almost unbearable.

The dream shifted then, and I was standing in front of him. I could feel my longing again, but this time as I stood in front of my love, the man I wanted more than any man I'd known before or since, was ridiculing me.

"You nasty fuck. If I didn't know my father would kick my ass, I'd fire your sorry ass, and force you to leave the mine, forever."

I was confused. I couldn't tell why he was so angry with me, until two of his buddies came out from around the stables. They beat me while he watched, smiling a seditious smile. As his friends beat me, all the feelings I'd had for him drained out. I'd been a fool. This man didn't love me. He only loved himself.

I fell over clutching my ribs. The man I'd loved with my entire heart leaned over me then, and said, "I told you to keep your perversion to your fucking self. You have no one to blame but yourself!"

He stood, kicked dirt into my face, and walked away.

I startled awake, feeling a lingering pain in my ribs. The dream had been so real. I knew instantly, this wasn't me or Howard Brice in the dream, it was a memory... Sampson's memory.

I didn't have Steve's gift. I couldn't see spirits, but I knew he was there.

"The son of a bitch, really fucked you up, didn't he?" I asked the silence. "Fuck him, he never deserved you!" I said, feeling his bitterness and sadness.

A gentle breeze brushed against me, as if telling me he appreciated my comment. I wished Steve was here, so I could communicate with him better. I wanted to express myself in a way that showed him exactly how much I empathized with him. I decided I'd just talk, and maybe I could associate with him in my own way.

"My wife, well, ex-wife was like him. I had given everything I had to her. Loved her with my entire heart, and she ended up stabbing me in the back, and throwing the love back in my face. I knew what it was like to hurt after that level of betrayal. I'm really sorry, Sampson," I said.

There was no acknowledgment this time, but I knew he'd heard me and related to what I'd said. I didn't know how, but I could just feel it.

I got up and started back toward the homestead. All four dogs came with me. Even Puddles had calmed down, no longer darting around me as she had. It was almost like they knew I needed time to think about the dream, and how closely Sampson's life and mine mirrored each other's.

By the time I got back, Steve was cleaning up and getting ready to go to the house for dinner. When he saw me, he stopped. "Are you okay?" he asked, and I turned to him.

"Sort of, but why would you ask?"

He shook his head. "Something's changed, I can feel it, but I can't put my finger on what."

I chuckled. "You have an odd gift, Steve."

His expression showed hurt, and I quickly went to him. "I didn't mean it that way. It just amazes me that you can discern shifts in the spirit world like you can. I had a run-in with Howard Brice this afternoon and ended up with a swollen hand to show for it."

"Really?" Steve looked alarmed. "What happened? Are you okay?"

"Yeah, I am, and I'll tell you about it when I tell the rest of the group. That wasn't the favorite part of my day, and probably not why you sensed a change in me. I went for a hike after I got back, and ended up hanging out on an old flat boulder Flex, Eddie and I used to play on when we were younger. Anyway, I think I fell asleep, because I had a... well, I'm not sure what you'd call it, maybe a vision or... the best way I can describe it is a memory, but the memory wasn't mine, it was Sampson's. I saw a man who looked like Brice, except more built. Sampson was in love with him, and I mean *really* in love with him.

In the first part of the memory, the built man and Sampson met me and we made love. It was definitely consensual, and I was so happy... rather, Sampson was. The entire memory seemed like it was happening to me, so it's easy to get confused. The dream shifted then, and the guy, the one Sampson was in love with, had set him up. Two men came around the stables and beat him really bad. I could feel the pain as they beat him. But, more than the physical, I could feel the pain of being betrayed. The asshole ended up calling Sampson a pervert." I chuckled at that, because Sampson was no more a pervert than him. "I woke up after the ass kicked dirt on him and walked away."

Steve sat next to me, putting his arm around me. "That gives us more answers then. I'm guessing since he looks so much like Howard Brice, he must've been the mine's owner, or his son."

I nodded. "Yeah, that was part of it too. Before he had his henchmen beat Sampson up, he said he'd have fired him if his dad would've let him. That must mean the owner liked him, and he was somehow important to the mine."

"Interesting, how do we verify that it's him in the mine?" Steve asked, and I smiled.

"Well, I think I'm as close to that as you can get. Before the asshole confronted me in the library, I'd managed to find evidence linking Sampson to the mine. Through a process of elimination, I can safely say, the only person known to have been a miner at Little Bird who I can't verify lived in the area after the mine collapsed was him. We can pretty much conclude that Sampson is the person in the mine."

Steve's eyes grew large. "Good job. You're good at chasing down leads. I researched that mine for months and never got that close. How'd you find this out?"

I chuckled. "Well, I followed a hunch, but let me get cleaned up for dinner. I'll tell you when I tell the rest of the crew."

Steve smiled, pulled me into a kiss, and held me for a moment. "I can think of better ways to celebrate," he said, and I laughed.

"I'll take a raincheck on that, but I'm honestly starving, and what I smelled coming out of Emma Jean's kitchen when I came back this afternoon made my stomach growl."

"Hmm, not sure I like competing with Emma Jean."

I kissed him smartly on the mouth, and laughed. "Baby, you can't compete with Emma Jean. You've heard the saying the way to a man's heart is through his stomach. I can attest to that, and the fact that Emma Jean is my first love!"

Steve leaned back with a full laugh, pinched my ass, then moved his hand to my crotch. "But, I'm the one who makes you squirm," he said, causing my body to shudder.

He let me go then, and grabbing his satchel that was sitting next to the door, he winked at me and said he'd see me over there.

17

Steve

A s Eric rehashed his day, starting with the discovery of the list of miners in the Little Bird Mine and how he'd managed to whittle down the list, until the only possible person who could be buried in the mine was Sampson. The group was ecstatic.

Things turned ugly, though, when he described how Mr. Brice had confronted him in the library, propositioned him, then threw his hand into the table when he said no. I had a hard time controlling my anger as he told the story. I'd love to have that son of a bitch in front of me right now. I was sure I could help him understand how to have better boundaries.

Finally, as he described the experience while hiking, I began to remember the first time *I* had met the entity we now knew as Sampson. As Eric explained, lying on the flat boulder, I remembered the entity leading me to the flat mesa next to the watering hole, and I knew that was where the two had met for their rendezvous.

"This makes sense now," I told the group. "When I first met Sampson, it was in the park, along a creek bed. He led me out along the creek to a flat mesa that had a beautiful vista of the area but was still concealed. From the Little Bird Mine, there's a lookout, and you can see the spot from there—although, just barely. I think that's where Sampson and his lover met before things turned for the worst."

"You think he was taking you there to show you?"

"It's hard to say, although it was the day I met you. Maybe he sensed that we were going to meet soon. Regardless, the puzzle pieces are beginning to come together."

"There was something else that was strange, and might be just me overanalyzing things, but before he asked me out, I said Sampson's name to Mr. Brice, and told him we'd narrowed down the list of miners to show that it was likely Sampson who had died in the mine. He looked... well, he looked upset about it. Is it possible he already knew, and that the family was keeping it a secret?"

We all sat quietly, thinking about it. "It's more than possible. If we're to assume Sampson was killed by the last of the gang of brothers who'd murdered the first two, and if we assume this guy's the one that killed him, then he'd have to be the last of the gang."

"That's easy enough to chase down," Mitch said. "The three brothers were wanted by the law. My ancestor Levy, had killed the first brother, the preacher, and had gotten a reward for it, so we should be able to trace down the name of the wanted man, and trace his family name. If the mine owner's sons were responsible for the Levy and Jack's deaths, and we already know those deaths were well known, then if the last son killed him and did it in the family's mine, it doesn't take much to assume they'd want to keep that quiet."

We all nodded, and I thought we'd all come to the same conclusion.

"I doubt it would've been too difficult at the time to pay off the paper regarding who was buried. By that time, Sampson really didn't have a family, so I doubt the paper would've cared one way or the other," I said, supporting Mitch's theory.

Mitch nodded, then added, "I'll go through my family's stuff again tomorrow. My family was really proud of our lawman ancestor, and his son, the judge. I'm sure there's a record some-where about who killed him. If not, I'm sure we can go through Texas history. The US Marshal would've had to document who he gave reward money to, and why. They'll still have a record of that, if nothing else."

Eric looked up. "I'll get back onto the ancestry part of this then and see if I can link us somehow. My dad is avoiding me, so I can't ask him, but I'm guessing since my mom's family is from this side of Texas, it's more likely that if I'm related, it's through her."

Flex looked over at Eric. "Why is your dad avoiding you?"

Eric shrugged. "They're upset because Lisa drove a wedge between us. They're saying I shouldn't have let her."

Flex made an annoyed sound. "Um, they could've tried harder. No offense, Eric, but your dad and brother are as dependable as my mom. They're only in this for themselves."

Eric looked sad. "I know, Flex, but they're the only relations I've got."

"Bullshit," Flex responded almost angry. "Dude, you, Effie and I are more family than any of our birth families ever were. Face it, dude, we're your *real* brothers. I know it's hard to let birth ties go, but ain't no use you letting them get to you, when you've got us."

Eddie sat across from Eric, smiling sadly. "We all know my mom is the bitch of the century. Flex is right, this is your family. It's mine too. So, stop pretending like you're an outsider."

I could tell Eric was touched, then he chuckled. "Why do I have a feeling this is about you wanting to pass chores onto me."

Eddie leaned back into a laugh. "Since you brought it up..."

Eric tossed his napkin at him, and the conversation turned to all the ways the three boys used to try to avoid working during the summers. The best one included the three of them darting out of the house when no one was looking and getting caught skinny-dipping in the river by a group of Catholic schoolgirls on an outing.

That night, we all sat around on the porch. Everyone had a busy morning the next day, so we didn't stay long, but Alex poured everyone a round of some costly tequila he'd brought with him from El Paso.

I wasn't much of a tequila drinker, and had honestly never had high grade before, but damn if I wouldn't want to from now on. The shots slid down our throats in a delightful way, and gave us all a nice buzz.

After taking Puddles for her evening walk, Eric came in and wrapped himself around my back. "I'm cashing in that raincheck," he said, and I couldn't help the smile that crossed my face.

The weather turned nasty the next day, and kept me from going back out to the documented sites as I'd planned. Instead, Eric and I worked side by side in the RV, as the thunder echoed around us.

Eric had taken Alex's information and, with more documentation from Alex's father, had shown Clifford Cox moved from Juarez to Laredo in the US. On his death certificate, his mother, Consuelo, had been named, so we could now assume Cox was indeed her son. It was easy to trace him after we could place him in Loredo.

I wasn't the least bit surprised to find out that Cox was my direct ancestor, especially as I'd found several ancestors between

Cox and me that had been admitted to various mental institutions.

"It seems my so-called gift has plagued a lot of my ancestors," I said to Eric, and he reached over to side hug me. "It's a shame they had to live in a time when those gifts would've been seen as mental illness."

"I can't say I'm too surprised, though. My great-grandmother reportedly died of a lobotomy gone wrong. Anyway, so now we know my connection, what's yours?" I asked Eric.

"I'm still chasing that down, but don't get your hopes up. I don't really know that I am. Maybe I'm just connected with Flex and Eddie, and that spurred this on."

"Possibly, but that doesn't feel right. It feels like you're connected in a more genetic way."

Eric shrugged. "We'll chase it down. Maybe Sampson had a child out of wedlock, and we'll never know one way or the other."

"Maybe, but we might as well go back through your family tree and see who was around at that time. That's probably the best way to pursue this. Do you have any leads there yet?"

Eric shook his head. "No, to be honest, I've been a little reticent to look. A big part of me wants to believe I really am a descendant of the same bloodline as the rest of them, but another part of me is afraid I'm not, and knowing will destroy the illusion. Flex and Eddie say I'm family, but it doesn't feel like I am, not really. It still feels like I'm alone. I know that's not fair to them. They've always embraced me, and so did their grandparents, but since my mom died, I've felt like I don't belong anywhere. It's silly…"

I looked over at him. The sadness from that night—the night I'd found him with the pills—was on his face again. "Listen to me, Eric, my parents aren't that great either. They cared a hell of a lot more about their image than they ever did about me. Hell, it's been years since I've even talked to them. I've lived my entire life alone, and even thought that's how I liked it, how I wanted it, but in just the short while we've been here, I've never felt so accepted, and I've never felt like I belong somewhere. That's different here. I feel like I can be connected with this group in a way I've never even considered before."

I chuckled self-consciously. "It's sure as hell not easy, and it's taken me a lot of internal work to manage my fears. Part of me still thinks it's only a matter of time before the other shoe drops, and one of them tells someone from my professional life that I'm insane and claim to see ghosts. I totally get why you're afraid to trust them, why you'd be afraid to look, in case you aren't somehow related, but seriously, you can't live your life that way, afraid the people you love will kick you to the curb. And, you're right, it isn't fair to Flex and Eddie, they weren't lying when they said you're family. I saw the truth of it in their expressions. They are yours too, at least, if you just let them be."

Emotions stirred through Eric, and he inconspicuously wiped away a tear. I almost said something about him not having to hide from me, but I decided against it. Even though it felt like Eric and I had been together for years, at this point, we were still new. We needed the time to bond before I started pushing him to remove all his barriers.

I thought up until that moment, I hadn't considered what we had going on could be something long-term. The thought almost choked me. All the old messages of not being someone who could be in relationships swept over me. Unfortunately, I flinched, and Eric sat back looking wounded.

"I'll go see if they need any help in the house, and give you some space," he said.

I jumped up and pulled him back into an embrace. "I'm sorry, wait. I just had a moment of clarity about the possibilities in our relationship, and it scared me for a second." I laughed. "Eric, you have no idea how hard it is for me to trust people, and all of a sudden, here you are getting past boundaries I didn't even know existed. Every so often, I'm going to freak a little, I'm sure."

Eric smiled in understanding and embraced me again. "It's okay. I'm scared too. We can work through it, though, right?"

I nodded, but I was truly feeling skeptical about that at the moment.

I changed the subject. "It's going to be wet and nasty tomorrow. Why don't I stay here and do your ancestral search? That way I'm the one doing it, and you don't have to deal with the anxiety. If, when I'm done, you aren't ready to hear it, I'll keep it to myself."

Eric laughed. "You know, once we have the information, my curiosity will win out over my fear."

I smiled and shrugged. "Probably, but at least it'll take the pressure off. Sometimes we need a choice, whether or not we already know what choice we're going to make."

That night when Eric announced that I was descended from Jack's daughter Consuelo, Alex jumped up, then winced from the pain. "Too early for that," he said. In his next breath, he said, "Primo! I could tell we were related the minute we met."

I couldn't help but laugh. "You do realize we're like fifth cousins or something like that."

"Oh, it doesn't matter. Until now, I didn't even know Jack's daughter had a son. Mi papá will be so excited."

I continued to chuckle and shook my head. "So, do you know if anyone in your family shares the same abilities as I have?"

"With the spirits? No, that would be something we'd have talked about. Mexican people don't have as much trouble with the other world as Americans do. We accept it as part of our lives and culture."

"It's definitely very much a part of my family," I said. "And it hasn't done any of them much good. The history of admissions to mental facilities has been fairly consistent through the generations."

Alex shook his head. "It could've come from Clifford on his papa's side. Do you know who his father was?"

I shook my head. "No, there's no evidence of that. Your great-whatever-aunt was listed on Cox's death certificate as his mother, but there was never a mention of his father, and Cox is too common of a name to trace it that way."

"Don't give up. I think you are meant to know about it now. That's why we're all together like this, so we can know the secrets of our ancestors."

I couldn't help but smile at Alex's optimism. I wasn't sure I agreed with his assessment, but it felt good to think it could be true, and life had reason and purpose, even if we didn't know what it was.

When dinner was over, Alex phoned his father on the house phone, turned on the speaker phone, and told him about our discovery. When he was done telling how I was descended from Clifford Cox, the old man exclaimed, no different from Alex, that we were cousins or primos, to be more accurate.

"How's your acting, or better yet, got experience with directing?"

When I looked questioningly at Alex, he burst out laughing. "Our film production company is family-owned, and mostly family-run. Papa's trying to figure out how to pull you into the fray."

I laughed. "Um, I'm afraid I'm an archeologist, señor Zitlal, and not the Indiana Jones kind. I'm not going to be much use to you in the film industry."

"No problema, primo. We'll find you a place. I'm sure Alex will recognize your hidden talents, and draw you in before the weekend is over."

I smiled, knowing I was being teased, but also that they were trying to make me feel accepted. It felt good. Maybe I could broach the subject of the family *gift*, and see if it had possibly come through this line.

As promised, the next day, I began going through Eric's maternal family line. What I found both astonished and confused me. Eric's grandmother lived in Toyah, a semi-ghost town outside Pecos, Texas. She owned a vast section of the desert there and did everything from running cattle to telling people's fortunes.

His grandfather had passed away many years earlier. She never remarried, and apparently became a businesswoman. Eliza, short for Elizabeth, had reams of information in the papers about her.

I read the articles, falling more and more in love with the eccentric Western woman. Most of the people in Toyah were both afraid and strongly bonded to the old woman. She did have some people who didn't like her, though. The paper quoted several through the years who called her a witch, or, more often, the Toyah Witch.

In one article from the early nineteen sixties that was intended to shine a negative light on her, she was rumored to speak to the dead. That was the part that confused me. If she had the ability, and the more I learned about her, the more I thought she probably did. I wondered how that related to me and my skills.

I printed the most illuminating articles about the Toyah Witch, including the negative one, and a couple that made me laugh, and then began my climb back through her ancestral line. Luckily, the family was Catholic, and I was easily able to find links through the Church's records. Eliza Drake was born in Toyah, and her husband was born in Odessa.

Because she reportedly had the same gift I did, I chose to pursue her family tree instead of her husband's.

Her mother was from Marfa before moving to Toyah, but her father was from Chihuahua, Mexico. It was already late in the day, Eric had left to help Flex and Mitch at the motel, and I really wanted to find a link for him before they arrived.

I decided the Marfa connection was the best route, since Marfa was just down the road from Alpine.

My instincts were right. Louisa Banks, maiden name Seawell, granddaughter to Levy Seawell, was the mother of both Mitch's and Eric's great-grandmothers.

There we had it, both of us were, in fact, linked to this family, albeit not in the way I would've assumed.

I spent the next few minutes creating a file and saving all the links with my research. I also drew a simple family tree that showed exactly how Mitch and Eric were related.

I highlighted Eliza on the tree, and decided I'd surprise them all with my findings of the Toyah Witch. Apparently, we shared some of the same traits, but unfortunately, for my family it ended up leading to mental hospitals, in Eric's it seemed to lead to notoriety.

I vowed to myself I'd visit Eliza's home and learn more about her, and now that I thought about it, get to the bottom of why Eric didn't know more about his grandmother.

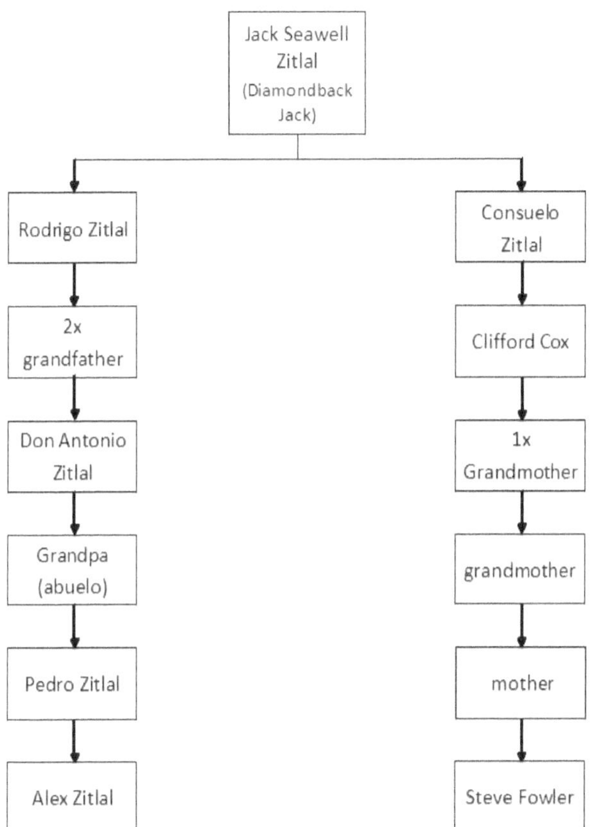

Jack Seawell Zitlal (Diamondback Jack)
Rodrigo Zitlal
Consuelo Zitlal
2x grandfather
Clifford Cox
Don Antonio Zitlal
1x Grandmother
Grandpa (abuelo)
grandmother
Pedro Zitlal
mother
Alex Zitlal
Steve Fowler

18

Eric

During breakfast, Flex and Mitch were talking about needing to do some work on a busted pipe running into the RV park, and knowing Steve was going to spend the day researching my family tree, I decided I'd rather keep my hands busy than sit around waiting for him to find out what I wasn't sure I wanted to know.

It ended up working out well because the pipe was located under some of Mitch's prized cactus gardens, and it took all morning for us to delicately, and by delicately, I mean like working with cacti that had thorns that went through thick leather gloves like they were made of silk.

By the time we got the cacti moved out of the way, the repairs were quick. Just had to find the broken pipe, cut it off, and replace it.

After an excruciating time replacing the cacti, and, of course, moving a couple to a different bed because Mitch said they were too big for the space now, I was ready for a break.

When we were finally done, I was hot, exhausted, more than a little irritable after a day of being a pin cushion, *and* I dreaded going back to the ranch and dealing with whatever Steve had found.

Regardless of my apprehension, arriving back at the ranch, I went into the RV, kissed Steve's head, and with as little discussion as possible, went into the bedroom and got a change of clothes. I decided to use the bathhouse instead of the RV, again mostly because I wanted to avoid Steve, but using the excuse that I was too dirty to use the RV.

The cool water of my bath calmed my nerves enough that when I came back into the RV, I was able to sit across from Steve without wanting to scream at him for absolutely nothing or run away like the coward I certainly felt like at the moment.

Steve finished up whatever he was working on, and leaned back, smiling.

"How was your day?" he asked, the smile never leaving his face.

"Shit, mostly. I've never been stuck so many times in my life. I love Mitch's cactus gardens, but damn, they suck if you have to move them!"

I looked at my hands, not wanting to know what Steve had found. He came over and sat next to me, bumping my shoulder. "You're related," he said, causing me to look up in shock.

"Really?" I asked, not sure how to define the plethora of emotions running through me.

"Really, so do you want me to show you now, or wait until dinner when we can tell the whole family?"

The most apparent emotion I felt was relief, followed by a return to exhaustion. "I think I'd like to take a nap, and let what you've just told me sink in. I'll wait until you tell the entire family. Hopefully, that'll give me time to get my wits about me."

Steve leaned over and kissed my cheek. "I'll let you nap alone, and go harass the rest of *your family*, then."

"Apparently, they're yours too."

"Way back, they're both of ours." Steve laughed. "Does this mean we're kissing cousins?"

I chuckled. "I'm not sure we count as cousins any longer, but if that's your kink, we can pretend."

Steve shuddered. "I don't think so, let's forget that part of it, shall we?"

I laughed. "Okay, go away, I want that nap now."

He kissed me again, then went to gather his things that I assumed he was going to show tonight at dinner, before heading out the door.

After he was gone, I lay on the bed and let my mind drift. I fell asleep fairly quickly and didn't wake up for over an hour. I wasn't one to take naps, but apparently, I'd started a new trend. The rest was what I needed to come to terms with, all the anxiety I'd felt about the process.

Now that Steve had told me I was related, I guessed I could admit, I always sort of knew. There was a connection to this place and these people that, in some way, went deeper than my immediate family. I belonged to this part of the world. Houston had felt wrong, Oregon had felt even less like home, but West Texas felt exactly right.

I headed to the homestead and saw Steve and Flex sitting on the porch. They were both smiling, and I couldn't help but wonder if Flex was now privy to my news. Part of me was jealous I wasn't the first to know, but of course, I'd sent Steve off without telling me. I couldn't begrudge him for letting the cat out of the bag.

I came up to them and sat on the swing next to Flex. "So, whatcha talking about?" I asked.

When both Flex and Steve blushed and looked uncomfortable, I laughed. "So, it was about me, I can tell."

Flex shrugged. "I might have been being a little overprotective of you these past few weeks. I was sort of apologizing to Steve for being an ass about it."

I didn't know what to make of that. "So, you two have made nice over me then?"

"We've made nice over our pissing contest," Flex admitted. "The truth is, I like Steve. I was jealous of his relationship with you. I guess I was afraid now that you liked guys, he'd come between us, like..."

"Like Lisa did," I said, and shook my head. "Flex, I can't apologize enough for that whole fiasco. Lisa was a bitch. I lost my way, thinking I had to make the relationship work, and ostracizing you and my other family to try to do that."

I looked over at Steve, then back at Flex, and said, "I've learned my lesson. I will never let someone I like romantically get in between my family and friends again. If I ever get married again, it'll be to someone who can accept y'all as a part of me."

Steve winked at me, and I turned to Flex. "I love you, Flex. You, Mitch, Eddie and Alex, and this entire West Texas family thing we've got going on."

Flex embraced me, and we hugged for several moments, until Mitch came out. "Hey, you're hugging up on my man there, buddy," he said, laughing.

"It's okay for brothers to hug, Mitch. Don't be a toxic male."

"Psst!" Mitch exclaimed. "So, y'all having a bonding moment? Should I let you have some space?"

"Nah," I said. "Join us, we're just talking about how I'm not going to let another relationship get in the way of ours."

Mitch smiled, but didn't respond. I got up and scooted in next to Steve, letting Mitch sit next to Flex.

We were talking about everything under the sun, when Eddie's two boys came running across the yard and onto the porch.

"I beat you, again," the oldest one, Drake, said.

"You didn't give me my head start, so that didn't count," his brother, Luke, responded.

They ended up sticking their tongues out at each other, and were about to burst into the house, when Emma Jean met them at the door.

"The two of you need to go wash up. I can smell the dirt coming off of you from here."

They grinned and did as she instructed.

Emma Jean smiled after them just as Alex turned up on the ATV.

After Alex turned the machine off, Emma Jean looked over at us. "I hope y'all are hungry. We're having fried chicken tonight, and I made more than I meant to. The grocery store was having a sale, so I bought some of those huge packs. Anyway, y'all get cleaned up too, and when Jimmy and Eddie come in, we'll eat.

Emma Jean made the best fried chicken in the world. I wasn't sure how, but it was crispy and not too greasy.

This was one of the meals she never showed me how to cook. Of course, that got my mind spinning. Emma Jean was getting older. I should start spending more time in her kitchen to see if I could learn how to cook the way she did. If I planned to stick around, I'd need to be more helpful, and the truth was, I wanted to stick around, more than I'd ever wanted anything.

Eddie and Alex's wedding was in the next couple weeks, and I'd agreed to stand up with Eddie along with Flex. All this meant, Eddie would be spending less time on the ranch, and I figured, that meant they'd need more help around the place.

I'd already decided I'd try to go back to school to finish my teaching certificate, then I'd see if I could get a job working at the local school district. If not, I'd need to figure something else out. Maybe even working with the parks department, but I'd probably need to go back to school for that as well.

My mind was wandering over these thoughts, while everyone talked about their days, and devoured their meals. When I looked over at what had started out as a huge pile of fried chicken on the buffet, I saw it was gone, except for a leg, and what appeared to be a thigh.

I laughed. "Emma Jean, you were worried about us not finishing off the chicken?" I said, pointing at the plate.

She smiled. "I shouldn't have been. Heck, Drake and Luke ate almost twice what you guys did."

The two boys smiled at us, each looking up from a piece of chicken.

"Boys have hollow legs," Jimmy said. No one really responded, since that was a fact each of us had intimate knowledge of, having been their age once ourselves.

The boys were in charge of cleaning the table tonight, so after Emma Jean helped them take the dishes into the kitchen, and got them started washing, she came back and sat down with the rest of us.

"I'm making homemade ice cream for dessert, but it'll be a moment before it's done," she said.

Steve smiled. "In that case, while we wait, I've had success in my research of Eric's family tree."

The entire room fell silent as everyone's attention turned toward Steve.

He looked at me and handed me a piece of paper, then gave an identical one to Mitch.

"It seems the two of you are distant cousins. The oldest brother, Levy, had a son, and that son had two daughters. As you can see from my crude drawings. Mitch is the descendant of one of the daughters and Eric is the descendant of the other's."

"Well, I'll be," Mitch exclaimed. "I always did wonder what happened to that line of the family. My grandpa was an only child, as were my mom and me, so we don't have family outside of us. I knew the judge had another daughter, but we lost track of her descendants long ago."

I smiled. I could feel myself becoming emotional as I followed the line up from my mom to grandma to Mitch's and my common ancestor.

"If you want," Mitch said, "next time you're at the motel, I'll show you the information I have about the judge we're both descended from. He was quite a character and known throughout the land. He was pretty notorious."

"Speaking of notoriety," Steve said, "I found some more information, something that might shed a little light on things."

He reached down next to him and pulled out several articles, and handed them to me.

"Your grandmother was Eliza Drake Hoge. As you can see in the articles, she was known as the Toyah Witch."

He paused to let me look over the article. When I looked back up at him, I could tell he was excited about what he'd found.

I read from the article, "The Toyah Witch, Eliza Hoge, claims she can see the dead and that they talk to her, giving her information to help those in need... It goes on to talk about her having the devil in her, but damn, Steve, she had the same gift as you."

He nodded. "That's what I'm gathering, and she used it to her benefit, holding seances, reading people's fortunes, all sorts of stuff that put her on the bad side of those who wrote that article."

"It also made her pretty infamous. That does explain a lot."

When I looked up, the entire group was watching me. I shook my head. "My mom and grandmother didn't like each other at all. My mom was a devout Catholic, and I'd heard her call her mother a witch more than once growing up. I never knew her. When my grandmother died, she was rather wealthy, having sold oil rights on land just outside of her town center to an oil company. I thought it was strange then that my grandmother, whom my mom hated, ended up buying our family's home, and eventually sent me to college. We still receive small payments from the oil company, which go into my brother's and my trust that was set up after my mom passed away."

"Did your mom ever talk about having the ability to see spirits?"

I shook my head. "No, and if she did, she'd never have told me or anyone else. She would've thought it was demonic."

"I think, because I have this skill, and many of my ancestors did as well, that it's a family trait that came through Levy, Sampson, and Jack's father. If it'd come through Jack's mother's side, which I originally suspected, your grandmother wouldn't have had it."

"So, we all could have the trait?" I asked, looking at Steve.

He shook his head. "No, Flex and Eddie aren't directly descended from the three brothers. Only Mitch, Alex, you and I are."

"I'm not sure I want to see spirits," Alex said. "No offense, Steve."

Steve smiled. "I'm not sure I do either, but it's not something I got to choose, and if you look at the horrors my ancestors have experienced since the turn of the nineteenth century, you'll see they'd have probably been happy to avoid it themselves if they could've."

"Well, now that we know where our connections all come from, where do we go now?" Flex asked.

"I'm guessing we can assume our enemy is Howard Brice. He's the one who's likely descended from the man who killed Sampson, and from what he did to Eric's hand, he's still a threat."

"How can we combat him?" I asked. "It's not like we can go to the sheriff and tell him our fifth-great-uncle came to us in a vision and told us to watch out for him."

Eddie chuckled. "Yeah, I sort of tried that when I suspected Alex, it didn't go over too well."

Alex smiled. "I think that's where I can be of assistance. I can have our company's security team do some digging. They might be able to get access to information about him that we've missed."

"Oh, that reminds me," Emma Jean said. "Flex, that's the same man that came around when you first came back to the ranch. He was interested in buying it from you."

Flex looked shocked. "I didn't know he'd come by."

Emma Jean blushed, and looked over at Jimmy. "We might have purposely neglected to tell you."

Flex burst out laughing. "I can't say I blame you. Anyway, a man also went to my mom's at about the same time. I wonder if he's the same guy." Flex looked over at Steve and asked, "Do you have a picture of this man? I'll send it to my mother to see what she knows."

Steve looked through his phone, found the man's photo, and passed it to Flex. "It's on his Facebook page. If you look it up, you can copy the picture and send it to your mother."

Flex did that as Emma Jean stood up and announced the ice cream was ready.

We'd all just sat down to eat, when Flex's phone dinged with a reply from his mom. She confirmed it was him.

Eddie sighed. "This isn't good news for my mother." He looked at Flex and shrugged. "Flex and I already figured my mother put this man up to trying to get the property. We still aren't sure why, but the way she lawyered up when the cops started asking questions indicates she's involved somehow."

Flex put his arm around his cousin's shoulder. "Dude, you can't blame yourself for this. Your mom... well, she's not you."

"I know," Eddie said, but the sadness didn't leave his face. "I wish this could all just be over. I'm tired of finding confirmation of her putting us all at risk. Fuck, now it's even affecting Eric!"

The boys came back into the room, went over to Eddie, and stood next to him. He rubbed their backs, and I could tell all three of them were having a moment. I didn't know Eddie's mom that well. She was always irritable and would send us all to Flex's house, saying we were under her feet. She was never really a pleasant woman, but I'd never thought of her as homicidal.

Emma Jean got up and scooped ice cream for the boys, and settled them back at the table.

The feeling was much more somber then, as we all finished our dessert and then dispersed to get ready for bed. I felt bad for Eddie and the boys. I'd heard some of the horrors they'd experienced since Flex and Eddie's grandfather had died. Mainly, the old bag that was Eddie's mom basically abandoned him and the boys, sued Flex, and fleeced Emma Jean and Jimmy. As far as I knew, Eddie was no longer in contact, but her meddling had continued to negatively impact us all, even me.

The next day was Saturday, and after breakfast, Flex announced we should all go to the cave where the mine entrance was. He and Mitch had decided we needed to do some sort of ceremony to connect with our common ancestors. Casting off evil spirits was the basic purpose. In reality, I think they just wanted to show Steve the cave.

Emma Jean, Alex, and Jimmy rode in the ATV, while the rest of us hiked.

I'd been to this spot a thousand times, but until I was out here with Alex's family when they'd come for Christmas, I'd never seen the entrance to the cave before. It was so perfectly hidden, I didn't think even if I'd been here another thousand times, I'd ever have found it on my own. If the legend that Jack had instinctively known where the mine was all those years ago was to be believed, there definitely had to be a little magic in our bloodline, and that magic had skipped me.

The cave was fascinating. It was really just an area where a lava tube probably used to be. The outside edge of the tube was mostly eroded away, but the effect was that there was a fairly good size recess into the mountain's side. The tube led up to where you could still see evidence of someone having once slept. I followed Alex and Steve as they explored the area. When we came to the end of the tube, Alex said to Steve, "This is actually where our ancestor slept all those years ago. It's bizarre to still have access to that."

Steve looked around in awe. Jack's personal things, although rusty and old, were scattered around the cave. "You can certainly feel his presence," Steve said.

When I looked at him, he smiled. "No, I can't see him here, but it's like the residue of him still remains. Do you know where he's buried?" Steve asked Alex.

Alex shook his head and looked over at Flex, who shrugged. "No, we've never known."

Steve closed his eyes for several long moments, then walked out of the cave and over to the edge where the shrubbery met the mountain's side.

"I think he's here," he said. "It feels like he was buried here."

There was no evidence anyone was buried there, except for where a few stones had been brought together, and what looked like the remains of wood between them. Steve pulled the wood out of the stones, and sure enough, before it crumbled, you could tell it had once been the pointed end of a cross."

Steve laid the crumbled wood back on the stones, and said, "His lover used to come to this place and mourn him. I can feel his sadness and loss. Inside the cave, though, I feel reunification. It feels recent, like they've been reunited here, and not long ago." Steve blushed then and shook his head. "Sorry, I'm going on like one of those TV personalities that say they can talk to the dead."

"Except, you really can," I said, causing Steve to blush deeper and smile.

"It's strange to be here. This area feels like a tomb, a sacred space, not just because Jack is buried here, but further back. I think this was a sacred place for the native people from around here as well. If I'm right, this cave was used by the Native medicine men and women. It's an auspicious place."

Our ceremony would've made the medicine folk of old frown with disappointment. It involved starting a fire in Jack's old fire ring, roasting hotdogs, and making smores with roasted marshmallows that Emma Jean had packed for the occasion.

Flex, Eddie, Alex and Steve went to the mine's opening, but didn't go far before they turned back.

"The mine isn't safe," Flex said, upon their return.

Eddie looked at his boys. "That mine is about to collapse, and you two shouldn't go anywhere near it. Do you understand?"

They both nodded, but if I were a betting man, I'd bet that both were already planning ways to get in there. The thought caused my heart to beat fast, and nerves flash with heat.

Eddie and Emma Jean exchanged a glance, before she said, "I think you boys probably need to collapse it yourselves—at least the entrance. It's too dangerous for it to be open. We're still getting stragglers who stay on the ranch from the article in that magazine in El Paso," she said.

That was true. Since Steve and I had arrived on the ranch, we'd had at least a dozen people check into the lodge, or travel the backcountry, citing the article in the El Paso gay rag, but I thought the need to blow the mine was less about the visitors to the ranch, and more about the boys.

When the sun began to get too hot, we all started back toward the ranch. I'd brought Puddles along with me again, and Flex had brought Ace. The two little dogs were leading the three stooges, as we'd all come to refer to the three bigger dogs that lived on the ranch, toward the homestead.

That afternoon, Steve helped Mitch with some of the chores around the lodge and bathhouse. I opened my laptop and began sketching out the family history, starting with the three brothers. Most of their stories had holes in them that I couldn't fill, so I made notes to see if Steve could help me flesh them out.

By the time Steve came back, letting me know that Emma Jean was telling us to come within the hour for dinner, I'd written enough that the story was beginning to take shape. I went to the back to get ready.

"I think we should preserve their stories, including my grandmother's," I said. "I'll let you decide how much of the family's special gifts we want to share, but for documentation purposes, it might be nice to at least allude to them." He looked sheepish.

Steve didn't respond, but read the document while I got cleaned up for dinner.

When I came out, Steve had a reserved smile on his face. "You have a gift for storytelling," he said, which made me blush a little.

"To be honest, I used to tell Emma Jean that I wanted to be a writer one day and tell the story of the ranch. I don't know why I never tried. Being in that cave today, feeling all the energy that surrounded it, and knowing that's our family, I couldn't help but put it down on paper. So, what do you think?"

"About the book? I think it's a great idea."

"But you aren't so sure about sharing that our family has a hereditary gift for seeing spirits?"

"Yeah, that makes me uncomfortable."

"No need, I don't have to include it. In fact, my grandmother's background is enough in and of itself to write a book just about her, and the mystery of whether she communed with the dead or not is enough to keep it interesting."

Steve leaned over and kissed me. "Ready to go?" he asked, and I understood he didn't want to talk any more on that subject.

I would never betray him, especially knowing what was at stake. We'd eventually get back around to discussing it, and when we did, I'd make sure he understood that clearly.

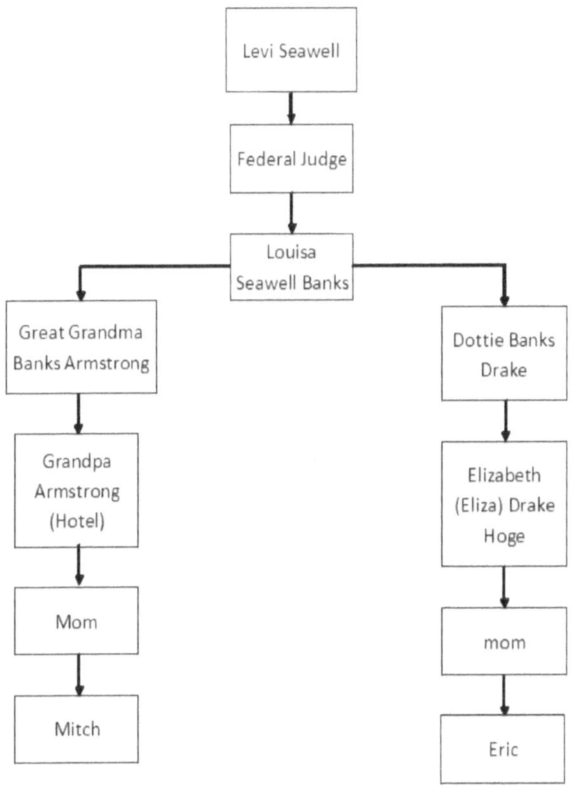

Levi Seawell
Federal Judge
Louisa Seawell Banks
Great Grandma Banks Armstrong
Dottie Banks Drake
Grandpa Armstrong (Hotel)
Elizabeth (Eliza) Drake Hoge
Mom
mom
Mitch
Eric

19

Steve

During dinner, my mind kept going back to Eric's book. He hadn't specifically mentioned his grandmother's abilities, and hadn't mentioned mine, but damn, the thought kept coming back to me, time and again. This was when I was going to be exposed.

I liked the book idea. I'd actually even thought about suggesting that to Eric myself, especially considering how good he was at research, but when I'd seen it for myself, in real life, everything was different.

After dinner, I excused myself and went back to the RV to throw myself into work. Eric was asleep before I allowed myself to stop and go lie down beside him, but sleep eluded me. I lay staring at the ceiling, my heart beating fast, sweat beading on my brows, as I thought of all the ways this book would end my career.

The next day, I told Eric I needed to be alone for a few days. I admitted I was freaking out, and that usually didn't stop until I had some alone time. The same sad expression I'd seen before I'd left for Mexico City crossed his face. He was expecting me to leave for good. I wanted to tell him that wasn't the case, that I wouldn't leave him hanging, that I wanted to be here for him, but even the thoughts sounded wrong. I was running away, and if history was any indication, I was running away for good.

He packed his belongings without saying much. When he'd moved them into the lodge, he came back to the RV, and said, "I will never write anything about you, Steve. Your gifts, your abilities... those are yours and yours alone. You don't have to fear anyone here either. Your secrets are safe with us."

He clipped Puddle's lead on, and left without kissing me, without even a look back toward me. I watched him walk away from the RV and go to the lodge, knowing I was doing the wrong thing. I knew I needed to go get him, pull him into my arms, and beg him to forgive my freaking out. Instead, I pulled the slides in, unhooked the connections to the RV, and drove off toward the park entrance, back to a life of loneliness and self-pity.

20

Eric

I SENSED HIS PULLING away after reading the beginning of my draft. I'd intentionally not mentioned his family in the introduction, determined to keep his part of the story silent, until he gave me permission to write about it.

Dinner had been mostly him staring at his food, and when I got back to the RV, he intentionally avoided having a conversation with me.

The next morning, I assumed we'd talk, but instead, he left. I couldn't help but feel betrayed again as memories surfaced of how Lisa had done the same thing. She'd built up my hopes, then dashed them. The difference between Lisa and Steve, however, was that I already felt more for Steve than I ever had for her.

We had clicked on a deeper level, had more in common, shared similar values, and our mutual interest in history had led to long and meaningful conversations. Despite that, I had to admit, I was waiting for him to go. Steve had been holding something back emotionally since we'd met. I was always all in, that was just my nature, but I could tell, every small part of him that he gave had cost him.

I also knew he was constantly battling an internal war between embracing my affection and running.

I hadn't really unpacked, so collecting my belongings didn't take long. I couldn't look him in the eye when I left. I'd already decided I wanted to remember him when he was allowing himself to feel love. I didn't want to see the fear, or even the possible loathing, in his face. It might all be a fantasy, but I preferred to live in it than to face a reality of utter rejection.

I didn't even cry when I got to the house, and into the kitchen with Emma Jean. I quickly called Mitch and told him I'd be staying in one of the lodge rooms for a couple nights, while I figured out what I was going to do after that.

Flex came on the line then, and surprised me by saying, "The hell you will. Move your stuff to our old bedroom in the main house."

"Flex, I don't want to be that much of a burden. I'm happy in the lodge."

"Dude, I'm getting pissed off just having this conversation. Why the hell would I leave you there, when you can be in a house that Mitch and I barely use? Stay there!"

I chuckled. "You're a bully, Fletcher Henry."

I could tell by the way Flex sounded that he was smiling. "On second thought, why don't you go sleep in the cave like your great-something-uncle did."

"Fuck you," I said, and I could hear Mitch laughing in the background. "Okay, asshole, I'll stay here, but I need to find something more permanent."

The silence held, and I was waiting for one of them to ask what happened to Steve. When they didn't, I sighed. "Yeah, he's gone, and no, I don't know if or when he'll be back."

"You okay?" Flex asked, and Emma Jean was now standing next to me.

"I'm fine, I guess. I sort of expected it, to be honest. I think I was the first person Steve ever got this close to. I think it finally just got to be too much."

Emma Jean put her hand over mine.

"Anyway, I think things feel different now. Steve gave me the best gift in the world. He gave me a connection, not just friendship, but also a familial one. I always felt like I belonged with y'all, now I know it."

Emma Jean chimed in then, "You always belonged, and would've even if you weren't related to those boys."

Flex heard her, and responded, "She's right. The family connection wasn't necessary for you to be one of us, Eric. You always have been."

I sighed, the emotion causing tears to sting the backs of my eyes. "Thanks. Just so you know, I'm going to spend the night in the lodge, and I'll move over tomorrow. For now, I think I just need to be alone."

After we hung up, Emma Jean embraced me. When she pulled back, she looked me in the eye, and said, "You got twenty-four hours to wallow. After that, I'm coming to get you, and you're gonna help me out in the kitchen."

I smiled and nodded. The fact that I'd wanted that very thing just a couple days ago made the moment feel that much better.

I left after that, went to the room in the lodge, and let the tears flow. They'd been threatening to since Flex pointed out what I probably already should've known. These people were my family. They were my family before they knew we were related, and they were my family now. It was just how things were.

Good to her word, like I knew she would be, Emma Jean was at my door the next morning, demanding I get a shower, then meet her in the kitchen.

My eyes were tired from the tears, and my head hurt from a night of self-recrimination and abuse. I was ready to leave that behind and get back to the living. Steve was becoming another person from my past, who didn't value me enough to fight for our relationship. Sure, I wanted him to stand up, to fight for me, but if I learned nothing else from my experience with Lisa, and even my father and brother, it was that you couldn't force people to love you, no matter what you did.

Emma Jean kept me busy, which was exactly what I needed. I could tell from what we were cooking, she knew it would be. I peeled and cut up potatoes, filleted a raw chicken, mixed up ingredients for a meringue pie, including making the meringue, and various other chores. When we were done with most of the prep work, Emma Jean sent me off to collect the rest of my things from the lodge and take Puddles for a walk.

I went up to the old room that Eddie, Flex, and I used to share when we'd visit during the summers and opened my laptop to the manuscript I'd started. I waited for the feeling that told me I didn't want to continue to wash over me. When it didn't, I began to type the stories from where I'd left off.

I was well into the zone, when Emma Jean called me down to help her set out the dinner service. I chuckled and thought to myself, *She's not going to let me spend too much time alone.* Under normal circumstances that would be a good thing, but now, there was a drive inside me that I couldn't describe, a need to write these stories, and acknowledge the men who'd sacrificed their lives in pursuit of love. As I wrote about Levy and his son, the federal judge, I felt a link to them. I knew I needed to do a lot more research and hoped that Mitch's family records would shed some light. I'd also need to go back to the library, and maybe even El Paso, and look up information about Mitch's and my most recent common ancestor.

I shuddered when I thought about running into Howard Brice again, and quickly decided I'd avoid that for the time being.

After dinner, I opened the laptop I'd brought with me, and began to read aloud what I'd written thus far. When I looked up, Emma Jean was beaming, and the rest of the table looked wrapped up in the story.

"So, what do you think? I feel like we should write these stories. They've been all but hidden for so long. I feel like sharing it. If we don't, it feels like it'd somehow be disrespectful to their memories."

Everyone at the table nodded, and Alex reached over and patted my shoulder. "When you're done, we can talk about movie rights." causing the rest of the table's occupants to laugh.

"Are you going to write about Steve's side of the family?" Mitch asked.

I shook my head. "No, not without his permission. There are plenty of other stories to be told. Even with just what we have, this is a mini-series, to say the least." I looked over and winked at Alex, who smiled.

"Mini-series, is it?"

"Hey, if we're talking the big time, let's go all the way!" I chuckled.

Mitch and Flex stayed at the house that night, and we stayed up late, rehashing what we knew thus far. The next morning,

I followed Mitch back to the motel, while Flex stayed back to help Eddie repair fences, where javelinas had ripped them open.

I was shocked when Mitch showed me his attic. It was full of stuff related to our family's lineage. I started going through the boxes of paperwork, and finally had to stop. There was so much here that I couldn't dream of getting through it in a day.

I came back down the stairs and told Mitch, causing him to chuckle. "To be honest, I'll need to get a printer and copier, and begin putting things in order, categorizing the documents relevant to ancestry, from the stuff your family kept for personal reasons. Do you know I found what appeared to be a school report card from nineteen hundred and nine up there?"

Mitch laughed. "My grandpa's mother didn't throw anything away, and they firmly believed everything pertaining to the judge was worth holding onto."

"Was that his report card?" I asked, and Mitch shrugged. "I have no idea, was there not a name on it?"

"No, it'd been torn off."

"Well, it probably was the judge's nonetheless. I don't think my great-grandmother kept much of anything of my grandfather's. *'The judge was the link to high society.'* That's the thing my grandpa would occasionally say when referencing the old man."

"Did he know him?"

Mitch nodded. "Yeah, the judge lived into his nineties. My grandpa didn't like him much, and vice versa. When his mom died, my grandpa inherited all the documents his parents had saved over the years. I was still little at the time, but I remember them bringing in all the boxes. I doubt he even looked at them, just shoved them in the attic to get them out of the way."

"Have you gone through them?" I asked, curious what level of interest Mitch had in all this.

"Nope, I looked through one box when I inherited the motel and house from my grandpa, and besides some old shot glasses I found in the process, I quickly decided it wasn't my kind of thing."

"Well, if you'll trust me, I'll go through and organize what you've got. Maybe I can even categorize it, and help you restore the important documents. Then, if you really aren't interested, you could consider donating them to the archives in Alpine or El Paso. I'm sure these things will eventually be important to people. Well, people like me," I said, grinning.

Mitch chuckled. "To be honest, it holds little value besides helping us solve the problems we already have. If you think it's of value, and know of an archive that would want it and preserve it, I'm probably game. So, if you've got that much to go through, would you prefer to stay here with us, instead of driving back and forth from the ranch?" he asked.

I looked at him skeptically. "I don't know. I've got Puddles, and I don't want to be an imposition to you and Flex. Y'all are still practically newlyweds after all."

"Gotta be married to be newlyweds, dude," Mitch said as he went into the kitchen. "I think it'd be fun to have you here. If you'd feel more comfortable, though, I can put you in one of the motel rooms. Do you want the honeymoon suite back? It's booked this weekend, but after that, it's open."

"That's totally up to you, I'm really easy going. I'm also happy to stay in the camper again if you prefer."

"I think you should stay in my guest bedroom. Besides, it's on the other side of the house, so it isn't like you'll disturb us, and you *probably* won't hear us."

Mitch's sly smile caused me to choke. "That camper's sounding better and better."

Mitch just laughed while he called Flex to tell him I was staying here, while I categorized the crap in his attic, as he called it.

I helped Mitch with dinner, took both Puddles and Flex's... or more accurately, Mitch's dog, Ace, out for a walk. When I returned, Flex was back, and laughed when I told him Mitch had strong-armed me into staying in the guest room.

Then, I looked Flex in the eye, and out of Mitch's hearing, I whispered, "I better not hear sex noises coming from your bedroom, or I'm going to move back into the camper again."

"Prude," Flex teased, and pushed me back into the house.

We finished eating dinner together, then Mitch showed me his grandpa's old study, a bedroom that had once belonged to his mother. There were tables around the walls, and a desk in the middle. "I've gotten rid of most of the stuff my grandpa kept in here. Most of it was junk he kept to keep my mom from moving back in," he said with a chuckle. "That was crazy, since she hated him with a passion before he died. She'll likely never set foot on the property again, even though he's long gone. Anyway, I think you could use this as your workspace. Flex, you and I can bring the boxes down and store them under the tables, then you can have the tops to organize it all."

"Wow, that would make it easier. I was going to ask for a table to take to the attic, and I'd have had to use the floor to organize, which would've been hard."

Flex and Mitch laughed. "Well, this is better, and I'm growing to like the idea of having my attic back to store stuff I want to keep, instead of old papers I haven't ever known what to do with."

"Sounds like a perfect plan then, huh?" I asked, and we spent the evening bringing old boxes down from the attic and storing them in the room.

That night was spent like all nights from then on. I'd lie awake, longing for Steve and forcing myself not to call him. I needed to be done chasing after people who didn't want me. Still, even with my resolve constantly reset, when I got deep into the documents, I'd run across something important or interesting, and I'd want to tell him, knowing he'd like the information I'd discovered.

That was something I'd grown to love, and painfully missed about Steve and me. He didn't mind my downloading at the end of the day. We'd snuggle, and I'd tell him what I'd found in my research. When we were working together, we'd occasionally stop and share a tidbit of information with one another, before getting back to work.

Fuck, I chastised myself, *you put the co in co-dependent*. Night after night I tried putting the man out of my head once and for all.

Finally, I decided to be proactive, and tried to talk to Flex and Mitch about the research I was doing. They acted interested, and sometimes that interest was valid, but for the most part, they were just being polite as I went through all my historically significant finds.

The judge was apparently a well-liked man and ran in important circles. I found multiple links between him and various governors of Texas. When I found a letter written to him from President Taft, I immediately went out to show Mitch.

From what I could tell, the judge had campaigned for Taft here in Texas. The letter was a thank you for his support. I remembered after I got back to the room, that Taft had been a chief justice after being president, so the two must've known each other through the law.

I made a side note to explore the relationship between them.

I found the letter of appointment to the Federal Judicial Branch by Theodore Roosevelt, and placed that in the pile of important files. I was already beginning to make a separate pile of documents I thought Mitch should keep, or at least donate to the Alpine archives, since the judge had been born in Brewster County.

The more I explored, the more excited I became. By the weekend, I was chomping at the bit to get back to my writing. I went back to the ranch without Mitch and Flex, thinking to give them a rest without me being underfoot, and hoping it would give me some time to play with my manuscript about the family.

I still needed to find out more about Levy, but I'd gathered as much data about him as an adult as was probably possible. I'd like to learn more about his life as a child, though, especially since up until this point, I had no idea where he was born, or how old he was when he'd died.

He was buried in the old Alamito Cemetery, and at some point, I needed to go to the gravesite and snap a picture of the stone. According to the documentation from Judge Seawell, he'd purchased a gravestone for both his mom and dad after his mother had passed away. She'd remarried and moved to El Paso, and was buried with her second husband there, but either there was no gravestone, or the judge had felt it inadequate, and had purchased one late in the nineteen teens for Levy.

To my relief, the ranch, for the most part, was deserted. Eddie and Alex had taken the boys to El Paso to prepare for their wedding. Flex had stayed over Saturday night, to get up the next morning and run the fences, and with no big crowd to feed, Emma Jean and Jimmy were tucked in their own duplex.

It should've felt lonely in the house by myself, but I was so bogged down writing, I didn't have time to think about it. I wrote late into the night Saturday.

I documented the family back as far as Levy on a family tree, starting with Mitch and climbing backward. Then I began to write out the details of the judge. If this turned into a book, it would most certainly be a book about him, since most of the data I had referenced him.

I'd found some information about Mitch's and my great-grandmothers, but the kids hadn't been as well documented as their grandfather, the judge had. Of course, there was a lot more information about Mitch's side of the family than mine, but since they were siblings, I would've thought maybe some correspondence had been kept. I still had several boxes to go through, and there were more things in the attic that Mitch said he didn't even know were there that could bring something to light, so there was still hope.

Now that I knew about my grandmother, though, and knew she was gifted and not the evil witch my mom had made her out to be, I was anxious and a little curious to chase down those leads. Still, my best bet was to find out what Mitch's attic yielded. Mitch's and my great-grandmothers were first cousins, after all. It seemed weird they didn't at least know each other.

Sunday night, I worked myself into utter exhaustion, mostly because I didn't want to lie in bed, feeling sorry for myself again, or wondering where Steve was.

I'd lost the battle with myself Saturday morning, and had texted Steve, but I knew he probably wouldn't get back to me. If he actually got a text out in the middle of nowhere, and even if he did, he was avoiding me. I knew it but couldn't help myself anyway.

When I eventually got to sleep Sunday night, I fell into another dream of Sampson's memories.

After being beaten, I avoided the man that looked like Howard Brice.

I kept thinking "Brice" in my head, that's what Sampson must've called him.

When he came into a room I was in, I'd find a way to inconspicuously excuse myself.

Brice's father had kept giving me administrative work to do. "Boy, you're too smart to waste down in the mine. I need someone to help me with all this damned paperwork," he'd said once, when I told him I preferred to work in the mine.

Unfortunately, I couldn't argue with him, so more and more, I was stuck in the house, helping the old man with his filing, and having to deal with the man I'd once loved, but had now learned to hate.

For the most part, Brice ignored me. Occasionally I'd look up and see him staring at me from across the room, but I refused to make eye contact. Just the look of him disgusted me now.

Months passed, and we'd all found some way to coexist, albeit strained, when Brice's father ran into trouble.

He hired a young attorney to represent him. Apparently, his other sons were outlaws and had been killed. There were questions about whether the old man and his sons were involved in smuggling, and since they'd had outlaw family, they were both under suspicion.

The attorney caught my eye the first day he was here. I could tell he was interested, but after my last relationship with Brice, I wasn't. I just wanted to do my work and earn enough money to get away from this place once and for all. My brother Jack had family in El Paso, and I thought it'd be nice to visit them. I hadn't really gotten to know his wife when she'd lived at the fort, but she seemed friendly enough, and family was family, even if it wasn't close.

When the attorney left the room, I was bringing some paperwork back to the old man that he'd requested. When I came out of his office, Brice was standing there staring at me, jealousy radiating from him.

Really, this man had me beaten to ensure I kept my mouth shut, and he was jealous? Fuck him! I thought. He'd lost any connection with me, and he damned well knew it.

Time went by, and the attorney left, but not before cornering me in a storeroom. When he came up behind me, turning me around and kissing me, I didn't resist. It felt good, to be honest, after all this time being forced to work with a man who had used me and then thrown me to the side.

When we came out, Brice was standing in the parlor. If he could've killed us, he would've, and I knew then, if I hoped to live, I'd need to leave soon.

I gave notice to the old man that afternoon, telling him I was moving back to El Paso to be with family. He didn't take it well and offered me a raise if I'd stay on. "No," I said. "My mind is made up."

That night we were all woken by the alarm bell they used when there was an emergency in the mine. I rushed out, ready to begin helping dig out any men that were buried.

Men were running everywhere when I spotted Brice. He seemed winded when he handed me a pick and told me to head into the mine. "The men are trapped in the right quad," he said.

Before I could go, he grabbed my arm, and said, "You shouldn't have done me dirty." Then, he let my arm go, and went in the other direction.

I rushed into the mine, curious why no one else was going in, then when I rounded the corner and saw the charges in the front area of the mine, I knew I'd been set up.

I turned to run, but it was too late. The explosion happened, and within moments, the mine collapsed around me.

I woke with a start, gasping for air. It was almost like I could feel the mine collapsing around me, like I'd been the one trapped underneath the rocks, like I was the one who'd died.

I got up, shaking off the nightmare, went to my laptop, and wrote down what I remembered from the dream. I was still shaking even after I was done. I went down to the kitchen to see if Emma Jean had left overs I could raid, knowing I wouldn't be able to get back to sleep anytime soon.

The moment I came down the stairs, I knew I wasn't alone. The hairs on the back of my neck were standing up, and I knew it wasn't Sampson in the room with me.

When I turned and saw the apparition sneering at me, challenging me, somehow, I could tell he knew I understood his story. "Leave," I said. "You have no right to be here. Leave and never come back."

The entity remained still for several moments, sneering at me. I yelled this time, "Leave me alone!"

Within seconds, he came toward me, my heart picking up speed even faster than it had been. I knew this thing intended me harm. Before it reached me, though, it stopped. When I turned around to see what had stopped him, I was staring into the face of all three brothers. They moved at once toward the other man, and when I turned back around, they were all gone.

I'd never seen ghosts before now. Instinctively, I knew something had shifted in me the afternoon I'd first seen the brothers. Like a veil that'd once been over my eyes had been lifted somehow. Damn, I'd love to know how to replace that veil about now!

I was shaking like a leaf. "*Fuck*," I said out loud, and looked around. I missed Steve. He'd know if I were safe.

"Be brave," I said to myself, and proceeded into the kitchen, got a glass of water, and sat on the stool facing the living room.

Despite it being ungodly early, and I knew I wouldn't be sleeping anymore, I decided I'd give Emma Jean the morning off and fix breakfast for everyone. Eddie and Alex planned to be back from their visit to the hacienda, as they called Alex's family home in El Paso, and the boys would be headed to school early. I could cook a breakfast casserole between now and when everyone would be stirring.

When I knew everyone was up, I radioed over to the duplex to tell them I'd cooked breakfast. When I mentioned I had bacon, the boys cheered in the background. For the first time since I'd seen the apparitions, I smiled. Children helped ground you better than anything else, and there was nothing more *of this world* than a couple pre-teens who had the appetite of a small army.

After the boys had eaten and caught their bus, Eddie had gotten back from the morning fence run, and was eating a chunk of casserole.

"I'm going to admit, I didn't make this just to be nice." I looked around the room and could tell everyone already suspected I had reasons for bringing them over.

"I had a nightmare or vision, or whatever you want to call it, last night. I saw how Sampson died and who killed him. It was deliberate, and like the prophesy Steve gave us, I think it was one of the Brice brothers from back then." I gave them the details of the dream as fast as I could, wishing I could just forget it.

"Dang, that's tough," Alex said. "Did he suffer?"

"No, I don't think so. It seemed sudden. But that's not all. Hell, it's not even the worst of it. I came downstairs to raid the refrigerator, and immediately felt like I wasn't alone. When I got to the foot of the stairs, the son of a bitch was here, staring at me. No, it was more of a creepy leer. I don't know what he intended to do, or even if he could've hurt me, but I knew he wanted to.

"He came at me, but before he reached me, he stopped. I turned to see what had stopped him, and the three brothers were there behind me. Before I knew what happened, they rushed him, and all four of them disappeared."

The group stared at me, no one saying a word. "That's scary as all fuck," Eddie said, and got a pop on the head from Emma Jean.

"Yeah, it is. Hell, I'm still sort of weak in the knees." Before I could help myself, I said, "I wish Steve was still here."

Emma Jean came over and pulled me into one of her comforting embraces, and before I knew it, we were all in a huge bear hug. I laughed as I was being smothered under all their arms.

When everyone pulled back, I sighed. "I'll be okay, but I'd rather not spend the night here alone again. I know I'm a coward, but shit, that was scary."

I almost expected to get a pop on the head from Emma Jean, but when I looked at her, she was just nodding.

When Steve didn't respond, I took that as a sign. We were over, and I could go on with my life. I acknowledged the pain, even embraced it.

I resolved to be fine being single. I could surround myself with friends and create my own family, but I wasn't cut out for modern dating. I got too attached too fast, and it set me up for this kind of pain. If this was any indication of what I was doomed to repeat every time I tried to date someone, I was so much better off without love.

Luckily, Alex and Eddie's wedding took my mind off of most of my own troubles. I knew Alex was wealthy, but I had absolutely no idea how wealthy until I saw the hacienda in El Paso. Regardless, the Zitlals were down to earth people and I immediately felt like one of them. Such a strange feeling after spending so many years feeling like I didn't belong anywhere.

The following week, the Zitlals descended on the ranch so Alex and Eddie could make their vows once again in Jack's old cave. Alex and Eddie dashed off then for their honeymoon, but Alex's parents agreed to stay at the ranch to help with the boys not wanting them to be out of school any longer than was necessary.

I stayed with Mitch and Flex, so I could finish the documentation of the items in Mitch's attic, and to be out of the way.

As I hoped I would, I finally found things from my side of the family, buried deep in one of the boxes.

It warmed my heart to see pictures of my great-great-grandmother holding my infant grandmother. Someone had scribbled their names on the back, *Dottie Seawell Drake holding Elizabeth Drake, age two.*

I'd loved to have known whose handwriting was on the picture. Was it my ancestor's or Mitch's? It didn't matter. Either way, someone in our family had written it.

I put the picture aside, intending to take this little treasure to a photo restorer and have it blown up. This was a whole section of my family I'd lost access to. I wished I could've known my grandmother, and I hoped maybe there'd be more pictures.

I ended up going through the online archives of the *Toyah Enterprise*, the local paper, and found every article I could about my grandmother. When I came to the obituaries, where it was announced she had died, I decided to search court records to see what eventually happened to her estate.

Unfortunately, I had no luck, so I bit the bullet once again and called my father. Of course, my brother answered, and proceeded to curse at me for continuing to harass them.

"Keith, I'm not going to fight you. I have questions about Mom and her family, and I need to talk to Dad."

When he refused, I said, "Fine, I'll just come to Houston and see him myself."

Keith was a stubborn asshole. From what I'd read about my grandmother, he'd certainly gotten that from her. Eliza was nothing if not a headstrong woman. Few, if any, of the towns-folk, like her or not, would've taken her on.

"What's so important?"

"Well, dickhead, I'm researching our family tree, and I want-ed to know what happened to our grandmother's things after she died."

"Dad," he yelled. "Eric, the destroyer of families, wants to know where our grandmother's things are?"

I heard talking in the background, and Dad responded, but I couldn't hear what he said.

"It's all stored in Toyah. Mom's mother had some arrange-ment with one of the storage units there to store her things in-definitely. What?" he asked Dad, who'd said something behind him.

"Dad says you can have it if you want it."

"Tell him I do. Does he have the keys?"

"Do you have the keys?"

I was frustrated. Why the hell wasn't I just able to talk to my own fucking father? Oh well, if I knew my brother, and trust me, I *did* know my brother, it was best to just let it flow and get to my grandmother's things, before challenging him.

"Dad said you don't need keys, just go to the Mayor's Office, and let them know you want access to Eliza Hoge's belongings.

Your name is listed on the paperwork, as is mine," Keith said in a huff.

Then a few seconds later. "Hey, is there valuable stuff in there?" That was directed at my dad.

"There's just paperwork and some of her old things, nothing of value," Keith said. I assumed he was repeating what my father was saying.

"Thanks, Keith. Hey, before I go, I'm sorry about Lisa, and me not being a good brother. I do love you and Dad. I just wanted to say that."

Keith didn't respond for a moment, but when he did, he said, "It's too late. You ditched us, and now, we don't want you back." Then, he hung up.

It hurt. I knew he was going to reject me again, but something told me that might be the last conversation I ever had with him. The stubbornness of my brother was a powerful thing. I was never strong enough to outmaneuver it. As a result, I just remembered a childhood with someone who was always pushing and never relenting. I was guessing Keith was dictating Dad's relationship with me as well, but that was on them. I'd tried, and that was all I could do.

I contacted the Mayor's Office in Toyah, and confirmed I had access to our grandmother's locker, then told them to expect me on Friday. I wanted to finish working through what I had here, and that gave me time to rent a U-Haul. I wanted to move whatever was in my grandmother's locker here, so I could go through it.

Mitch seemed excited to see what was in her locker. The Toyah Witch had become something everyone was interested in learning more about. He told me that once I had all his family stuff sorted, we could keep her stuff here as we went through it. "Provided it isn't infested with mice or scorpions," he said, and shuddered.

"Agreed!" I said, and was a bit put off by the scorpions thought myself. If her stuff was being stored in one of those outdoor storage units, I could only imagine what shape it was in.

As the week went on, I became more and more excited about going through my grandmother's things. It was like going to meet her for the first time.

Mitch's family stuff had been well categorized, and I showed him the things I thought he should donate to the Alpine Library, the stuff that should probably go to our ancestor's alma mater, the law school in Waco, TX. I also encouraged him to scan and put the less relevant stuff online for future generations to be able to research.

There was also a lot of stuff that had no real value and could be tossed, making room for my grandmother's things.

On Friday, I got up early and drove the moving van the two and a half hours to Toyah, excited about seeing my grandmother's belongings. I went into the Mayor's Office and was immediately surrounded by smiling people.

When the mayor came out, he shook my hand, and told me how excited they were to finally meet me.

"I'm confused. I'm just here to pick up my grandmother's things," I told them.

With that, there was a bit of a gasp behind me, and I turned around, the confusion becoming stronger.

"Well, that might be a problem," the mayor said. "Here, let me show you."

He escorted me and several of his staff down the hall and then down two flights of stairs into the basement. He flipped on a light and turned to me with a big smile. "This is your grandmother's estate," he said. "It's been converted into a museum."

I didn't know what to say. I began moving around the room, looking at the items on display.

"My father said they were being stored by the city, but he didn't say you'd turned it into a museum," I said, trying to figure out how I was supposed to react to all this.

"Well, when we first spoke to your mother, maybe twenty years ago, it was all in storage. It was here in the basement just like it is now, but no one had organized it or made it accessible. Your mom made it clear she didn't want the stuff, although technically, it does belong to your family."

"Why, um... well, why is it here in the first place?" I asked.

The mayor and the women standing behind him looked stunned. "You don't know?" he asked.

"No, I honestly don't know anything about her. This is a fact-finding mission for me. I... yeah," I said, still totally flabbergasted.

An older woman came around the stalls from somewhere in the back. "Well, I can be of some help with that mission of yours," she said, and I turned toward her.

"Your grandmother donated the money to build this town hall in the early nineteen sixties." The woman chuckled then, and said, "She kept the deed to the place though, and when she died, she demanded in her will that her items be kept in the basement of the town hall. That way she'd be able to haunt the place properly."

The mayor chuckled behind me. "Your grandmother was a character. She loved to poke at the holier-than-thou people who at the time gave her a great deal of grief regarding her... well, her skills."

"Anyway," the mayor continued, "after your mom refused the items, Mrs. Clifton here petitioned the City Council to let her use the basement as a museum in your grandmother's honor. She's run the museum ever since."

"Damn," I said, shaking my head, and then I apologized. "I'm sorry for my language. I'm just overwhelmed."

Mrs. Clifton burst out laughing. "Son, if you're apologizing for saying a cuss word, you really didn't know your grandmother at all. The woman cussed like a sailor."

I looked at the people in the room, and all of them had expressions on their faces that demonstrated how much they cared about her.

"Well, I'd like to spend some time in the museum, and I may have some questions for you all."

I turned to move into the stacks, when I stopped. "If you're worried about what I said earlier, don't be. I won't be taking anything with me. I thought this was all rotting away in some storage unit. I was already planning to donate what I didn't want to some archive somewhere. If the city is willing to care for the stuff and even display it like this, that is more than I could've asked for."

The mayor smiled, and told me Mrs. Clifton would show me around, and that when I was done, I could interview anyone here, that they all had their own special memories of my grandmother.

The museum was fun and colorful. It displayed things my grandmother clearly cherished, including scarves from India, and Spanish heirlooms. There were tons and tons of items that gave a nod to the occult, like an old crystal ball, stowed in a room and surrounded by what appeared to be beads from the nineteen sixties.

As we toured the museum, Mrs. Clifton chattered on in her tour voice, talking about how Eliza was a documented medium, and could tell you exactly what your loved one was like, without asking questions about the individual. Her most famous phrase, though, was, "If the spirits want to talk, I can tell you what they are saying, but if they don't, you can't make them."

Of course, experts had called her a fraud because she couldn't read everyone. But, from my discussions with Steve, if a spirit had transitioned, they simply weren't there to get information from.

Mrs. Clifton showed me what she said was her most famous reading. "It was for a woman whose husband and son had disappeared," she told me. "The reading was done in public, and the county sheriff was sitting in the audience. Eliza listened for a couple moments, cleared the room, forced the cameras to be turned off, and asked that the sheriff remain with her and the woman. She told the woman her husband was dead, but said the son was still alive. He was seriously injured. With Eliza's lead, they found the boy and caught the man who'd kidnapped them. Eliza was also able to tell the sheriff where the bodies of the man's other victims were buried."

"Cool," I exclaimed, causing Mrs. Clifton to chuckle.

"You really didn't know about any of this?" she asked, surprised.

I shook my head. "No, my mom didn't care for my grand-mother at all. I didn't know anything about her, until recently when I began to do some research."

"Well, you should know your grandmother is both revered and passionately hated by the people in Toyah." She chuckled again. "It was always that way with her. You either adored her or despised her."

"I'm guessing you were on the adoring side?"

Mrs. Clifton smiled. "Your grandmother took me in when I was a wayward teenage girl. My mom and dad were strict, you might say. I left home and was living on the streets, after they'd found out I was pregnant and refused to give the child up for adoption. She found me hiding inside an old, abandoned building. When I asked her how she knew I was there, she said, 'Your Grandpa Joseph told me where to find you.'" The woman smiled. "My grandfather had died a couple years before. He'd been my friend and advocate against my tyrannical parents. I'm sure all this sounds odd to you, unless..." The woman looked at me strangely, and I laughed.

"I'm sorry to disappoint. I didn't inherit her gifts."

Mrs. Clifton smiled and shook her head. "They were a gift too. You'll never know how many people like me your grand-mother saved. She's our heroine."

After I'd finished the tour, I admitted that I was a historian and wanted to write a book about my ancestral line, all the way back to the federal judge.

"Yeah, I believe your grandmother predicted that, but the information about all that is stored in her home. That's not really my territory, though. You'll have to ask the mayor and Jim Pete about that. He runs the house museum."

"There's another museum?" I asked, surprised.

She shrugged. "Well... sort of. Not like this. It's occasionally open to the public, but mostly it's used for public meetings, and sometimes people rent it for gatherings and such."

"I'd like to see it," I replied, again surprised by what I was learning.

Mrs. Clifton assured me I had only to call if I needed documentation for the book, and she'd forward me anything I needed, then she took me back up the stairs to the Mayor's Office. When she told him I wanted to see the house, he smiled. "Of course, I'll take you over there myself."

I expected we'd get into a car and drive there. Instead, I followed the mayor out the front door of the building, turned right, and walked right up to a sprawling western-style, turn-of-the-century home with a wraparound porch. "This is where my grandmother lived?" I asked.

"Yep, she owned a good portion of downtown, buying property as people moved out. We had a resurgence in the sixties, and that's why she decided to build the town hall next to her home. Well, and because up until sixty-nine, she was the de facto mayor."

I looked at him oddly, and he smiled. "The population had fallen so low that the city stopped electing mayors. Your grandmother was too stubborn to leave, so she began running the city, at least until we held an election again in sixty-nine. She happily handed over the reins though... well, sort of." He chuckled.

The mayor unlocked the residence, and I stood in the opening and stared. The house was beautiful. We stood in a long entryway with a large staircase that rose up from the middle and looked as if it ended at an upstairs bathroom. Dark walnut hardwood floors gleamed throughout the house. The furniture was immaculate, as if someone was still living here and taking care of it.

I was surprised that I didn't find dust. I'd spent a lot of time in West Texas, and dust was a reality of life. Even with Emma Jean's intense attention, there was often dust covering the furniture in the ranch house.

When I ran my finger across a gleaming piece of furniture, the mayor chuckled. "Your grandmother never tolerated dust in her house."

"How'd she manage to keep it out? Can I patent the technology?"

"You'll have to take that up with her," he said.

Without explaining what he meant, he led me through the home. "It looks like she still lives here. I don't understand. I thought all her stuff had been moved to storage."

"Well, all her papers and many of her knick-knacks were. The stuff she said you wouldn't want to deal with was removed."

"That I wouldn't want to deal with?" I asked.

"Yeah, your grandmother predicted her grandson would eventually want her stuff, and in her will, she gave the property to the city, stating that all her belongings must remain in the house, and the property must be maintained, until you decided what to do with it."

It seemed surreal. Firstly, that she'd predicted I'd come, knowing how much my mom hated her. Secondly, that I had no idea who she was. Also, what city followed strange rules like that?

It was too much to really process, but I wanted to know more about what my grandmother had in store for me regarding the book.

"Mrs. Clifton said something along the lines of my grandmother predicting I'd be writing a book?"

"She did actually. We all thought it was because she'd started having problems with dementia, but even when she was close to ninety years old, no one would dare question her. There's a box labeled 'Grandson' in her study. It's locked, and she said if anyone opened it, they'd be cursed, so naturally, none of us have ever had the gumption to try."

I chuckled. "Sounds like she had you all wrapped around her little finger."

Something fell in the room next to us, and the mayor blanched a bit. "It's best you don't antagonize her too much."

I looked over at where the noise came from, and back at the mayor, shaking my head. Again, I wished Steve were here. If my grandmother was still lurking around, and I had no doubt from the expression on the mayor's face that she was, I'd love to have been able to talk to her, or at least understood what she wanted.

When we finished touring the downstairs, he led me to the upper rooms. The roof came up at a slant, so there were really only two bedrooms. One had obviously been my mom's bedroom growing up, and I went inside and perused the items. It was decorated for a young girl, and I could tell my grandmother hadn't removed anything since she'd left. I felt sad that the two of them had never reconnected, then thought of my brother and me.

When I went into my grandmother's room, I was met with the smell of fresh lavender. I knew then that she was still in the house, and the feel of her spirit was light and happy. I smiled as the mayor led me around the bed and into a small side room.

"This was her study," he said. "And here is where she kept your box. I'll leave you alone now, so you can open it, and see what she left you."

"When you're done, I'd appreciate it if you'd come to the office. We have paperwork to discuss, and I'm sure the city attorney would like to meet with you."

I shook my head at how strange things were here. I walked around the room, feeling my grandmother's presence even stronger in here than I had in the bedroom. There were books ranging from romance to Zane Grey's Westerns. There were also some books that were clearly very old, and when I touched them, I knew they'd belonged to the judge.

I was about to pull one out, when the box on her desk scooted toward me. Even knowing that my grandmother meant me no harm, having a box move on its own was disconcerting, so I just nodded. "Okay, I'm going," I said, and sat down at the desk.

I found the key in the front drawer and unlocked the box.

The box was in what they called the waterfall design, clearly from the nineteen forties, like some of the old furniture my father occasionally restored as a hobby in his workshop behind our home.

I opened it and saw a letter with the word "Grandson" written on it.

I exhaled, more to alleviate the beating of my heart than out of frustration and opened the letter. The writing was wobbly, as if it'd been written by an older person who'd lost some of her motor function.

Grandson,

There are many things I wish I could say to you in person, but your mother wouldn't permit it. I dreamed last night that you'd eventually come to my home searching for me, or at least what's left of me. I will do what I can to preserve some of your heritage for you, including the items in this box.

I dreamed you'd become a writer, telling the story of my great-grandfather, but also the story of the gifts that have passed down through our family. I couldn't tell if you'd inherited these gifts in the dream, but if you have, I warn you to stand strong against the currents. They will sweep you away if you let them.

If you stand up to them, however, people will accept you for what you are, and eventually even embrace you, as they have with me.

I've left my great-grandfather's journal in this box. It's what he wrote when he was a young man, while his mother was still alive. There are things in this box that would embarrass our family, including a detailed account his mother gave him of her life as a prostitute, and a love affair his father had with his mother's brother before he married her.

I'm not sure why it was important for you to have this journal, but the spirits were adamant that I should ensure that you do. As with our gifts, the currents against a man loving another man, even in our modern times, is something that can carry you away. By the time you see this, things might be different, but even if they are, be cautious with this information.

I've left various other things, including information about my cousin. If he's still alive when you find this, his side of the family possess most of the information about our great-grand-father. Part of me thinks maybe you'll already know this, but if you don't, you'll be able to find him with the information I've left you.

Finally, some of my dreams weren't always clear. I saw images more than I was given direction. These types of dreams are the hardest to discern, so I can only tell you what I've seen, and hope when you read this, it'll become clear to you.

I saw you with two handsome men. One was good, the other evil.

When I looked at the two men, I saw two souls in each of them. It was almost as if they'd both lived before, and were both reliving their lives again, fighting the same battles as before.

The evil man killed the good one, and it felt like it was over you.

I can't remember much more, except that before the dream concluded, you were in a cave, or maybe an old mine. You were surrounded by explosives, and the evil man was standing in front of you, laughing and saying that he'd finally kill you for good.

Grandson, I'm sorry, but in the dream, he succeeded. However, my eye was directed to a small opening. A place where if you had acted quickly, you could've been saved from the blast. This opening stretched deep inside the cave, and although you can't escape through it, you would be able to get air.

If by chance you are in that situation, find the opening and hide in it. It could save your life.

In conclusion, there are legal issues for you to handle. I've left the home to the city, because I see your life isn't here, and the home can be used for a greater purpose. I've seen they will need to expand the town hall, and this property is perfect for their needs.

I've also seen you need a connection to what was taken from you. I was never able to find a way back into your mom's heart after her father died. I think she blamed me for not being able to save him, but I promise you, he was the love of my life, and if I could've saved him, I would've.

Regardless, the items in my home, along with several acres that should be rather valuable by the time you're ready to inherit it, will become yours once my will has been completed.

I sense hostility between your brother and you. For that reason, I've given the property to you alone. The firstborn will inherit all my belongings. That being said, I'd ask that you split the revenue from the sale of the property with your brother. This will bring you both back on good terms. I know I don't know you, and probably don't have the right to ask things from you, but if you would do this for me, reuniting with your brother would be a gift.

With all my love, grandson. I mourn and regret much in my life, but nothing so much as I regret never knowing you and your brother.

The people of Toyah will do what they can to support you. I feel that as well. Have a good life, grandson, and I hope what I've left you gives you peace and prosperity.

With All My Love,

Your Grandma Eliza.

When I finished reading, I leaned back, wiping at a tear that'd slipped past my defenses. A whiff of lavender fell on me again, making me smile.

"Thank you, Grandma," I said to the room, and felt happiness surround me, warm like a hug.

The mayor and city attorney went over my grandmother's will. She had predicted almost to the year when I'd come to town looking for information on her. She specified in her will, the home could be used for the town's purposes, and had allotted money for upkeep on it until I came.

It was bizarre, but when I asked the attorney about it, he laughed. "Well, legally, no matter how strange it was, we couldn't do much about it. If we'd tried to overpower her wishes, you and your brother could've sued us. Besides, if you hadn't shown up as predicted, we would've reached out to you anyway to settle the estate. When the home is transferred to us, you will inherit a hundred acres of oil-rich land just east of town. Your grandmother was tough, and knew how to lock land down so no one could touch it. There have been multiple suits filed against the property, which I've had to defend over the years. The will was ironclad, which means the oil companies are chomping at the bit to get their hands on it. When you're ready to sell, you can almost bet you'll have a bidding war on your hands."

"That's a good thing?" I asked, not knowing anything about real estate other than how to buy, fix up, then lose a tiny house in Portland, Oregon, to a hateful ex-wife.

"Yeah, it's a good thing. You'll be a very wealthy man when it's all said and done."

I sighed in contentment. Like anyone, money was a needed commodity to survive, but it hadn't ever been something I chased, not like Lisa had. Regardless of that, I could use the revenue to survive my unemployment.

I asked what the value was, thinking maybe a million, which was a little more than what was split between my brother and me in our trust left to us by our mom. But when the attorney showed me the estimated value, I almost passed out.

"Seriously, desert land is worth that much?"

He smiled. "No, son, *oil land* is worth that much."

"Shit, okay... well, my brother will be happy."

The attorney looked at me oddly. "Aren't you the firstborn?"

I nodded. "Yeah, but..." I pulled the letter out of my pocket and showed it to the attorney. "My grandmother asked me to share the loot."

He laughed. "That sounds like her. She was always setting folks up to be better people. Well, that's up to you, but I'll be happy to help you set up a sale of the site. I wouldn't recommend keeping the land. It's not only valuable, but once you own it, the oil companies will push eminent domain on you, and force you to sell anyway. They've done that again and again in these parts. You'll be better off selling it by auction."

"I'll sell it. It's what my grandmother expected anyway."

When he looked at me questioningly, I pointed to the letter again, and he smiled.

Before I left, I arranged to spend some time in my grandmother's home, before I had to give it up. I just wanted to be here and get to know the town and the stuff she loved, before I left for good.

The attorney said he could give me a year from the transfer before I had to remove the belongings and surrender the home to the town. That was perfect, I thought, and I was about to leave when I decided I'd use the attorney for one more thing.

"Can you write up a quick will, in case something happens to me between now and when the year is up?"

The man nodded but didn't ask my reasoning.

I had him write my will to say that if I died, my half of the property would be given to Flex and Eddie equally. I also said that my brother should inherit the rest of the property, or the proceeds from its sale.

I'd donate my grandmother's things to the basement museum, to be managed by Mrs. Clifton. Finally, I had my part of the trust given to Eddie's boys. That way, I could ensure they'd get into college and have a secure future.

I thought about giving the letter to Steve, knowing the advice my grandmother gave would serve him better than me, but that didn't feel right, so I left that part out.

I signed the will and drove the U-Haul back to Alpine. It might be empty, but what I'd acquired from my trip to Toyah was greater than anything I could've put into the back of a U-Haul anyway.

21

Steve

THE NIGHTMARES STARTED A week after I left the ranch. Okay, after I left Eric.

I threw myself into work, sailing through the sites along the Rio Grande, and up into where streams at one time must've flowed all year long.

I was too distracted to use my abilities to see or feel anything, but I didn't let that stop me. I concentrated on the archeological evidence, researched what I didn't have readily available through the Department of the Interior, and continued my discussions with the Museum of Anthropology in Mexico City.

I missed Eric every minute of every day, but I managed to convince myself this was all a scam, that I was being taken. Somehow, our connections were faked, in an elaborate scheme to discredit me.

I knew I was lying to myself, but it made it easier for me to justify how I'd left, and why I needed to stay away. The more time passed, the more I fed into my own conspiracy.

I was in the field all day Saturday, but the minute my Wi-Fi connected with my phone, it dinged. I knew it was him, and I almost looked at his message. Almost, but I knew if I did, I'd text him back, or worse, go running to him with my tail between my legs.

I deleted the message instead and got to work cataloging what I'd found during the day.

That night, I dreamed of monsters lurking around the RV, each trying to get to me. The next night, I dreamed of Eric being eaten by the monsters, and worse, me walking away and letting them have him.

Every night the nightmares grew more intense, and more focused on Eric's death.

By the following weekend, I'd had all I could take. I picked my phone up and called him.

He didn't answer, and I couldn't blame him. I put the phone down and buried my head in my hands. I was such a stupid ass. A selfish, stupid ass. I'd had the real thing, something I had never imagined I would have a chance at, and I'd tossed him aside like I didn't care.

I began packing up the RV, and decided to head over to the ranch, find him, and if I had to, beg for his forgiveness.

I went outside to stow my equipment when I was grabbed from behind. I felt the sting as a needle penetrated my neck, then darkness descended around me.

22

Eric

I T WAS LATE WHEN I got back to Alpine and returned the U-Haul. I was in such a good mood as I rehashed the events in Toyah in my head again. I couldn't believe all that had happened to me there.

I got my car and drove back toward the ranch. When I called Flex and Mitch, they told me they were staying there tonight, and that I should come to the ranch instead of Alamito. I'd shared some of the news about Toyah with them, and they were as astonished as me.

I was looking forward to the meal Emma Jean said she'd save for me. Toyah had been a whole lot of information and I was totally on overload.

I parked the car behind Flex's truck and rushed up to the lodge to freshen up before going back to the house for dinner. I was just about to go inside, when I felt something hit me on the back of the head.

I woke up to an excruciating headache and blurry vision. As my eyesight started to refocus, I started to make out some more details. My heart started to race as I began to realize my grandmother's visions were on-point. I was in a cave, an old mine by the looks of it.

"Fuck," I said out loud to myself, and heard a nasty laugh behind me.

Howard Brice walked out of the shadows and into view. "Well, well, how the mighty have fallen," he said. "Now, I bet you wouldn't mind taking me up on my offer."

"What?" I asked, confused about what he was talking about.

"You think you're so smart running to the fucking sheriff, telling him I'm a faggot who can't keep my hands off of you. Like you're worth that much," he said, and spat on the ground next to him.

When I just stared at him, he said, "What? The know-it-all don't have anything to say now? Well, that's okay, I'm going to shut your flytrap up for good," he said, and laughed wickedly.

"Why are you doing this? Just because I said no to dinner?" I asked, and he whirled back on me.

"No, not because you said no to dinner. *Because*, you fucked that scientist, but wanted nothing to do with me. I'm better than him. You should've been mine. You *are* mine, and he is nothing."

I stared at him again, not sure what the hell he was talking about. The confusion that crossed his face made me think maybe he didn't either. At this point, I could only assume he was possessed, or something. Nothing else made any sense.

I tried to reason with him, hoping to express some sort of logic that might cause him to snap out of it.

"How am I yours? Mr. Brice, seriously, I don't know you. We just met a couple times. Why are you doing this?"

"We know each other," he said, the confusion leaving his face. "You put your pretty ass out there and want men to fawn over it. I know what you are."

With that, he began fooling with wires, and I could tell they were connected to explosives. With him distracted, I began looking around the mine for the opening my grandma had talked about in her letter.

At first, I didn't see anything, but then I spotted something in the shadows that appeared to be a possibility. When I continued looking around, there was nowhere else it could be.

Howard Brice came back into the room and laughed at me. "You're looking for an escape. There's no escape. You can look all you want, but this is your grave, you little slut, just like the Little Bird Mine is the grave of the man who led my ancestor on."

When I looked surprised, he smiled. "You think we didn't already know who was down there? The son of a bitch's brothers had killed my ancestor's kin. He'd led him on, and set it up so he could bury him, along with evidence that our family had been smuggling. Thanks to him, we got off scot-free, and got rid of his ass as well."

"Why did you have Steve do the research then?" I asked, my curiosity momentarily overriding my fear.

"Dr. Fowler was a tool. I wanted to find out if there was any evidence out there about who was buried down in that pit. If not, I'd be able to say it was rumor, and reopen the mine."

"Why would you want to do that?" I asked. The evidence was that the mine was empty.

Brice laughed again. "It was empty of quicksilver, but full of uranium. There's a hella lot of things you can do with uranium."

I shuddered at the thought of what he meant, but before I could ask any more questions, he turned to leave.

He then turned to me and shot me an evil grin, before saying, "Don't worry, your death should be fast. At least, I think it will."

This time when he laughed, it sounded different... like it was someone besides Howard doing the laughing.

As soon as I heard his footsteps trailing off into the distance, I did my best to hurry toward the spot I thought might be the opening my grandmother had mentioned.

My feet and hands were tied, making it hard to move, but I managed to wiggle toward the area, and thanked the universe my suspicions had been correct, and there was indeed an opening into the space. I managed to wedge myself as far as I could into the small alcove where the opening was, hoping my grandmother was right again, and this would keep me safe.

Boom! There was a quick flash before everything went black, and the shockwave hit me. I woke up later, unsure how long it'd been. Dust was still whirling in the air. I could feel it coating my tongue, a combination of earthy dirt, and the burnt, taste of gunpowder. I started coughing and craned my neck, so I could breathe some of the fresh air coming in down through the opening.

In the distance, I could hear voices.

"Hello, is anyone in there?" I yelled as loud as I could, despite the coughing fits.

"Is someone down there?" It was Flex's voice. "Flex, it's me, it's me, Eric!" I yelled.

"Fuck," I heard. "Eric, what happened?"

"Howard Brice tried to kill me. He blew up whatever mine this is."

"You're at the volcano," he said. "How'd you survive?"

"I'm in some sort of opening. I think it narrows up in front of me, but at least I have air coming in." I coughed as I strained to yell, my throat and lungs taking in more of the dust and soot.

It was silent for a moment, and I could hear the radio.

"The sheriff is going to be here in a moment, and we'll get you out. He wants to know if you're injured."

It didn't feel like I was, other than my head hurt where I'd been hit.

"Not much, but I'm tied up, Flex. I can't do much other than lie here."

"Okay, keep talking. I'll wait here until help arrives."

It seemed like it took forever for anyone to get to the mountain. I could hear people talking, but it was too indistinct to make much out.

I eventually fell asleep, the adrenaline and initial shock of the whole thing wearing off, leaving my exhausted body helpless against it. Somehow, between the letter and the prediction that I'd be okay if I found the opening, I knew I would be, eventually.

I was awoken by the sound of a helicopter, or something, coming in for a landing, and taking off again. When I called out, though, no one answered. I felt myself panicking at that point and began yelling.

Finally, a voice I didn't recognize called out to me. "It's okay, Mr. Anderson, we're here, we just couldn't hear you over the helicopter."

"Why did a helicopter come?"

"We found someone who'd been given a heavy dose of something, and the helicopter was here to take him to the hospital."

"Do you know who it was?"

I heard another voice talking then, and then answered, "Do you know a Steve Fowler?" I was asked.

I shuddered. "Steve was drugged? Yes, I know him."

"It appears he was the one who set the charges and then took an overdose to kill himself."

"No," I said. "That was Howard Brice. He was acting crazy, like he'd lost all reality and wanted to kill me for not being his. I'm not sure why he was so angry, but it wasn't Steve. I haven't seen him in weeks."

There was more talking, then the man responded. "Okay, that's good to know."

The voices left then, and a while later, someone called my name. "Mr. Anderson?" they asked.

"Yeah, I'm here," I said, but weariness was coming over me.

"We're going to start drilling toward you. It's going to take some time, but we're going to try to figure out where this opening leads and hopefully get to you sooner. Can you cover your mouth and nose?" the person asked.

"No, I'm tied up," I said.

There was more chatter, then the voice came back. "Okay, we'll try to keep the dust at a minimum, but we'll check on you every few minutes?"

"Okay," I answered, but I was weary and exhausted already.

The dust from the drilling was worse than the dust created by the explosion. At one point, I couldn't breathe at all, and even passed out.

When I woke up, I was lying on my back, and it was daylight. They were trying to put some sort of mask on me, and when I tried to talk, I coughed up mucus instead.

"Shh, lie back," a paramedic said as she pushed me back on the cot. "You inhaled a lot of dust. Don't try to talk."

I began coughing again, and the paramedic gave me a shot of something, which helped me calm down a bit.

I remained conscious as they airlifted me out, not unlike they had Steve earlier, I thought. I wondered if he was okay, and more importantly, why he was on the property to begin with.

When I got to the hospital, I was wheeled into the ER, and very soon afterward, given another shot that put me to sleep.

When I woke up again, I was extremely groggy, but alive.

My lungs screamed with pain, and it didn't feel like I could get a good breath, even with the oxygen tube they had attached to my nose.

When a nurse came in, I said, "Can't breathe." And she left, returning a moment later with a doctor.

He checked me over and gave me another shot that put me out again.

The next time I woke up, I was lying on my side. I saw Flex and Mitch sitting in the chairs next to my bed. When they saw me wake up, they both got up and came over to the bed, asking if I was alright.

"No," I whispered, my lungs still hurting from breathing in too much dust. "I feel like shit!"

"Steve?" I asked, and both Mitch and Flex looked concerned.

"He's not stable yet," they said. "But, we haven't been given much information, since we aren't family."

I shook my head, still confused about all this. Why had Howard Brice wanted to kill me? Why had he used the mine?

Hell, how did he even know about the mine, and what was Steve's involvement?

For a moment, I thought maybe Steve had told him about it. Maybe Steve was playing this somehow, but I shook my head. I didn't know why, but I knew that wasn't the case.

The doctor came in a moment later, looked over my charts, and said he thought I'd recover without any long-lasting issues. The x-ray of my lungs didn't show settling of the dust particles, meaning I probably wouldn't have pneumoconiosis. Although I had no idea what that was, I was glad I didn't have it.

"Steve?" I asked, before going into another coughing fit.

The doctor hesitated a moment, then I could tell he decided to ignore protocol, and said, "He's going to be fine."

I nodded, and whispered, "Thank you."

The doctor smiled. "We're going to give you something to help ease the pain and help you sleep. We want to make sure you don't end up with pneumonia, before we send you home."

The nurse came and put something in the IV, and told Flex and Mitch that I'd fall asleep and probably wouldn't wake up until morning, and if they wanted to head home, visiting hours were almost over.

"I'd like to stay with him," I heard Flex say, and the nurse replied that only family was allowed.

I heard Mitch quickly say, "I'm his cousin."

I fell back to sleep smiling, thinking to myself that we had to be like several times removed.

23

Steve

I woke up to an empty room. My head ached, like I'd just had a night of serious drinking and not drinking any water afterward. I leaned up in bed, and realized my hands were handcuffed to the bedframe.

"Hello?" I called, confused and beginning to panic about maybe being in a mental institution. Many nightmares I'd had since learning of my family's history started just like this.

A moment later, a uniformed officer came into my room. Behind her was another woman I assumed was the nurse.

I lifted my hand the little I could, and asked, "What's going on?"

"I'm Deputy Farnsworth, I need to ask you some questions, Dr. Fowler," she replied as the nurse came over to check my vitals.

"Do you know a Howard Brice?" she asked.

I nodded. "Yes, I did some work for him, researching the history of a mine his family owned."

"Do you know his whereabouts?" she asked.

I shook my head, which only made the throbbing headache worse.

I lay back until the pain subsided, then said with my eyes still closed, "I'm sorry, I haven't seen him in weeks."

"Can you tell us why you were on Flex Henry's property last night?"

"No, but Flex is a friend," I responded. "The last thing I remember was setting my RV up to move it from the national park to his ranch, when someone attacked me from behind." I lifted my hands, forgetting I was handcuffed.

I let my hand fall back and opened my eyes again, looking at the deputy. "I remember being stuck in the neck with a needle. Was I drugged?"

The deputy looked over at the nurse, who said, "Yes, almost fatally. You were found with gamma-hydroxybutyric acid in your system."

"Have you ever used liquid ecstasy before?" she asked.

I answered honestly, "No, I've never used illegal drugs before."

The cop nodded as if she didn't believe me.

"I'm confused. I was attacked, and now I'm lying in a hospital handcuffed to a bed. I need some answers fast, or else I'm going to need to speak to my attorney about who's really the bad guy here."

"You were found outside of a crime scene, Dr. Fowler, where someone tried to kill an Eric Anderson."

"What?" I asked, sitting up despite the pain in my head. "Tried to kill Eric? Is he okay?"

Deputy Farnsworth stared at me a long time, before she asked, "So, you don't know how you ended up there?"

"No, but I'm going to ask you again, is Eric okay?"

"Dr. Fowler, I'm not going to speak with you about the victim, but you need to tell me what you know about this situation."

"I've told you what I know. I was attacked, I woke up here." I was getting more agitated now, concerned how Eric was. I was freaking out. "Get me my fucking attorney!"

Fuck, at least maybe he could force them to tell me about Eric. I needed to get to him. Fuck me, I'd deserted him… I needed to fix this. I needed to get to him *now*!

The deputy shook her head and left the room.

"Is Eric here?" I asked the nurse, who refused to look me in the eye.

"Eric!" I yelled. No one responded, so I yelled again. "Eric, are you in here?"

Several nurses came in and told me I needed to stop yelling and calm down. Instead, I screamed louder. They shut the door, but that just made things worse. I screamed until I completely broke down. I was crying in the bed, still calling for him, when a different deputy came in and undid the handcuffs.

"You are free to go, Dr. Fowler, *after* you're discharged, that is. But, we'll have more questions for you, once you recover."

"Is he dead?" I asked, unable to manage the tears. "Is Eric dead? Is that why you won't tell me?"

The man looked at me, shook his head, but didn't respond, leaving me lying in a puddle of my own tears.

A little while later, a doctor came in, but he had what looked like security with him. He checked me over, then discharged me. The entire time I felt like I was a pariah.

I was escorted out of the hospital. A taxi was waiting for me and drove me from Alpine back to my RV at Big Bend.

I found my phone lying in the dirt outside the RV, and was frustrated that it no longer had any charge. I rushed into the RV, plugged it in, and when I finally got service, tried calling Eric.

There was no answer, and I assumed that meant the worst.

I wanted to drive to the ranch, or at least call, but after everything with the sheriff's deputies, I had no idea what Flex or Mitch, or even Eddie, might think, so instead I called an attorney friend of mine from Austin.

"I need you to represent me, Jason," I told him, and he immediately agreed.

We did the retainer thing, him saying he couldn't speak to me until that was handled, then he said we could do the rest later on.

"I'll call the sheriff's department and let you know what I find out," he said, and hung up.

About an hour later, he rang me back and told me I was a suspect in an attempted murder case.

"*Attempted* murder, so he's okay?"

"Well, he's not dead, but I don't know much more than that."

I couldn't hold back the tears. "Thank God," I said. "Thank God, he's alive."

"I have to know what happened, Steve, if I'm going to defend you."

"I came out of my RV and was attacked from behind. Someone stuck me with a needle, and I woke up in the hospital. I don't remember anything else."

"Did you see your attacker?" he asked.

"No, it happened too fast."

Jason sighed. "They found some evidence that incriminates you. A letter that says if you couldn't have him, then no one would. They think it's an attempted murder-suicide."

"Shit, I didn't write a letter, Jason, and he didn't break up with me, I broke up with him. Well, that's not true either... I left and didn't call him back. We didn't technically break up, cause we weren't technically together."

"Why did you leave?" Jason asked.

"Because I'm a coward and an idiot," I said, finally admitting the truth. "Jason, I was actually going back to find him. I'd been having nightmares since I left. I couldn't get him off my mind, and I was going to go back and beg his forgiveness. I was prepping the RV to leave when I was attacked."

Jason chuckled. "So, the mysterious Steve Fowler finally found someone who caused him to open up then?"

"Yeah, but I've fucked it up, and now all this."

"Well, I'm sure he'll be able to give a statement. Maybe that'll exonerate you."

"I hope so. Meanwhile, I need to be safe, and out here, I'm a sitting duck. I'm going to drive the RV into Marfa for a few days."

"That's fine, but Steve? Don't try to find Eric. Stay put until things settle down."

I nodded, then said "okay" into the phone, although I didn't want to stay put, nor not see Eric. If he was injured, I wanted to see him more than ever.

I drove the RV over to a little campground I knew was private and out of the way. The roads from Big Bend to Marfa were mostly empty, so I could tell no one had followed me. I felt completely paranoid now and decided to take the sim card out of my phone, afraid whoever had attacked me might be able to trace me with it. On the way to the campground, I stopped at a store and bought a crappy prepaid plan to get me by for now.

I phoned my attorney with the number and told him I was in hiding until I knew I was safe, and if anything came up, to let me know.

I hid for a week, surrounded only by the spirits of Marfa. The spirits didn't pay much attention to me, however, and their constant milling about made me feel somewhat comforted.

At the end of the week, I'd had enough. I needed to find out about Eric, so I phoned my attorney, who told me he hadn't heard anything on the case, but he agreed to speak to the sheriff's department.

I got the phone call back a little later, and Jason was clearly relieved. "You're off the hook. Eric confirmed it wasn't you and identified Howard Brice as his attempted murderer. When the sheriff went through his home, they found the printer the note had been printed on, and the fingerprints they found on the letter even matched his. They found his body too. When the blast went off, it collapsed the area where he was sitting, killing him instantly. In fact, he'd moved you just outside the entrance. Somehow, you narrowly escaped the collapse, some sort of miracle, the sheriff said."

"Why didn't they reach out to tell us."

"Apparently, they tried to call you instead of me, and they said your phone wasn't working."

"Well, no, I have the sim card out. Like I told you."

"Well, if you're free, they have some follow-up questions for you. I can fly out there if you want me, but they've assured me you are no longer a person of interest. They want to see you, because they want to know about your attack. They're afraid more people were involved in the attacks against Eric and you."

"I think I'll be fine but keep your phone on. If they start accusing me of anything, I'll want to have you on the line."

Jason agreed, and we disconnected.

I decided to drive over to Alpine. Somehow, knowing Howard Brice was dead made me feel safer about everything.

The sheriff met me at the front desk and escorted me into an interview room. I noticed both the male and female deputies, who'd questioned me in the hospital, sitting at their desks. Each of them watched me with accusatory expressions as I went back.

"Sir, I was told I was no longer under investigation, but from the looks of those two deputies out there, that's not the case. If I'm still a suspect, I need my attorney present."

He chuckled. "You aren't a suspect, and my deputies are just protective of Flex and Eddie. Those poor boys have been through hell. Eric is one of theirs, so naturally, they're feeling protective over him too."

I sighed. "Well, I can't deny that sort of makes me feel better, actually. If any of them are still in danger, I'd prefer they were well protected."

The sheriff regarded me for a long moment. "You're attached to them too, aren't you?"

The question caught me off guard. "I'm a loner, or at least I usually am, but yeah, I care about them, more than I ever thought I could."

"And one in particular?"

I couldn't hold back the tears. "I've been so worried, Sheriff. I hurt him..." The sheriff stiffened, and I shook my head. "No, not physically, but I left him without a good reason. I hadn't talked to him for a couple weeks before all this happened. I was going to go apologize when I was attacked. Now I doubt he'll ever want to see me again."

The sheriff handed me a tissue, and I tried to clean myself up.

"Well, if it's any consolation, Eric has called me almost every day since he got back from the hospital, asking if we'd heard from you, and if you were okay."

I wiped at the tears that escaped my eyes, and asked, shocked, "Really?"

The sheriff looked at me. "You know people's love lives aren't really part of my specialty, but it sounds like he misses you, and is worried about you."

I sighed and chuckled a watery laugh. "I should go check on him."

"Yeah, you should, but first, let me get this out of the way."

The sheriff asked me again to rehash my story, which wasn't any different than what I'd said before. However, when I told him about the first time Eric and Howard Brice met, he nodded. "That sounds about right. We found correspondence in his personal effects that indicates he was involved with the scheme to get the ranch property from Flex right from the beginning, and it all appears it was because he wanted the mine."

"I thought the mine was abandoned."

"It was, but we also found evidence that ties Howard Brice to a smuggling operation between Mexico and here. I'm guessing they wanted the abandoned mine to store drugs after bringing them across the Rio Grande."

I shook my head. "I didn't have a clue about any of this. I was hired to investigate the Little Bird Mine, but he never told me why. The entire mine had been collapsed, though, so he couldn't hide anything in that one. Do Eric and the others know about all this?"

The sheriff nodded and smiled. "That and a couple of other surprises, which I'm not at liberty to tell you."

"If you're done with me, Sheriff, I'd like to drive over there and check on them myself."

"I think that's a good idea, son, and if you remember anything else, let me know."

I nodded, but there wasn't much more to tell. I could've mentioned knowing Sampson was buried in the mine, but I couldn't see what the relevance was, so I left that out.

I pulled into the ranch's driveway just over an hour later. The place appeared abandoned until I put my car in park.

Before I was all the way out of the car, Eric burst from the house and flew into my arms.

We were both weeping as we clung to one another.

"I was so afraid," I kept telling him. When he pulled back, I continued, "In the hospital, they wouldn't tell me if you were okay. They led me to believe you'd been killed, Eric. I thought my world had ended."

He just nodded and snuggled into my embrace.

I pulled away slightly and looked him over. "So, you're okay, nothing permanent?"

"I'm fine," he said, his voice hoarse.

"You don't sound fine, what's wrong with your voice?"

"He inhaled a lot of dust," Flex said. I hadn't even noticed he and Mitch had come out on the porch with him.

"I'll be alright, just need time for my lungs to heal."

I nodded, and then wiped back a few tears.

"Are you okay?" Flex asked, and the tears flowed again.

"No, not really," I said, and looked at Eric. "I was coming here when I was attacked and drugged. I was going to come and beg you to forgive me and give me a second chance. Is it too late, Eric? Am I too late?"

Eric pulled me in for a kiss that could've melted steel. Instead, it melted all the coarse spots inside me, and caused my world to line up right again.

When Eric pulled back, he said, "I love you, Steve. I know it's too early, but I love you anyway. No, it's not too late."

More tears fell, and I held onto him like my life depended on it, because in more ways than one, it probably did.

24

Eric

A DOUBLE WEDDING? WHAT the hell are you talking about, Flex?" I asked, but I couldn't resist the smile.

"It would be so perfect, and it's not like you and Steve haven't already professed your undying love. Hell, the two of you are practically inseparable since he came back into your life."

I hugged my friend. "No, it's too early for us. Besides, I think your mom would kill us all if we took her son's wedding away from her."

Flex sighed. "Yeah, probably, but it's such a good idea. So, tell me this, if he asked you to marry him, would you say yes?" Flex asked, and I shoved him.

"Have you proposed to Mitch then?" I asked, trying to take the heat off me.

Flex blushed and smiled. "Yeah, a couple weeks ago. He said yes, but we've been enjoying that information being between the two of us, and not sharing with the world yet. You know how my mom can be."

"Speaking of moms, how's Eddie doing with his mom's admission that she was involved all along?"

"We really haven't spoken about it, but luckily, she wasn't the one behind trying to have us all killed. She set the ball in motion, and when things got ugly, she tried to pull back, but her life was threatened by the gang."

It'd been a while since everything had gone down. The entire thing had happened because Eddie's mom wanted the land for the mine. She'd admitted she didn't know where it was, but she'd been aware of the legend and was convince she was going to strike it rich when she found it.

When she'd lost in court, she'd recruited Howard Brice to help her acquire it. She'd known him because she'd dated Howard's dad when she was in high school. After Eddie's dad left her, she rekindled their relationship.

What she hadn't known was that Howard had been involved with smuggling drugs across the border. The fact that Eddie's ex-wife was marrying Howard's drug-running partner, just seemed to make things worse. When she voluntarily gave her testimony about what had happened, as a plea bargain for parole, instead of hard time, she'd admitted the preacher in Alamito had sought Howard Brice out too, in an effort to exact revenge on Mitch for ruining his church.

When the sheriff and his deputies went through Howard Brice's house, they found incriminating evidence against her, and she agreed to testify if they didn't send her to jail.

The prosecutor agreed, since what they really wanted was the men who'd worked with Brice and his partner Princeton. She testified what she knew, which wasn't much, but with her testimony, Eddie's ex's testimony, and the stuff they found in the Brice home, they were able to round up the rest of the smugglers and drug runners, which apparently, wasn't too hard now that the two main players had been killed, and the Juarez cartel had ostracized them.

We all breathed a sigh of relief when the prosecutor made part of the agreement that Eddie's horrible mother was never to contact any of us again. If she ever came close to the property where Flex and Eddie lived, she'd be arrested, and a predetermined sentence behind bars would begin.

"I feel bad for Eddie," I admitted. "Family can be hurtful, but at the end of the day, they're... family."

Flex smiled, and ignoring my comment, asked, "So, you're getting along better with your brother and dad then?"

"Yeah, I guess there'll always be a wedge between us, but at least I'm not being ostracized any longer."

"The millions you gave your brother might have something to do with that," Flex said, smiling.

I chuckled. "Yeah, he seems to be pleased with his new life as a millionaire."

"Speaking of millionaires, what are you gonna do with all your new-found wealth?" I asked.

Flex shook his head. "As you already know, we still don't know how much is there."

When they were pulling me out of the collapsed mine, several rocks they removed were found to be laced with gold and silver. Steve had a friend and a fellow professor that was adept in geology. He'd connected them with a reliable and ethical mining company, located in this part of the country. They were still doing surveys, but from what we'd learned, they thought there was a significant amount of gold still to be mined.

"I hate that the explosion destroyed Jack's cave."

"Yeah, me too," Flex said.

"I can't help but feel guilty about a lot of this. I know it was all Howard Brice and his gang of thugs, but I still struggle with bringing him here onto your property. If I hadn't..."

Flex held up his hand to stop me. "You've got to stop all this. Howard Brice is to blame, and Eddie's mom, but not any of us. We were just living our lives, and bad people took advantage of us. There's nothing we could've done except what we did, and in the end, Eric, all of us came out on top. Can't you see that?"

I nodded. "Yeah, I guess I do, but that doesn't mean I don't feel responsible."

Flex got up and came over to sit next to me. "You've always been one to take on too much responsibility. It's sort of just who you are, but know this, we all feel blessed that you're part of our lives, and besides, if it hadn't been for you getting trapped in that mine, Eddie and I wouldn't be headed toward gold-mine wealth."

We sat for a long moment, just enjoying the cool spring breeze. "Yeah, in answer to your question earlier, if Steve decided he wanted to spend the rest of his life attached to me, I'd say yeah."

Flex smiled at me and winked. "Then we *could* have a double wedding?"

25

Steve

I PACED ACROSS THE floor for the hundredth time, looking over to where Flex sat next to Mitch, and sighed. "Are you sure this will work?"

"Yep, I've tested the field, and I think he's open to it," Flex said.

"You don't think I should do this alone?"

"Nope, Eric will like that we're here."

"It's not too early?" I asked again.

Mitch laughed. "Dude, I've not known Eric that long, but even I know there's no such thing as too early for Eric Anderson. If you love him, this is the time to tell him."

"When are Alex and Eddie gonna be here?"

Emma Jean came out of the kitchen shaking her head. "Son, none of us are willing to miss this. Have faith, and we'll all be here for you and Eric when the time comes."

I fell into the old recliner where Jimmy usually sat. The moment I was in the chair, I remembered him, and turned to Emma Jean to ask how he was.

"He's doing fine," she said, before I could ask. "The doctors have all given him the thumbs up, and since we avoided an attack, there isn't any damage. The stents should do their thing and get the blood flowing to all the right places, but..." she said, looking at Flex. "He *is* going to have to take it easy."

Flex chuckled. "That'll be like trying to hold the wind down."

"More like a fart," Mitch mumbled, which earned him a look from Emma Jean. Still, she wasn't able to hold back a chuckle.

She walked over to me and patted my shoulder. "He'll ride over with Alex, Eddie, and the boys when they get here."

A few nights ago, I'd woken up to the sounds of someone gasping, and even though no one was there, I knew immediately that Jimmy was in trouble. That morning I all but demanded they take him to the doctor, and sure enough, there was a significant blockage of his arteries.

"Had you not told us in time, they said a heart attack could've killed him," Emma Jean told me that night. He was scheduled for surgery right away but had demanded they let him sleep in his own bed before they poked and prodded him.

"The spirits aren't ready for you to join them yet," I told Jimmy, and was confident that was the truth.

Jimmy just shrugged, but I could see there was relief in his face, which told me he wasn't ready to join them yet either.

The ranch's spirit brothers, as I'd begun referring to them, hadn't been around in a while. Eric had insisted I go with him to his grandmother's house in Toyah. He wanted to speak to his grandmother, who he all but swore to me still occupied her house.

He wasn't wrong. The woman showed up within seconds of us going into the house. She smiled the moment she saw her grandson, and although I couldn't hear her, she motioned in ways that made it clear she was happy to see him.

We visited for some time, and I was able to assure him she could hear the stuff he told her. I played interpreter most of the day, and we were preparing to leave and stay in a hotel just off the interstate, when she pointed toward her bed.

"She wants us to stay here," I said.

"Is she going to come in while we're sleeping?" he asked.

When I looked at the spirit of his grandmother, she smiled and shrugged, then mouthed, "Maybe."

When I told Eric, he laughed. "Promise you won't come into the room while we're asleep, and we'll stay."

The woman clearly laughed, crossed her heart, and nodded.

"She promises, crosses her heart, and hoped to die too…" I said, causing Eric to laugh out loud.

"Too late for that, Grandma," he said.

It warmed my heart that I was able to connect the two of them. Eric let me read her letter too, and the part where she talked about standing up to the currents spoke volumes to me.

I figured she'd written that part for me, although there was no way to tell. I decided to accept that part on faith, instead of asking her directly.

I stopped being so afraid that people would ask questions about me. I'd got so much done on the grant project while avoiding Eric that I'd managed to finish most of the Archaic period research. And, because I was so involved with the research on Eric's and my family tree, I had a good portion of it done for modern times as well. When I reported this to my oversight committee, they were beyond pleased. I also gave myself permission to help Eric research my own familial line, so he could include that in his book.

When I presented him with all the details of my family being institutionalized through the ages, he seemed shocked. "Don't you want to hide this part?" he asked.

"No, that was just my fear talking. My ancestors, who'd been tortured for their gifts, deserve the truth to be known. No one can fault my work, as it's been thoroughly documented with historical references. I have never been one for conjecture without definitive proof to back it up, so it's time to stop hiding. Not that I want to tell the world I'm a medium, or anything like that. I don't really want to have to do readings and shit," I exclaimed, causing Eric to laugh.

"No, I think your scientific mind would explode," he said, giggling.

"Definitely," I agreed.

I came out of the kitchen, where I'd been helping Emma Jean with something, when Mitch, Alex and the boys rushed into the room in a flurry of noise and excitement. "You're gonna propose to Uncle Eric?" Luke asked.

I chuckled. "I guess, but don't tell him when you see him. It's gotta be a surprise."

Luke's eyes were wide, and he nodded. "I promise, Uncle Steve, I won't say nothing."

Emma Jean corrected him. "You won't say anything. It's not Spanish you're speaking here, so one negative is all we use in every sentence."

Luke acknowledged her, but only enough to prevent himself from getting a lecture.

I was literally shaking when Eric came in. He came over and kissed me, then turned to the group, telling them about all he'd gotten accomplished that day.

When he sat on the dining chair Emma Jean always pulled over when we were all together, I went over to where he was sitting, and got on one knee.

He turned to me, surprised, and I could tell he was thinking I was about to pull a prank on him. I was pleased to see he didn't even anticipate the proposal.

"Eric," I began, and the room fell silent. Eric looked around the room, then at me, and I could tell, it was beginning to register for him what was happening.

"I know it's only been a few months, but I'm totally and completely in love with you. Here, in front of your family and friends, I want to ask, will you consider being my husband, and loving me for..."

Before I could get the rest out, Eric leapt out of the chair and into my arms. "Oh, my God, are you serious? Are you really proposing to me? Like, wanting to get married? Flex didn't put you up to this, did he?"

I leaned into him and kissed him, causing him to fall silent. When I leaned back, I said, "Eric, no one had to put me up to this. I want you with every fiber of my being. Are you strong enough to be my man?"

The "*Are you strong enough to be my man?*" song lyric was one I couldn't resist referencing. Eric had been dancing around the RV every evening for the past week, teasing me with the Sheryl Crow song.

Tears flowed from his eyes, and he nodded. "I want you more than I can say." He kissed me deep and long, clearly forgetting our entire little tribe was surrounding us.

When he pulled back, I smiled. "So?"

"Oh, yeah... Yes... Yes, Steve. Oh, my God, I can't believe this is happening. Yes, I'll marry you!"

The entire room erupted in applause, and Eric jumped and turned back around toward the group.

"Time to celebrate?" he asked, looking embarrassed.

"You bet your ass," Alex said, reaching behind him, pulling out the tequila, thrusting it in the air, and saying, "To my primo-in-law!"

The rest of the night, we celebrated and kicked up a huge ruckus.

Jimmy, Emma Jean and Mitch sang love songs, and the kids danced around us acting silly, and making the dogs bark and run back and forth among all the adults.

When we got back to the RV, we were both rather tipsy. Eric leaned over and whispered the song lyrics, *"I'd be the last to help you understand. Are you strong enough to be my man?"*

I smiled at him, and although I couldn't sing and didn't try, whispered back, "I have a face I cannot show. I make the rules up as I go. Just try and love me if you can. Are you strong enough to be my man?"

Eric nodded. "I am, you know... I *am* strong enough to be your man."

"I know. That's why I proposed."

"We're really getting married?" he asked, and I nodded.

"That's what you agreed to."

"Fuck," he said, and jumped back. "I wanna do it here, like with flowers, and I want to have a big tent, with lots of people you work with, and maybe I can invite my grandmother's friends from Toyah..."

I laughed. "Whatever you want. Just as long as I get to have you when this is all done."

"You already have me."

That made me crack a big, wide grin. "But I want you forever, like the brothers have their men."

"What did you see?" Eric asked.

"It's what I haven't seen," I said. I couldn't be sure, but it was very possible they had transitioned, and Eric took my statement as confirmation.

"I'm glad, but I wanted Sampson to see us officially tie the knot. I wanted him to see us get the happily ever after that he'd never had," Eric said.

"He knows, and as you just said, you're already mine. It's what he needed. I think seeing their descendants happy in relationships with other men that they love is what they all needed." He nodded. "I still want to do something special for them, at the wedding, I mean."

"No doubt, maybe we could all dress in old-time cowboy gear, with cowboy boots and spurs, and…"

Eric shut me up with a kiss, and when he pulled back, I tried to keep going, and he kissed me again. I began tickling him, and we ended up back on the bed.

After making love, we cuddled in each other's arms. I was dozing off, when Eric said, "No cowboy boots or spurs, or any such nonsense, but I'd like to have the photo of them we found in Fort Davis blown up. We can put that behind the altar and honor them that way."

"Mmm," was all I said, but he knew I agreed. For all I cared, we could get married naked as long as he continued to agree to be mine. Eric Anderson had closed all the sad loops in my soul, and I'd do whatever it took for him to be happy.

26

Epilogue: Eric

THE ENTIRE AREA UNDER the cottonwood trees was decked out in wedding stuff. There was a gentle breeze that fluffed up the white ribbons and lifted the white tablecloths into balloon-like shapes.

Guests had been steadily arriving since this morning, and Emma Jean was in the house, lecturing the caterers on what needed to go where. We'd all managed to persuade her that she needed to be a guest, instead of cooking. Now, we all realized as the caterers looked over at each other and crossed their eyes, maybe we should've just let her do it.

We had the brothers' picture colorized and blown up, so it looked almost like a modern picture. They stood so handsome and proud behind the altar.

The crowd began congregating around the chairs, and Eddie had the boys go coax Emma Jean out of the kitchen, and toward the event. When the music began, Jimmy walked Flex and Mitch down the aisle, and positioned them on the side where Eddie stood waiting. Then Emma Jean escorted Steve and me down the aisle and placed us next to Alex.

The minister motioned for the attendees to sit, and announced the wedding.

We each said our vows, having written them beforehand. Already fighting back tears, when Steve slipped the ring on my finger, I bawled like a toddler.

When we came to the part where the minister pronounced us spouses for life, Alex and Eddie moved behind us and joined hands.

"We are gathered here on this is an auspicious occasion as the six of you, all related by long-passed ancestors..." the minister pointed toward the picture behind him. "...but also by recent events that you've had to overcome and survive. The men whose picture stands behind me are those who came before, linking each of you together. If you try hard enough, you can feel their presence here, along with all those who've come before us. Through them, you are, and through yourselves, you will continue to be. With that being said, and with the power vested in me by the great state of Texas, I now pronounce you husbands and spouses for life."

When Steve embraced me, he was shivering.

"Are you okay?" I whispered in his ear.

"So, so okay!" he sighed, and I chuckled as we kissed.

As we walked back down the aisle, I felt lightheaded, like I'd drunk a glass of champagne too quickly.

When we were all down the aisle, all six of us turned back toward the crowd. Where we had been standing, were our ancestors, the three brothers along with Levy and Jack's lovers. Sampson looked back at us, a sad smile on his face.

"He's alone," I said, and drew in a shaky breath.

Steve took my arm in his. "No, no, you're wrong, he isn't alone. None of them are. I was wrong, they just hadn't transitioned. They've been with us, a part of us, at least until now. Eric, Sampson was able to feel love through us. They've all experienced their love, acknowledged through us."

I turned again, and the brothers and their lovers were facing us. The oldest brother, Levy, pulled Sampson to his side, and as we watched them, they grew bright, like something had cast a light onto them.

They turned then and disappeared into the light.

When I looked over at Steve, he was crying. "They are gone now... they've transitioned."

I sighed, and when I looked at Eddie, Mitch, Flex and Alex, they were also wiping at tears.

The rest of the evening was a whirlwind of food, drinks, dancing and people. Finally, after the crowd was gone, we all sat around on the porch, happy, exhausted, and enjoying each other's company in silence. It was a perfect wedding, and perfect day.

The next morning, Flex and Mitch were headed to Seattle and the San Juan Islands for a honeymoon, and Steve and I were flying to Europe for ours, but for now, we were just enjoying hanging out together.

Finally, Flex broke the ice about the brothers, when he said, "So, they stuck around for our big day."

Steve nodded. "More like they *were* a part of us until that big day. I think we sort of fulfilled their destiny. We dared to love and overcome all the same sort of obstacles they faced, but we survived it."

Mitch cleared his throat. "We did more than survive, we built on top of that love, and now, we've made it to the relationship finish line," he said, chuckling.

Flex ribbed him, but then leaned over and kissed him on the mouth.

"So, that's it then? We won't be seeing them again?" Alex asked.

Steve shook his head. "No, they're no longer here."

He sighed. "Well, if that means no one is trying to kill us any longer, that's okay with me, but I think I'm going to miss having an ancestor hanging around."

Steve chuckled and looked at me. "Well, I wouldn't say that. Eric's grandmother seems to have taken a shine to the new place."

He looked over my shoulder and blanched. "But that's a really good thing," he said, and the expression on his face made it clear she'd shown him exactly how she felt about his teasing.

We all got up to say our goodbyes, when the boys came running outside, telling us we couldn't leave yet.

"Why not?" Eddie asked.

"The three brothers told us a secret that we were supposed to share with you once it's all over."

Eddie looked at them curiously. "Which three brothers?" he asked.

"You know," Luke said. "Levy, Sampson and Jack."

"You talked to them?" Steve asked, and boys both nodded enthusiastically.

"So, what did they say?" I asked.

"They said you and Uncle Steve would have two, and that Uncle Flex and Uncle Mitch could expect one, but she was going to be a little girl, and we had to help take care of her."

All of us looked at the boys like they'd grown horns. "How is that supposed to happen?" Mitch asked, laughing.

"They said it'll just happen when it's time."

We left laughing, thinking the boys had maybe had a bit too much excitement with all the brother ghosts, and wanted to add their own part.

Six months to the day later, Flex got a call from his mother, who was all excited. "My neighbor is expecting triplets, but her boyfriend told her he didn't want them, and she told me she wants to give them up for adoption. When I told her about you boys, she got so excited, saying she already thought how amazing it would be if her babies could be raised by gay men."

That night Flex and Mitch came in telling the story, and we all laughed. Drake came in, and said, "That's what they were saying. Some woman by the name of Abigale would have triplets, and that she'd want you to raise her babies for her."

"Flex," I said, feeling nervous. "Did your mom tell you the name of the woman?"

He shook his head and texted his mom, then we all waited with bated breath for her to respond.

When the ding came from his phone, he looked down, and physically paled.

"Yeah, her name is Abigale... Abigale Smith. Oh, and Mom said she's our cousin somehow... like she's somehow related to us."

Emma Jean snorted. "Well, can't say I didn't see that coming. Guess you boys better get to practicing your diaper changing."

"Wait," I said. "It can't be that easy. Adopting children is tough. There are families that've been on waiting lists for years."

Emma Jean just shrugged and went into the kitchen.

Three months and a ridiculous amount of paperwork later, Samantha, Mitch and Flex's little girl, and Jack and Levy, the two boys we'd agreed to adopt, came into our lives like three torpedoes. I always wondered if they had the personalities of the brothers they were named after.

When Abigale announced she wanted us to have the babies, we all drove to meet her, and we all fell for her right away. She spent the last month of her pregnancy at the ranch with us, since she didn't really have a good place to stay, and we'd all agreed we wanted her to be a part of the babies' lives. Too many of us knew what it was like to lose a parent, and if the woman was willing to be a part of the kids' lives, we were all one hundred percent for it.

Abigale moved in with Katherine, Flex's mom, after that, so she could help her back on her feet. "That's how I can be a part of my grandbabies' lives, without having to go to that cursed place," she announced, when she agreed to take Abigale on.

Something magical happened between Katherine and Abigale, and the woman managed to get Katherine to start coming out to the ranch regularly. She still insisted she hated the place, but she'd become ridiculously attached to her three grandbabies. Yes, even our boys were hers.

We were an odd little family, but it somehow worked. Drake and Luke were amazing babysitters, and Alex's nieces and nephews were constant visitors as well. The little ones grew up thinking of them all as their cousins.

Steve was immediately asked to become a National Historian for the Department of the Interior, after completing the history of Big Bend. In the summer, the boys and I would join him on the road as we explored and documented the historical sites throughout the national parks.

I completed the books detailing the lives and history of our families. There was too much to tell to write only one, so each family got their own book. As a result, I was hired to speak at several conventions around the nation about the history of West Texas, because when the books were done, they really were a history of the area as much as they were about us.

The university in Alamito hired me as well, and with Steve's help, I finally got my Ph.D., even though before I met Steve, I didn't really even know I wanted it.

Mitch and Flex ended up moving full-time to Mitch's house at the motel. I guessed we all knew that was coming, but what we didn't know was that he was going to ask Steve and me to take over the ranch house.

"Eric, you're taking more and more of the burden from Emma Jean, and I need to be stable for little Sam," he said to me one day, as he began convincing me the homestead should be where we lived to raise our boys.

"Besides, you need Emma Jean's firm hand as you learn to raise two boys, and no one is more expert in that than her."

I finally agreed, and Steve and I moved into the old farmhouse full-time.

Eddie and Alex stayed in the duplex for several years, until Alex convinced him to build a proper house next to it. They tore the wall out between the duplexes and expanded Emma Jean and Jimmy's living space. That was the best solution, since all the kids ended up there almost every afternoon after school was out.

Emma Jean no longer cooked for all of us, but she was still the matriarch of the place, and the kids needed Emma Jean and Jimmy time at least once every day.

I did most of the cooking for our expanded family. Emma Jean finally relented and taught me her most prized recipes, such as her fried chicken, as well as all of her Mexican recipes.

Jimmy passed when the little ones had just turned ten. He pulled Steve aside a month before he died, and told him he knew it was his time, and that he planned to stick around until Emma Jean was ready to leave as well. "I'll need you to help me communicate," he said, causing Steve to laugh.

"You've never had trouble communicating before. I doubt death is gonna stop you."

That made Jimmy chuckle.

According to Steve, though, he was as good as his word, and after he passed, he would come and go, keeping an eye on our family.

Emma Jean was in no hurry to leave us, though, and was in her nineties when she finally passed, long after the kids were all grown, and had started lives and families of their own.

The gold in the volcano was significant, especially for this part of the world. It took ten years for the mining company to completely mine the veins. When it closed, we agreed we wanted the entire mine blown up, to ensure there would never be another person caught in a cave-in. Having experienced that firsthand, I knew just how scary it could be.

The mining company was reluctant, but luckily, Flex had retained all the rights to the property, and when he insisted, there was no choice but to concede.

Alex's family used the ranch numerous times for filming, and his Juarez studios became well known in the US for creating period films, not just in Mexico, but in the US as well.

We never saw the brothers again. However, without them, we all knew we would've never survived. They were our protectors and our guides, and it almost felt like they had set up and created what they'd all yearned for, but never had.

As the years passed and grey began to pepper all of our hair, we continued to sit around the wide front porch and talk about the times when we met and fell in love with our husbands.

Every time we discussed this, no matter how often we did so, the conversation always ended with how lucky we'd been and how grateful we'd always be to the ghosts of Levy, Sampson, and Jack. Not only had the three kept us alive, but they'd prompted and supported the love that became the bedrock of our lives. What better gifts could anyone ask for?

Genealogy
Appendix

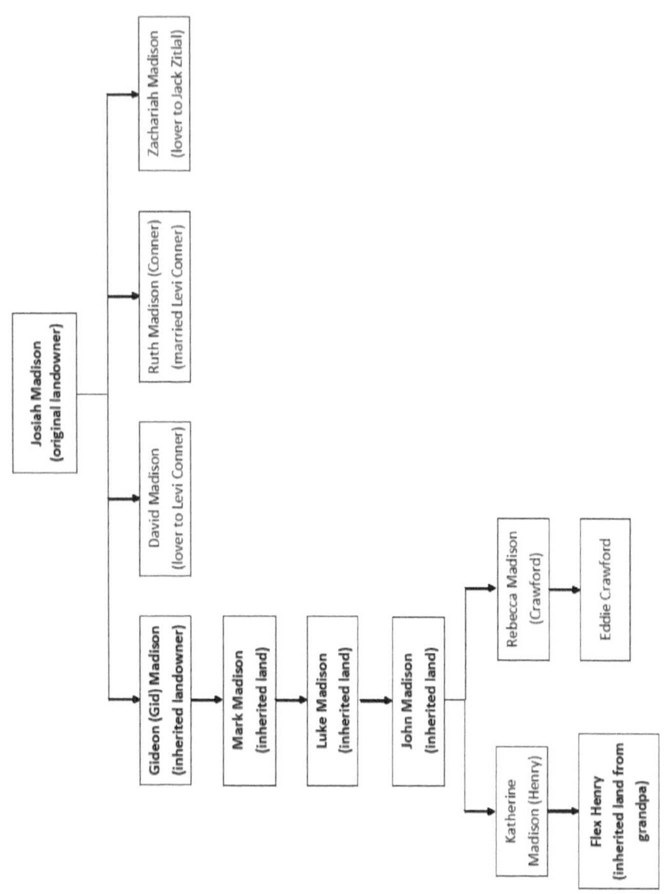

Josiah Madison (original landowner)
David Madison (lover to Levi Conner)
Ruth Madison (Conner) (married Levi Conner)
Zachariah Madison (lover to Jack Zitlal)
Gideon (Gid) Madison (inherited landowner)
Mark Madison (inherited land)
Luke Madison (inherited land)
John Madison (inherited land)
Rebecca Madison (Crawford)
Eddie Crawford
Katherine Madison (Henry)
Flex Henry (inherited land from grandpa)

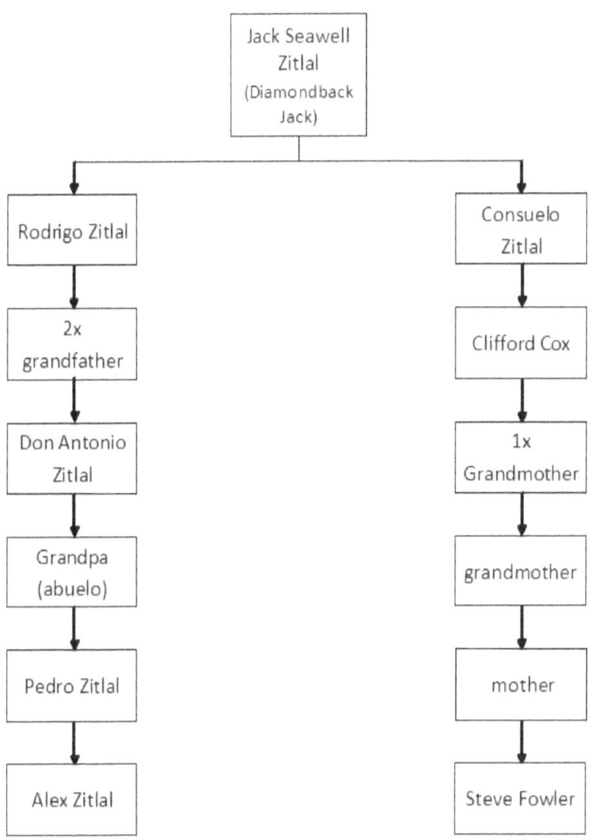

Jack Seawell Zitlal (Diamondback Jack)
Rodrigo Zitlal
Consuelo Zitlal
2x grandfather
Clifford Cox
Don Antonio Zitlal
1x Grandmother
Grandpa (abuelo)
grandmother
Pedro Zitlal
mother
Alex Zitlal
Steve Fowler

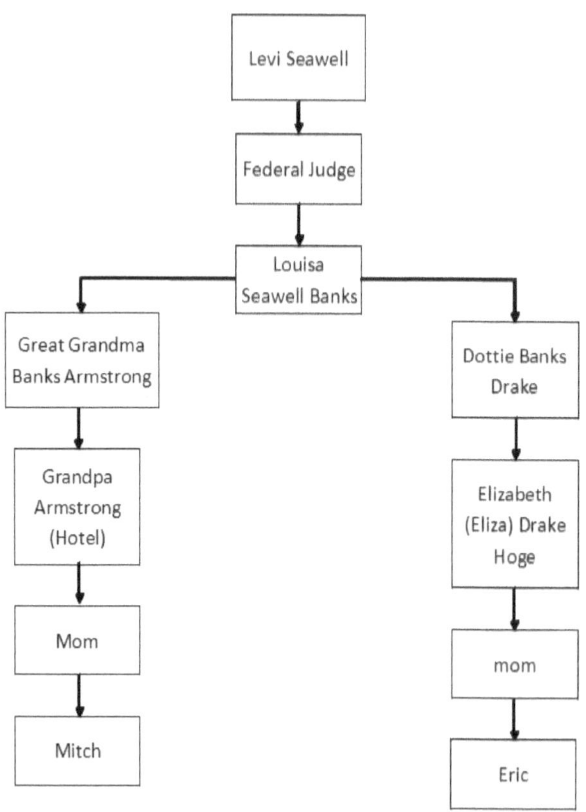

Levi Seawell
Federal Judge
Louisa
Seawell Banks
Great Grandma
Banks Armstrong
Dottie Banks
Drake
Grandpa
Armstrong
(Hotel)
Elizabeth
(Eliza) Drake
Hoge
Mom
mom
Mitch
Eric

Cursed to never find love, Crea is shocked when he finds the perfect man. Choosing to fight the curse could cost him everything, including his life.

Emerald Earth **by Adam J. Ridley**

Available at your favorite bookseller

Join Blake's email list to get advance notice of new books and receive his occasional newsletter:

www.blakeallwood.com

MM Romance
By Blake Allwood

Transitions Series
Aiden Inspired
Suzie Empowered (MF Romance)
Bobby Transformed

Chance Series
Love By Chance
Another Chance With Love
Taking A Chance For Love

Romantic Series
Romantic Renovations (1)
Romantic Rescue (2)
Romantic Recon (3)

Melody Series
Melody of the Heart
Melody of the Snow

Road to Rocktoberfest Anthology
Changing His Tune - 2022

Coming Home Series (2023)
A Long Way Home
Family Home
Down Home
…and many more

Novellas
Tenacious
Moon's Place

Romantic Fantasy
By Adam J. Ridley

Big Bend Series
Love's Legacy (1)
Love's Heirloom (2)
Love's Bequest (3)

The Witch Brothers Series
Emerald Earth
Diamond Air
Ruby Fire
Sapphire Water

Blake Allwood was born in west Tennessee, then moved to Kansas City MO after earning a degree in Early Childhood Education from Graceland College in Lamoni, Iowa. He met his husband Shaun in 1995 and they officially married in 2015, once gay marriage was legalized; although they still consider Valentines Day 1995 as their true "anniversary date". Twenty-two years later (2017), after fostering 12 children together, he and his husband sold their home, purchased an RV and began traveling the country with their two dogs.

Typically, Blake can be found relaxing in the RV or by the fire with his laptop and their Jack Russell Terrier, Buddy, curled up between his legs demanding attention. Denver, their Siberian Husky mix is often asleep at his feet or playing tug of war with Blake's husband.

Most of Blake's stories are inspired by the places they have visited in their ongoing travels. His first book, *Aiden Inspired*, was released in 2019 and he has now written over 20 books. In

2023 he is releasing the ***Coming Home*** series which is comprised of ten-plus sweet contemporary romance novels that are based on a fictional town in his home state of Tennessee.

Blake also writes under the pen name of Adam J. Ridley for his urban fantasy fans looking for stories revolving around gay characters. His first series is The Witch Brothers Saga, starting with ***Emerald Earth***.

biblilopride.com

Books by LGBTQ+
authors